MW00761012

# Survivors of the Chaos

## *A Sci-Fi Thriller*

Steven M. Moore

ISBN 0-7414-6583-3

Printed in the United States of America

This is a work of fiction set in the future. Although some references may be made to public persons, institutions, places, and real events, these references are only intended to establish a historical backdrop for the fictional story presented herein. Any other names of characters found herein corresponding to persons living or dead is purely coincidental

Published May 2011

**INFINITY PUBLISHING**
1094 New DeHaven Street, Suite 100
West Conshohocken, PA 19428-2713
Toll-free (877) BUY BOOK
Local Phone (610) 941-9999

## Dedication

To the creative thinkers and gifted engineers of NASA's Apollo program. Like those used by the designers of the pyramids, your skills lifted humanity to great heights. That these skills will be lost to the ages is a great human tragedy. Perhaps one day others like you—not robots or probes—will carry the torch of adventure and show the way to the stars.

# Part I

## Zebediah

*To survive it is often necessary to fight and to fight you have to dirty yourself.*

— George Orwell

# Chapter One

The marauders swept down on Jesse Lane. Wild spirits bent on revenge, their outlines ill formed in the snow squall, they used their wide-brimmed hats to pummel their steeds, urging them on towards the rancher.

He knew them—such gangs were blights on the Midwest. These Devil's minions preyed on honest farmers and ranchers that tried to scratch out a living in a lawless land. The marauders robbed, raped, maimed, and killed.

Always on the lookout for them, he had killed one of their scouts some years back, but this time events favored them. You need two arms to drag a calf out of a mud hole.

At the sound of the horses' hooves and the savage yells, he let go of the bawling calf and spun to face them.

There was no time to reach for the rifle stashed in the saddle scabbard on his mare. Their bullets ripped through him. He staggered backwards and nearly fell into the ashy, slick mass that imprisoned the calf.

His horse reared and bolted. Two marauders whipped their steeds to give pursuit. Two more lassoed the calf. The other five turned their mounts towards the ranch house.

*Please God, be merciful. May Zeb already be there to protect the rest of the family.*

Battling pain and the growing darkness of death, he propped himself up on an elbow and watched them ride off. Hats pulled low and slickers streaming in the wind, all soiled and stained by years of weather and neglect, their attire mimicked the souls of his killers.

The leader of the main group carried the infamous square pennant, once white but now equally soiled. They had sewn a red cross to the banner, a faded cross that recalled historical origins to a few but bloody savageries to many.

Lane's strength failed. He eased his head back onto the mud, ready to yield to the dark.

3

Some say you see your entire life when you die. He only had the one memory....

***

Lane listened to his wife's screams.

*How do they do it? How can they stand the pain? And then do it again?*

He could butcher a cow or a pig, but he couldn't bear to watch his wife giving birth. He couldn't stand to see her suffering. He also knew that he wouldn't be able to tolerate the pain she experienced.

He leaned back in the threadbare chair, closed his eyes, and prayed. His calloused hands gripped the armrests. His muscles tensed and relaxed with every scream.

He wasn't sure how this thing with God worked, but he was sure going to try to communicate with the Old Fellow. He picked up his Bible, its worn leather cover nearly a match for his weathered face. A faded red ribbon marked a favorite passage, the Sermon on the Mount.

*This here's a good woman, Lord,* he prayed. *You damn well better take care of her. You certainly don't want to take her yet. She'll argue with you for eternity.*

Abruptly there was silence. Lane's prayer stopped in mid-thought. He probed the silence. He wet his lips and hoped. Had he been too rough with his Lord?

A baby's cry interrupted his thoughts. Another Lane was born. Mother and son were fine.

They called the boy Zebediah. Family and friends often shortened it to Zeb. Some criticized the name as too egotistical—wasn't every child a gift of God? Others criticized it as too Old Testament, but Lane knew that the Zebediah that mattered was the father of the apostles John and James.

Moreover, Lane didn't care too much about what most people thought.

A tall man with a full beard, he managed to look well dressed even in patched pants and soiled shirt. Through his veins coursed the blood of generations of independent-minded yet God-fearing ranchers. He was poor and proud, a man whose main goal in life was to provide for his family and live in peace with his neighbors.

4

While many men had a lot to say and others liked to listen, he paid more attention to what the Earth had to say. He was an actor on a stage controlled by the weather and seasons, by backbreaking work and long hours. For him, becoming close to the Earth was becoming close to God, for the Earth was God's gift to man.

***

Zeb turned Jefferson towards home. He and his horse moved against the wind. It was slow going with forty-plus pelts stacked behind the rider. He hunched down to minimize the wind resistance, but Jefferson forged ahead, not needing the help.

It took longer than he thought. He knew his mother would be worried, but he wasn't about to abuse his horse. Jefferson was a partner in life that he had come to love and respect.

Zeb cursed when it started to snow, but then turned his face skyward, asking the Lord's forgiveness and sucking in some flakes to cure his thirst. The storm would slow them more.

He was not dressed for a storm. Threadbare jeans and a cotton work shirt were not enough to keep him from shivering. It didn't help that his feet were bare and the jeans were wet from the knee down. He had stashed his boots away in the middle of the pile of pelts and waded out to his beaver traps.

Finally, he could make out some of the distant home lights, shimmering through the light snowfall. Home always looked better embraced by new snow. He felt like one of the kings heading for Bethlehem. He scratched the stubble on his chin and smiled.

*I need a heavier beard, I suppose. Like Pa's.*

Abruptly Jefferson reared. Zeb had all he could do to bring the horse under control. He managed to keep the pelts from sliding off.

He saw what was making the stallion skittish. He slid off his mount and approached the still figure on the ground. Already partially covered with snow, Jesse Lane lay on his back, eyes wide open and staring at the sky. The pool of thickening blood by him and the gunshot wounds told the tale of violence.

Sobbing, Zeb dropped to his knees.

*Marauders,* he thought. *They've murdered my family.*

A terrible coldness gripped his heart, causing it to race with fear of danger and the unknown. He brought his emotions under control, replacing the fear with a thirst for revenge that no snowflakes could cure.

He closed his father's eyes. He struggled to his feet and looked homeward.

*Even if I die trying, Lord, help me take some of them with me.*

He went to Jefferson and took the heavy pile of pelts off his back. Their value seemed to have vanished in the cold wind. He put them beside his father's still body. He planned his attack strategy while he put his boots on. He then mounted, removed his rifle from its scabbard, and turned the horse toward the distant lights.

He slowed the horse to a walk and entered the area between the outbuildings and the house. Usually the bustling center for many ranch activities, it was now drained of life. When he passed the pen, he noticed the hogs were gone. The same story held for the milk cows in the barn. All was quiet.

He left Jefferson in his barn stall munching some oats, readied his gun, and walked towards the house. Up the gravel path and onto the wide front porch, sweat beading on his forehead in spite of the cold, he found the front door ajar.

*Not a good sign. Where is everybody?*

He pushed the door open with the barrel of the rifle and peered inside. Nobody. There were signs of struggle everywhere, but the kitchen had suffered the most damage. He frowned upon seeing the blood spatters.

Upstairs he found his mother and sister on his parents' bed. They were naked and their throats were slashed. One of his sister's legs was twisted at an odd angle, a jagged and bloody bone protruding from the break. Some of his mother's long, beautiful hair lay loose on the sheets, ripped out by the roots.

The bruises on their bodies and the blood under their nails told him that they had not made it easy for the men that had raped them repeatedly.

He rushed to the bathroom. Vomiting and sobbing, he thought he would lose his mind. He sank to the floor. All energy had left him. He was an empty husk. Driving out rational thought, the image of his slaughtered family burned into his brain.

It took him two days to bury them and put the ranch into some semblance of order. He found some loose livestock that had somehow escaped the marauders and secured the animals in the barn with enough feed and water to last for several days.

On the morning of the third day, he secured the main house the best he could, mounted Jefferson, and began his quest. He would hunt the marauders down and kill them.

He hadn't eaten much in those three days. He was feeding on the raw emotion of revenge.

It was his birthday. He had turned twenty-one.

# Chapter Two

"The Chair recognizes the Honorable Senator from Mid-Atlantic Pharma. Mr. Martinez, you now have the floor."

Fabio Martinez put his computer tablet on pause and looked up. He didn't particularly want the floor. The Chair of the Acquisitions Committee was in a meeting room that looked austere, dark, and smelly. He assumed the floor was also dirty and smelly. He rarely appeared at meetings in person for that reason.

His private joke aside, in his office he got down to business. Speaking a command to his AI, he took direct control of his avatar as a VR presence at the meeting. Others in the Committee were also present using only their electronic surrogates. They often carried out the business of the Senate of the Mid-Atlantic Union that way.

*Yes, the moldy old building is showing its age,* he thought, looking at the wood trim and furnishings of the committee room in Philadelphia. *It shows that the Union government is broke, but that's not news. I become rich while it goes broke.*

Martinez didn't like anything about Philly. He preferred to stay secluded in his penthouse in New York unless he was off skiing in either Bariloche or Switzerland. Many thought he was a recluse, but modern corporate CEOs were often that way. It saved on security costs.

Philadelphia was the capital of the Union, a country that contained most of Maryland, the old District of Columbia (now in ruins and returning to swamp land), Virginia, Delaware, New Jersey, and the southern portion of the state of New York, including New York City, the commercial capital.

The Union was wealthy as nations go in the world of 2131, its wealth based on pharmaceuticals and electronics. Yet there was a wide range of personal fortunes too, from people like Martinez, who had business interests all over the planet and beyond, to a poor and struggling underclass that lived on the street, many without jobs, healthcare, or food.

Those lucky enough to have jobs often sat in factories twelve to fifteen hours per day performing mundane tasks that were not worth the expense of automation. When they became sick, they often died. Their captors harvested body parts for the good organs before they threw the rest of their bodies into a recycling bin. Hospitals and cemeteries were only for the rich.

"Mr. Chairman, I'm willing to meet the Senator from LMRB Technologies half way," said Martinez via his avatar.

LMRB stood for Lockheed-Martin-Raytheon-Boeing. Their Senator represented a company even bigger than Martinez' GenCorp L.T.D., which owned Mid-Atlantic Pharma. His people had brokered a deal with LMRB.

"My constituents will support the bill for the acquisition of ten stealth scramjets if the good Senator will support our request for trials of the new drug Good Times to be carried out on the homeless populations of Philadelphia, Baltimore, and New York City."

"That might diminish the tendency for those populations to protest and riot," observed the Chair.

"Yes, that might be one of the drug's positive side effects."

"Senator?" The Chair raised a furry eyebrow, an implicit question for the good Senator from LMRB Technologies

"Works for me," he said.

Martinez looked across at the Senator from WorldNet, his main competitor. Martinez had done her a favor the week before. Denise Andersen nodded without showing any expression on her face.

*Works for everybody,* thought Martinez. *She's probably screwing her current lover. Completely disinterested in this meeting, she's leaving everything to the AI-controlled avatar.*

Each year Martinez' company, GenCorp, had profits larger than most countries' GDP. The subsidiary, Mid-Atlantic Pharma, was hoping that Good Times would be another money producer. Its introductory price would be high. He might reduce the price in the future, but only to increase the volume of sales—he had little concern for the desperate millions of people that needed his drugs.

*I practically gave away the aids cure. Wasn't that enough?*

Mid-Atlantic Pharma and the other pharmaceutical companies under the GenCorp umbrella had specialized early in exotic drugs, many of them developed in micro-g environments at the International Space Station, on Farside, and on Phobos, one of the

Martian moons. One thing led to another. Now GenCorp was much more than a conglomerate of drug firms, selling everything from plant fertilizers to huge earth-moving equipment.

Its only serious competitors in size were LMRB Technologies, a conglomerate with little in common with GenCorp, and WorldNet, a true competitor in almost everything GenCorp laid its hands on. All three companies, like many other worldwide corporations, had their own security forces to protect themselves against attempts at industrial espionage. Such threats were common, as were protests from the rabble, another threat during the time of the Chaos.

Born in Argentina, Martinez' lower middle class parents had possessed limited access to most of the new genetic treatments for their son. While he was as healthy as a *pampas* bull, his swarthy and hirsute skin and his short, compact, ovoid body made him unattractive to most women. Learning to work around that, he discovered at an early age that money could buy him about any woman he wanted.

Andersen was an exception.

The AI put through a message to his avatar's tablet that was as virtual as the avatar but more controlled by the AI. Bryce had more candidates. That was good. He made a nice piece of change on that side business. Fortunately, with the Chaos, officials poorly kept records, another consequence of the fact that most countries were on the brink of bankruptcy. He had a great deal of freedom to practice his entrepreneurship.

"We're adjourning," said the Chairman after an aide whispered something in his ear. "There's a riot outside. I'd suggest those here physically retreat in the company of their bodyguards. The rest should have your AIs sign off for security reasons."

Martinez frowned. The rabble was becoming more and more vociferous and demanding as the world economy soured. What little order existed was due to private security firms.

*That's why it's called the Chaos.*

He left the VR world and returned to his real office, a secluded workaholic's retreat that represented about fifteen per cent of the floor area in his New York penthouse. He still found the jump a little disconcerting, but it was a lot better than subjecting himself to protestors. Or dirty rooms and floors.

*I've always hated crowds, especially those that might be violent. Speaking of which....*

"I want that asshole Ruffini on the phone," he told the AI. "He thinks I'm going to give a speech tomorrow, but I'll be damned if I'm flying to Gettysburg in this weather and with hostile crowds. He can either figure out how to do an out-of-doors VR or forget about me being there."

Martinez' AI was already connecting to Ruffini's AI.

# Chapter Three

The marauders made no effort to cover their trail. Following the footprints in the new snow, Zeb headed southeast. The marauders were obviously not worried about him, even if they knew of his existence.

He found other ranches they had plundered and buried the victims.

He also found a young girl that had survived by hiding in a trunk in the cellar of her house. She was malnourished and dying of thirst. He took her to the nearest town where an old doctor promised to do his best.

"You trying to catch them bastards?" asked the doctor.

"They killed my parents and my sister. What would you do?"

The doctor looked at his daughter, a twelve-year-old, who was sewing buttons on one of his shirts. He shook his head sadly.

"She needs me. So does the waif you brought in."

"Well, no one needs me, so I plan to hunt them down, or die trying."

The doctor went over to an old wooden desk, opened a drawer, and rummaged around in it. He handed Zeb a leather cartridge belt and holster, a revolver, and several boxes of ammo.

"Then I suspect you'll need this more than me. It's a mite handier than a rifle."

"I can't take it. It cost you a lot of money."

"I make a good living. People usually can't pay much, if anything, but they give me produce and livestock instead of cash. No one much uses cash anymore. I can't recall when I last seen hard currency." He scratched behind his head as if that would stimulate a memory. "There was a time when we paid taxes. The government hired constables to protect us from killers like your marauders. Not anymore. Some damn fools started calling it socialism." He lowered his suspenders and put on the shirt that his daughter had handed to him. "The cities are worse, I hear."

Zeb's attention notched upwards. "Can you tell me about the cities?"

Years earlier, he had asked his father the same question....

\*\*\*

Jesse Lane received a steaming mug of coffee from his son but continued to stare into the embers of the fire in a way that made Zeb hesitate. Finally, the boy's courage peaked.

"What was it like before, Pa?"

Jesse was startled but smiled at his son. The boy's temerity amused him.

*Maybe we're too stern with the kids.*

"Out here someone might kill you for interrupting his daydreams, boy."

"But it's night, not day," said Zeb with a wink squinted enough to be discernible in the waning firelight.

"So it is, son, so it is." Jesse laughed and then became more serious. "In that case, though, they be nightmares." Having filtered out some grounds through his mustache and teeth, he spit the coffee residue into the fire. "Before what?"

"Well, before, like when we were just one country. I heard we stretched from coast to coast."

"One big country. Too big, maybe. We weren't satisfied either." Zeb's father looked into the darkness, seeing the spirits of the past. "Always meddlin' in foreign affairs, not taking proper care of our own problems. I've never been to either coast. Can't say that I want to visit them. Lots of sin in the eastern and western cities."

"You mean killings, like here, with the marauders?"

"Some of that, with gangs everywhere, worse than marauders, but lots of dirty, indecent shit too. Men doing it to men, women to women, and trading around like it was some kind of game. It's a wonder the good Lord doesn't do something about it."

"I guess I don't understand what that means. But I wanted to ask about the cities. Were they full of tall buildings?"

"I suppose they still are. Don't know for sure. Out here we don't receive much news about the rest of the world." He stared at the sky, wondering if that space station was still there. *Zeb wouldn't be able to handle that concept,* he figured. *I have a hard time myself.* "The whole business broke down, you know.

13

Different parts of the country went their separate ways. People grouped together with others they were comfortable with and broke off with those that were disagreeable to them. Sometimes violently. Washington couldn't hold it all together. Not bad by itself, I suppose, but the greatness of the whole country was lost. It is what it is. The Lord works in mysterious ways."

"Who was Washington?"

"I'm referring to a place where all the national leaders lived. I guess Washington was also some historical fellow too, but I don't remember much about him. I left school a long time ago."

"At least you could go. I'd like to get schooled and learn things too."

"Nothin' useful in schools, boy. They don't teach you anything 'bout runnin' a ranch. Just useless facts that are mostly lies anyway. Be content with your lot in life. The Lord is good to us."

"I know that, Pa. I'm just curious, that's all."

\*\*\*

The marauders turned more to the east. Jefferson was stronger than all their horses, so Zeb was gaining ground. He figured he was only a half day behind when he came upon campfire ashes that were still warm.

The weather had turned temperate again. The thin snow cover was gone. Nevertheless, the wind blowing off the prairie had a bite to it that made him keep the collar of his slicker turned up around his neck.

The following morning he found what was left of the marauders. At his parents' ranch, he had counted nine sets of tracks. Clustered around a fire, its embers still hot, were nine marauders and their steeds, all dead. He walked around the site, shaking his head, trying to figure out what happened.

The vultures and coyotes had already done good work on the cadavers, but he could see that most of the marauders had many wounds. The same was true of the horses. Even the ground was riddled with bullet holes.

"Jefferson, I'd say that the Lord's wrath came down on these devils. How, I don't know. It's very strange."

More than perplexed, he felt cheated. Someone had done what he had set out to do, yearned to do, in order to avenge his family.

14

He mounted Jefferson and turned him back the way they had come. It was a lonely ride. The desire for vengeance had kept him going. Now he felt drained, without purpose.

After a long day, he made twilight camp by a small creek. Although the water was only a little above freezing, it was clean. He decided to wash off some of the grime before starting a fire. He stripped to the waist. The cold water on tense and tired muscles offered relief. It also pumped him full of resolve.

He made an oath to return to the family ranch and make it the best ranch around. He would find a good woman and raise a family, keeping the Lane name alive for many more years. He prayed to the Lord to give him the strength to keep that oath.

A thump-thump-thump in the distance interrupted his thoughts. A running herd of buffalo, all in synchronized step, seemed headed his way.

He ran to Jefferson, removed the rifle from the scabbard, and retrieved from the saddle horn the gun and cartridge belt the old doctor had given him. The sound was now oppressive.

A huge flying machine rose over the crest of a nearby hill. A bright light turned the fading twilight into high noon. The monster machine was painted black along the bottom; the forward part was dark and shiny glass. He could just make out that there were men inside.

Four blades made the thumping noise and whirled around the top. Something like a windmill was on the machine's tail, spinning so fast it was a blur. Spread along its front were cannons of various sizes. Underneath were sled rails and wheels.

He threw the rifle down and shielded his eyes with his left hand while he waved the pistol skyward, trying to take aim in the glare. A net dropped on him.

He knew all about nets. He used them more in fishing than in trapping. This one was huge and he became tangled. They had designed it to fish for humans.

# Chapter Four

Denise Andersen was not happy with the compromise she had brokered with Martinez. Pleasure, however, sometimes trumps business, even for someone as involved in her business as much as she was, so her dissatisfaction was transient. It helped that she was off-line.

While her avatar attended the Committee meeting, she was relaxing in a hot tub in Sydney. It used more water than the average person's monthly allotment, a luxury whose cost was irrelevant to her. She had been present in the flesh at the opening of a new art museum but was now tired of both people and travel.

It had been good to come, though. Both the Man and Isha Bai were present. She intended to maintain good relations with the U.N.

*It's powerless. The Man is a token figurehead. I don't think that's particularly good.*

Her guest for the trip was a Metropolitan opera mezzo-soprano that specialized in the role of Carmen. She was reading a historical novel when Denise joined her in bed.

The next morning, she boarded her personal scramjet and returned to New York City.

\*\*\*

Andersen was a product of expensive genetic engineering. Her perfect body, the unblemished face, and indeterminate racial characteristics were common among the sons and daughters of the rich.

She was born into a powerful South Asian family. Her parents spared no expense in making her the genetically perfect human being. They raised her in a way that resulted in her thinking she could have anything she wanted. At twenty-five she ousted her CEO father in a bitter corporate takeover and stayed on the prowl ever since.

In spite of her privileged upbringing, she cursed in several languages while she watched the scene that her security cameras had recorded the night before on the eve of her return.

A gang had hit one of her warehouses in Tribeca. After killing four security guards, they made off with over twenty million in exotic designer drugs.

Moreover, that was the wholesale price. Their sale to the rich bastards that could still afford a decent healthcare plan would be worth many millions more.

She pounded her desk. Her Chief of Security Peter Bradford, accustomed to her tantrums, patiently watched pens and pencils jump up and down. He waited for her to say something.

***

When Andersen finally turned off the TV monitor with a voice command, Bradford sighed. He knew what was coming.

"I'm not going to miss those guards," she informed Bradford. "They must have been incompetent. Why in the hell did you hire them?"

"They were all tempered under fire in the N.Y.P.D.," he countered.

He knew she was never content with what modern gene splicing gave her. Instead of her mother's long blond hair, she shaved her head, except for the fashionable two tufts over her ears.

The diamond hanging from her nose wasn't artificial, but it wasn't ostentatious either. A tight fitting jerkin accentuated her cleavage and contrasted with the baggy, multicolored pants that she had tucked into calf-high fake seal leather boots. This was no bow to animal rights people—this particular seal was extinct. A matching belt carried a taser on the left and a vibrablade on the right.

"N.Y.P.D.? N.Y.P.D.?" He watched the redness creep from her breasts, up her neck, and into her face, making it all the uniform hue of unbridled anger. "Cops are targets for the gangs nowadays. Is that what you mean by tempered under fire?" The last question was a scream.

She stood and waggled her finger at him. She was five centimeters taller than Bradford was and he was not short. He figured she would intimidate anyone.

"These were all good men," he said.

"And now I suppose their families will all receive good life insurance payouts." She walked over to the office windows overlooking the East River. In the pregnant silence he could hear her breathing return to a more normal state. "Somehow I have to figure out a way to stop this. It happens too often."

"We do everything that is possible within the law and a little that is questionably legal besides. I'm at a loss. We need fresh ideas."

"Well, here's one. Let's work outside the law for a change. What's wrong with that? Other countries don't pussyfoot around with these criminals. Why should we?"

"Because some of your operations are in the Mid-Atlantic Union. Moreover, like Fabio Martinez, you enjoy certain privileges with the U.N. Space Agency."

"The privileges come because I fund a lot of their operations. And it's not just the R&D that benefits me. But, back to my question: can we go the vigilante route?"

"We could try. You already spy on Martinez to gather intel on what he's doing."

"I'm sure he's doing the same to me. Right now, I think he's pulling a fast one on Farside, but I can't figure it out. The authorities don't know about any of it."

"They probably suspect."

She went to him and looked into his eyes. Once they had been lovers, she a precocious college student, he her father's man. However, she grew tired of him.

She grabbed his genitals and squeezed. When he winced, she let go, laughing.

"I just wanted to make sure you hadn't become a dickless wonder, love." She walked to the desk and sat. "Now go away. I believe I have come up with a solution, so I must think about the detailed implementation."

"I can help with that."

"Oh, you will. Or you'll be wishing you were one of those security guards."

Bradford turned and left her to her scheming.

\*\*\*

Bradford's office was nearly the size of Andersen's. It hadn't changed when she grew tired of him. He had secure lines that she didn't know about.

"She's up to something," he said into a videophone.

No picture transmitted, none received. The voice signal was encoded with a key that was decipherable by only the newest quantum computers. There was not much chance that anyone listening in would have one of those—they were still experimental.

"She's always up to something," came the reply. "So am I. Why is this any different?"

"She's going to try something illegal to stop the pilfering."

"Illegality is always relative. They sanction murder in several of the new countries to keep down the population. Who's going to say what she's doing is illegal?"

"Since I don't know what it is, I don't know who would say it. Probably the Mid-Atlantic Union."

"Probably not. Ruffini knows who's keeping him afloat. It would have to be something egregious where the rabble needs a scapegoat. Keep me posted, though. This could be amusing."

# Chapter Five

The men strapped him in a chair. Muscles rippling, he strained at the leather bonds. One of the men laughed at his struggles, so Zeb spit in his face. The man punched him. The blow split his lip. Blood started to drip down onto his bare chest.

"Wilson, don't damage the goods!"

Zeb was pleased but otherwise surprised when Bryce stepped out of the shadows. He used Zeb's rifle to club Wilson. The giant fell and cowered at Zeb's feet.

Bryce was the leader. He bossed the pilot of the helicopter, the name of the machine that had swooped down on Zeb. He also led the rest of the group. They didn't need a bath as much as Wilson did, who even smelled of urine, but they weren't presentable for Sunday services either.

Zeb had learned that these men killed the marauders.

*They stole my revenge; now they steal my freedom.*

Bryce patted him on the cheek.

"A young Apollo, my boys. Lots of good, healthy farm food and fine fresh, country air went into making him. Mr. Martinez will make a nice profit." He kicked at Wilson's ribs, who scooted away on all fours. "We can't sell damaged goods, you idiot!" He waved something that looked like a gun close to Zeb's face. "Now, *Monsieur* Zebediah Lane, you are mine to sell, trade, or barter, as legal representative of Fabio Martinez." The others, excepting Wilson, guffawed. "This little instrument will make it so. It's not a gun, but it will hurt like hell if you move." He winked at Zeb. "I'm going to put it against your left shoulder. If you stay nice and still, you will experience the slight prick of a needle. Do you understand?"

Zeb nodded. When Bryce shot the gun, Zeb still strained once more against the leather. As promised, his shoulder hurt like hell.

"It's not surprising, but you have muscles for brains too." Bryce tossed the instrument to one of the men. "I will explain what I did, Mr. Lane. If you ever think of escaping and you happen to succeed, what is in your shoulder will allow us, or anyone in Mr. Martinez's employ, to track you down. I know it's hard for you to grasp the concept, but that's what it does. It's more powerful magic, like the helicopter."

"What did you mean when you said that I am yours to sell?"

"Well, just that. I know these aren't foreign concepts to you. You ranchers do it all the time with your livestock. Consider yourself my livestock now." He winked at the other men. They all laughed again. "There's some rich dude in New York City who's going to fall in love with all those muscles." Bryce squeezed Zeb's biceps. "Not to mention your package."

While the rest was a mystery, Zeb did understand the concept of livestock....

*** 

"You want a horse, son, you gotta earn it. What you offerin' me?"

Zeb looked at his father, half hidden in the glare of the red orb on the horizon, his long hair blowing in the cold wind from the north. Lane's mare shuffled back and forth, the vapor from her nostrils streaming out like some ancient dragon's breath.

"I can do a lot more trappin', Pa. There's a big demand for real furs for the dandies in St. Louis. I figure they will take all I can deliver."

Lane dismounted. He handed the reins to Zeb.

"Not a bad idea. You're good at finding the right places to lay your traps. But I need you to keep up with your other work, too. Your sister and mother have all they can do around the ranch house."

"I can do all that needs to get done. Just name it. I only have to stretch my day a little."

"OK, I'll see what I can do. There's an auction in three weeks down in Cheyenne. You and I will take a little ride down there on Sally. Maybe you'll ride back with me on a new steed. But right now take this old mare to her barn and make her comfy for the night while I scout out what your Ma is cookin' for dinner."

Zeb led the mare away while Jesse Lane walked towards the house.

The trip to Cheyenne was an epiphany for Zeb. He had never seen so many people at one time together in one place. They had mounted huge TV screens above the auction floor so people could see the livestock and the bids on them no matter where they sat. He had never seen TV before.

"Believe it or not, this is nothing," said Jesse. They sat high in the bleachers that surrounded one of the livestock auction corrals. "World's probably still full of too many people. They just ain't here, that's all. Many are on our two coasts. I don't know about the rest. Used to be that the slant-eyes numbered in the billions. I don't know if they still do. I don't really care."

"Slant-eyes?"

"Chinks. Japs. All those Asian people."

"Why are they called slant-eyes?"

Jesse used his two index fingers to pull up the corner of his eyes.

"'Cause they look like that. I suppose they're God's people too, but there were billions of them, and they owned America."

"America?"

"Our whole country was called the United States of America. It fell apart because we weren't united enough, I guess." Jesse pointed to the arena. "Now there's a spirited one."

The conversation changed to horses when the auction began. The fat woman on the left side of Jesse participated enthusiastically. The older man waited patiently.

"What about that one?" Zeb asked once.

"He has a lazy look to him, son. You don't want a lazy steed. We're workin' people."

The tenth horse attracted his father's attention. It was taller than the average and a little skittish.

"Know anything about that one?" Jesse asked the woman.

"Comes from Parker's ranch. Ken Parker saddle broke him. Looks a little wild to me still, but Ken generally does a good job."

"I heard that the horse went lame a while back. Ken must be a good nurse too."

"You don't say."

The woman didn't bid on the horse. Two others did, along with Jesse. Zeb's father won the bid.

When they went down the bleachers to claim the horse, Zeb muddled over a new concept.

"I guess it's all right to lie when you want a good horse, right Pa?"

"I didn't lie. It's part of bartering. I made her think that the young horse wasn't as good as she might have thought originally. The horse did go lame while back. That's no big deal, but she thought so. If she really wanted him, she would have bid. So, truth be told, she really didn't want him." He clutched at Zeb's shoulder, nearly at the level of his own now, although the boy was only fifteen. "Wha'cha going to name him?"

"Jefferson. I think there was someone important named Jefferson once. I like the name."

"Actually, he was one of the first presidents of the United States of America. I can't remember which one, but he wrote something called the Declaration of Independence."

"Would he be insulted to have a horse named after him?"

Jesse Lane laughed his deep baritone laugh.

"Well, I think you'll just have to ask him that when you meet him beyond those Pearly Gates."

\*\*\*

They left Zeb alone with Wilson. He wondered if the man would try something, considering that Bryce had embarrassed him. Instead, he became talkative.

"I guess you're wondering what's happening to you?" he asked Zeb. There was a light but cold breeze still whipping through the room, but Zeb was upwind from the slovenly giant.

"You think? Am I just cattle to you people?"

"To Bryce, maybe. And not cattle. More like a stallion. You have family?"

"I did. The marauders killed them all."

"No shit! I'd hunt the bastards down and kill them. What we're doing to you is nothing in comparison."

Zeb strained at his bonds. They had strapped them on wet, so the leather was cinching up tight as they dried.

"I did go after them. You fellows killed them."

"Oh, those. We always take out them bastards when we can. They're animals."

"No argument there," muttered Zeb, feeling the irony. "Can you loosen the straps a little? They're cutting off my circulation."

Wilson checked and confirmed that. He started to adjust the bonds one by one. Zeb went into action when his right arm came free. A hardened fist hit Wilson in the solar plexus, taking the air right out of him. A mighty right cross paid him back for the earlier encounter.

Wilson went down for the count.

Zeb struggled to loosen the bonds on his left hand and feet, but soon he was free of the chair. He went to the door of the small room and peered out. A darkened corridor looked like it might lead to freedom. Still shirtless, he hurried to the door at its end, opened it, and looked out across a desolate landscape filled with run-down buildings and iron rails crisscrossing on the ground.

He wondered what happened to Jefferson. Without the horse, he wouldn't stand a chance of putting distance between him and his captors. He went from building to building, working his way across the area.

"Hold it!"

Zeb froze. One of Bryce's men had a rifle pointed right at him.

"Smart ass, aren't you? Bryce!"

Bryce came out of one of the buildings Zeb had already passed, rubbing his eyes but furious in spite of his sleepiness.

"Where's Wilson?"

Another of Bryce's men went to fetch Zeb's guard. The man was still groggy from Zeb's punch.

"Idiot!" Bryce shook him. "You almost lost this month's best take. You are one royal fuck-up."

"Sorry," mumbled Wilson. "It won't happen again."

Bryce drew his revolver and shot Wilson between the eyes.

"You're damn right it won't!" The others laughed but quieted when Bryce glowered at them. "Any of you that fucks up will get the same treatment." He went back to his cabin.

# Chapter Six

"Cal, I've known you for a few years now. I trust and value your opinions. How likely is it that these accidents are unrelated?"

Calvin Fuller, head of U.N.S.A. Security's Farside Office, watched his friend swing into her Yoga position, head on a thick pillow, feet and legs resting easily against the gym's wall. Her only attire was a monokini and an old U.S. silver dollar that usually rested between her breasts. It now rested on the pillow.

He was used to his friend's idiosyncrasies. While Looney attire was informal, Downy customs and religions still influenced Looney society. Scientists and support staff came and went, especially to Farside, where many projects and even some industries took advantage of the lighter gravity or the absence of light pollution from Earth.

However, the two of them were from Mars. Martian living was even more informal and was more in tune with a completely controlled artificial environment.

"Fortunately, I'm a happily married man," Fuller said. "Other Loonies might find this distracting. If you did this in Times Square, you'd certainly start a riot."

She laughed. "And who would start it? The men or the women?"

"Given New York City, hard to tell."

"Well, you should be used to it. Any ideas in regard to my question?"

Fuller hesitated while her thoughts returned to her childhood on the Red Planet....

\*\*\*

"Jenny, Jenny, where are you?"

She left the small room that served as the family bedroom for three people and study area for her.

"I'm doing my homework, Mother."

25

"Come! China Inc. is no more. There is rioting."

"Here? On Mars?"

The family had been listening for some time to the news that the infamous Chinese empire, that juggernaut of unrestrained fascist capitalism, was imploding. Multiple regions were declaring their independence. The split roughly corresponded to languages—the English of Hong Kong, the Mandarin of the north, the Cantonese of the south, and the Mongolian of the plains. However, there were even smaller divisions based on dialects of these major languages.

To Jenny it seemed like the gods had dropped an expensive porcelain bowl from some ancient dynasty, causing it to be shattered into pieces.

Her mother straightened the collar that covered her neck and patted down the rest of the gray, drab uniform she wore, habits long ago acquired in their haste to fit in as immigrants in the straight-laced society of China's most important colony. Jenny knew that to her way of thinking, the planet had gone mad.

Jenny's father rushed through the door, stopping when he saw them standing there.

"Please, what are you doing? We must leave. The rioting is more widespread. There are casualties. Do you understand? We must leave. People are already filling the tunnels in panic."

"Then why add to it?" asked Jenny. She assumed a martial arts pose. "I am ready to defend us."

Her mother laughed. "You cannot stop them, Mei-Xing. It's like when someone yells 'fire!' in a theater. The mob has a mind of its own. But where will we go?" The last question was directed at her husband.

"The university. I know some safe places. Hurry."

They were soon on their way, running when they could, but most of the time pushing through the flow of the crowds. Jenny was amazed at their actions.

Old timers were even stripping off their company uniforms and dancing in their underwear with the younger Martians. Many of the latter were completely naked. Her mother covered Jenny's eyes as they hurried by public orgies. Fights broke out when men went after women, men after men, and women after women. Emotions unleashed after decades of Puritan control trumped rational thought at every turn in the corridors.

Some corridors mercifully had lights knocked out. In others, someone would try to attack her mother. Her father did a good job of defending his wife, but Jenny also contributed.

At the university, her father had to beg to gain entry. The various levels of the university were calm and quiet compared to the craziness they had left behind.

"Are we safe here?" asked Jenny.

"We can only hope," said her father.

***

Fuller studied his colleague for a moment. She was a tall woman, her perfect figure hiding a muscle tone that was a weapon in itself. She looked to be more Latino than Chinese, her facial expressions at times carrying some of that intriguing indigenous mystery of a Bolivian or Peruvian.

Their common past, when the tsunami from the Chaos hit Mars, was nearly irrelevant. He decided he was more Looney now than Martian. He wasn't so sure about Wong.

*The world is such a melting pot now. And we're the better for it.*

The epicanthic fold of his eyes was more pronounced than hers. Yet his name was Fuller. The correlation between race and names was becoming weaker as the decades marched by. There were still bigots and racists, but most people largely ignored those with mental perturbations.

***

"I'm not a great believer in coincidences," Fuller finally responded. "I believe at least one of the accidents is murder."

"I'm here to think out of the box, so let me do so." She flipped out of the Yoga position with a push of her hands. She landed nimbly on her feet as if she were an Olympic gymnast, not easy to do even in the low gravity. "I need to connect to a work station that has access to all your databases."

"All? Even the scientific stuff?"

"Especially that. You know I'm cleared for everything dealing with U.N.S.A. I want to be free to explore any possible avenue."

27

"Well, good luck on understanding some of it. Many of the Farside projects are weird and esoteric. They make my head hurt and I'm constantly around them."

"I'll yell if I need help."

\*\*\*

It was three hours after her ship landed that Wong started to work. She did not stop until 53 hours and 22 minutes later when she buzzed Fuller's office. He let her in.

"Justin Bloch. He's your man. At least here. His handler Earthside is another question. We can sweat the name out of him."

"Bloch? He's one of our most trusted employees. He runs a tight ship over at Imports and Exports." Fuller's bushy eyebrows were dancing in surprise. "I find it hard to believe."

"It wasn't easy to track down. I made some calls. We also broke some old laws about medical records, I'm afraid, but they were Downy laws, not Looney laws." She plopped down in his guest chair and crossed those magnificent legs. "Bloch was blackmailed. The accidents started shortly after he returned from Earth after visiting his family. He's divorced but maintains a good relationship with his ex and their children." Her voice took on a sad timbre. "Monica Bloch, the oldest child, is dying from cancer. No one in the family could afford the super expensive drug needed to control it. For some reason, they now can. Believe it or not, the funds are routed here and then back to Earth. I can't trace their real origin."

"I hate to go after a man in those circumstances," Fuller said.

"Normally I'd say 'don't,' since I want the handler. Nonetheless, a murder was committed, Cal. While the handler is the real bad ass here, I can't exonerate Justin Bloch. Maybe we could turn him if we offered to pay for Monica's drug while he's in the slammer."

Wong saw that Fuller liked that idea. Bloch had an office down the hall from Fuller, so they decided to confront Bloch.

\*\*\*

After pleasantries, Fuller became all business.

"Justin, we know. We need the name of your handler."

To Fuller's astonishment, Wong leapt over Bloch's desk and grabbed his hand, not a spectacular feat in gravity one-sixth of Earth's, but a fine display of reflexes nonetheless.

She held his right arm immobile with her left hand while she used the right to pry the syringe out of his clenched fingers. She tossed the syringe across the office into a trash receptacle, another amazing feat considering that she instinctively had to recalculate that same parabolic trajectory in the weak gravity of Luna.

She knew Justin Bloch was a strong man but he cried all the same. Wong stood by him. She squeezed his shoulder, trying to comfort him.

"Want to tell us about it?" asked Fuller.

"They approached me on my last trip Earthside. They said they were from GenCorp and only wanted information. They'll kill my daughter if they find out."

"By cutting off her meds?"

They now understood. A GenCorp pharmacy subsidiary, GenMeds, still had thirty-seven years to go on the fifty-year patent for the drug Bloch's daughter was taking. The increase in worldwide patent times was yet another concession the big corporations obtained when they agreed to help hapless governments quench the looting, rioting, and vandalism associated with the Chaos. Monica Bloch would be dead before her cancer drug became generic.

GenCorp's CEO was the Argentine Fabio Martinez. It was the largest of the system-wide corporations. Martinez was probably the most ruthless of their CEOs.

"So, what were you giving them, Justin?"

"I want a deal. Otherwise, I'm not talking."

"There are ways to make you talk," Wong said.

"You can't torture me here. Luna is a U.N.S.A.-protected colony still."

Fuller looked at Wong with a frown. "I guess we could send him to Mars. They still work under many of the same old laws as the first Chinese colony."

"You—you can't do that!"

"I'm sure there's a big rig pulling out of LEO real soon," said Fuller.

"That's 'Low Earth Orbit' to you," said Wong.

"I know that! I may be ready to lose my mind, but I'm not stupid."

"So let's make a deal," said Wong. "We'll keep you from the needle and we'll make sure Monica is supplied with her drug. I don't think we can promise much more, right, Cal?"

Fuller shook his head.

∗∗∗

They appeared before the Luna colony's Farside Court two weeks later. During the interim Wong enjoyed being the house guest of Fuller and his partner, Jorge Leon Benavides, an astrophysicist working on dark matter, something that had baffled scientists for over a century.

They had Bloch's testimony that it was a case of industrial espionage. GenCorp only wanted information on one of U.N.S.A.'s top-secret research programs that was taking place at Farside. However, the panel of five magistrates threw that part of the case out since it was Bloch's word against an important and powerful corporation. Such were the ways of modern courts.

Wong was used to a court decision going the wrong way. She had learned to shrug it off. It wasn't her fault. She didn't count court decisions in her personal scoring system. In her opinion, no case had ever stumped her. She had a perfect record.

"I bet they know GenCorp is guilty," said Wong the night after the hearing.

"Of course they do," said Benavides, "and I'm inclined to disagree with the verdict. Bloch will spend thirty years of hard labor in Alaska and GenCorp gets off free. Life sure isn't fair."

"They used him," said Fuller.

"So did we," said Wong. "But it wasn't enough. I would like to bring GenCorp to its knees, but it isn't going to happen this time."

"Maybe some other time," said Fuller. "To your health, my friends."

They raised their glasses.

"To Monica," said Wong.

# Chapter Seven

"Say, aren't you a pretty one!"

Zeb picked himself off the floor of the cattle car. After a long trip in the helicopter, they had shoved him inside and locked the heavy door. He went to it. He kicked and shook it.

"Calm down in there," said Bryce from outside. "Save your strength, Zebediah. You'll need it. And don't go wasting your energy with the women. You don't know what kind of diseases they might have."

Zeb heard guffaws from the rest of Bryce's troop.

"He's so full of shit."

Zeb turned to face the woman. She was young, late teens or early twenties. The rest, a mix of fourteen men and women, sat on the floor of the car, backs against the opposite wall, their heads bowed.

They were in various stages of dress. Two women wore only shoes. Zeb figured this was not the moment to be embarrassed.

"I'm Zeb," he announced. "What is this place?"

At that moment, there was a thump and a lurch when they connected the car to a train. The screech of iron wheels on old tracks announced motion. The train left the siding. The smell of diesel permeated the car.

"My name's Sandra, short for Alexandra," the woman said when she recovered her balance. "This is an old train car and we're headin' down them old tracks straight to hell."

"Ain't no such place," said one of the women who wore only shoes. "This train's goin' to New York City."

"And you're...?"

"Bev." She scowled at Sandra. "Short for Beverly."

"How long will it take?" asked Zeb.

"A few days," said one of the men. He was dressed in a dirty cotton flannel shirt and underwear. He rose to his feet, adjusted to the swaying motion of the car, and crossed over to Zeb,

31

his hand outstretched. "Luke Johnson. Sandra, she be Alexandra Simpson. Bev, she be Beverly Pratt." Luke introduced the others. Some weakly nodded. None rose to shake Zeb's hand. "We're all tired," Luke explained. "We don't receive much food or water. Have anything to eat on you?"

Zeb pulled out some jerky from his pants pocket.

"It's all I have. You folks can have it. I had breakfast this morning. Uh, where do you do your business?"

Luke pointed to a corner of the car.

"There's a hole in the floor back there. Use the straw for cleaning if it's number two."

"Not much privacy for the ladies," Zeb commented.

Bev laughed. It was a dry laugh followed by a coughing fit. Zeb waited until she could speak.

"I don't think Bryce imagines a future for us as ladies. We'll be lucky if a pimp wants to take care of us as his whores."

"What do you mean?"

"She means that we're part of the skin trade," said Luke. "I've heard about it all my life but didn't know it was for real 'til now. That's what Sandra meant when she said we'd be going to hell."

Sandra punched Zeb lightly in his bare belly.

"Don't worry. You're quite the looker. You'll be taken care of."

"I don't want to be taken care of. I want to stay right where I am."

"I don't think any of us has any choice in the matter," said Luke. "We'll be sold in the underground marketplace." He pointed at the small wound on Zeb's shoulder. "And you can't run away. They'll always find you."

Zeb began to have a glimmer about what was happening to him.

*First, I lose my family and now this.*

He joined the rest sitting against the wall of the car opposite from the door.

"What if we jump them when they open the door to give us food?" he asked.

"They only put people in through the door," said Sandra, sitting down beside him. She pointed to the opposite end of the car from the makeshift lavatory. "They drop food and water through a hatch there. Not much food and the water's dirty, but we survive. They don't want us damaged too much."

The daylight that filtered through the slats in the old cattle car dimmed. They made no new stops. Night came and Sandra slept, resting her head on Zeb's shoulder. Bev stretched out, her head in Luke's lap.

"This must be hard on the women," whispered Zeb.

"I think they tolerate it better than we do. But we're all frustrated and depressed, to say the least."

\*\*\*

The next morning before the others stirred, Zeb removed his pants, ripped out the seams and, with his belt, hung the pants like a curtain, providing privacy for the makeshift bathroom. The women were appreciative. The men were stone-faced.

"You're a real gentleman," said Sandra. "Now, cowboy, if you could just find me a dress, I'd go to the dance with you."

The makeshift curtain fell down a couple of times, though, which brought guffaws from the men and Zeb's hurried repair.

"You be a little wet behind the ears?" asked Luke some time later.

"You mean innocent?" asked Zeb. "I suppose so. Only women I've ever seen in underwear were my mother and sister. I was taught to avoid the temptations of the flesh."

"Yeah, guessed that. You come from good God-fearing folk, I betcha. This has to be hard for you. But think of Pru over there. She's Mennonite, and still Bryce don't care any 'bout her feelings. We're all livestock to him." He spat on the floor of the car. "Ever I get the chance, I'm takin' out that evil SOB."

"Bryce? He hardly seems worth it."

"No, not Bryce. His boss. The big man. The devil behind all our misery."

"Who might that be?" asked Zeb. The car lurched again.

"Some asshole called Martinez. Sounds foreign to me. But them cities're all filled with foreigners."

"They're all God's children," said Zeb with conviction.

"Don't be a fool, boy. There's evil in the world." Zeb nodded. "We must have done something mighty bad to piss the Lord off this much."

"You have quite a tongue, old man."

"Call it experience."

\*\*\*

Night came again. The constant lurching of the car and metal-on-metal screech of its wheels made it difficult to sleep. Some of the group told stories or described their previous lives to pass the time. One woman sat off to the side, wringing her hands and singing nursery songs, all sanity fleeing into the lost nights of her captivity.

The car began to smell like a pigsty. Somewhere in the still hours before daylight the train stopped. The door opened. Several men with rifles looked in on them, frowning at the stench.

The group crowded to the opposite side of the car, afraid of the guns. Zeb, now down to his underwear, stood between his new friends and his enemies, daring the men to enter.

"Bath time!" said the apparent leader. The others laughed.

A man with only one eye entered the car, dragging a fire hose. He pointed it at the group.

"Let it rip, you mother-fuckers!"

The water was so cold it would have stung even without the high pressure. They all sunk to the floor.

Zeb reveled in the soaking. The water was clean and pure and carried away his aches and pains.

The others were not so appreciative nor took the bath very well. One woman, who had become sick during the night, drowned. When the water stopped, two of the men dragged her out of the car and threw her into an old trash bin.

It gave Zeb an opportunity to stick his head out and look around before they clubbed him into submission.

They were at a deserted train station. The sign announcing the train stop, rotting and swinging by one nail, said Topeka. He strained his eyes, looking into the dark for a way to escape. There was none.

When the train started again, Zeb wiped the blood away from the wound in his head. He asked where Topeka was. Luke shook his head. He had no idea.

# Chapter Eight

Jenny Wong returned to Earth with Bloch in tow. A quick hop from LEO and through customs and they were in the newest U.N.S.A. spaceport.

Nestled close to the old Colombian pueblo of Villa de Leyva, the new spaceport was only partially finished. She delivered her prisoner to U.N.S.A. Security and decided in favor of some R&R. The jumps through time zones and from space had caught up with her.

After a few hours sleep, Wong was summoned to the Director's office.

***

Dressed conservatively in a powder-blue day suit, Isha Bai looked like any other executive that worked in the new office-building complex at the spaceport. Although she was head of U.N.S.A., she was unfamiliar to Downies and Spacers alike, since she rarely appeared in public.

Among those that knew her, though, she was not always popular as she tried to balance her organization on the three-legged stool where Downies and Spacers were two of the legs and the huge Earth companies represented the third. While sometimes sensing that the stool was tottering one way or the other, it was nevertheless true that she wielded immense power in a world every day more dependent on raw products and spinoffs from space exploration. If people thought of her at all, they first thought of that power; they rarely thought of her origins.

The Indian subcontinent was now the most densely populated area in the world. Even the ravages of three major wars, two with the Muslims led by Pakistan and one with China, had not stopped population growth run amok. While modern technology permitted the average Indian family to dream their lives away plugged into the latest virtual reality channel, for the most part it was still squalor and filth they lived in.

She had been lucky. More than lucky. Blessed. That was the correct word. Her father had been a regional governor and amateur astronomer who was more than pleased that his only child had wanted to study astrophysics, although she was not the son he longed to have. He had been willing to make the sacrifices necessary to finance her early education.

She traveled to MIT at sixteen where she started her career with a double major in astrophysics and political science. She only returned to India for her father's funeral. At twenty-six, she had a PhD in astrophysics, a post-doc at Cornell, a law degree from Yale, and an MBA from Wharton. She then started her career in N.A.S.A. During her nine years at U.N.S.A., she had changed it into a powerful institution while the rest of the world struggled through the Chaos.

Bai's tactic during those years was to work closely with hundreds of companies, making sure that the agency was no longer dependent on donations from reluctant governments, something that had hobbled most U.N. agencies and the old space programs. The three-legged stool was at first much more stable than the original model with two legs. Recently, however, the leg corresponding to private industry seemed to be growing fatter and longer than the other two.

*Have I gone too far?*

Statistics for world industry universally gave credence to the now standard formula: every credit invested in space research and development came back a hundred-fold to the industries supplying the venture capital.

*But did they want more?*

Recently she had been working to tip the balance the other way, thinking that U.N.S.A. was in danger of becoming dependent on the companies that supported them.

*Have they decided that U.N.S.A.'s piece of the action was no longer necessary, not even for political correctness?*

\*\*\*

Denise Andersen was also with the Director.

"Good job on the Farside case," said Bai. "Unfortunately we don't have enough to go after Martinez."

"I'm sure he enjoys that. Am I interrupting something or is Senator Andersen here for something that relates to me?"

"I'm not here in my official capacity," said Andersen. "The Mid-Atlantic Union is too piss-poor to receive special treatment from U.N.S.A." She sat down, a surprising move since the woman was even taller than Jenny and towered above the diminutive Bai. Many type-A personalities would have used that height advantage to their benefit. "WorldNet, on the other hand, puts butter on your bread, Agent Wong. Are we clear on that?"

Bai indicated that Wong should sit. The Director followed suit. Wong noted that she didn't space themselves equally around the conference table. The Director sat closer to Wong so that they both faced Andersen.

"You answer my question first," said Wong. Isha Bai squirmed a little in her chair in reaction to the tone in her agent's voice. "Since I rarely eat bread, let alone put butter on it, your clichés not only sound old-fashioned, they leave me cold. Tell me what's on your mind, directly, and without veiled threats."

"My, aren't we edgy?" said Andersen. "Let me put what I said differently. I pump enough money into U.N.S.A. that I expect some return on that money. Take that as a threat if you want."

"No, not a threat," said Bai, "but way too strong since you have come to essentially ask Agent Wong a favor." She winked at Wong. "U.N.S.A. is not here at your beck and call, Senator. We accept the money you volunteer because I decided to build the relationship with the corporations in that manner. It guarantees you nothing and is based on mutual trust and benefit. You don't own a percentage of stock in a corporation called U.N.S.A. Is that clear?"

Andersen shrugged. "We are wasting time puffing ourselves up like strutting peacocks while the peahens are waiting to be fucked. We've already talked about what I want and it seems you agree." She looked from Bai to Wong and back. "Now we just need Agent Wong to go along."

"I said it might be a good idea," said Bai, "but my agent's decision is final."

"What are you proposing?" asked Wong. She was tired of the posturing of two powerful women. Her world was much simpler; there was no place in it for superegos.

"I have a crime problem in New York City. In other cities too, for that matter, but New York is critical. It's still the center of the universe. The Chaos has spawned gangs and other criminal elements that make a laughing stock out of my security forces. N.Y.P.D. is helpless. I need someone undercover that can at least provide timely intel to my security forces or N.Y.P.D. so we can achieve some semblance of order.

"I'm not a cop," said Wong. "I'm also not a mercenary. Besides, U.N.S.A. has no business becoming involved in local crime fighting."

"I beg to differ," said Bai. "Recently Denise lost a large shipment of drugs that would have helped many people. These were designer drugs that came from our R&D efforts in space."

Wong thought a moment. She could see all kinds of potential problems. She could also see dying patients. That most of these were rich—they couldn't afford the drugs otherwise—made no difference.

*There are good people that are rich.*

The problems had to do with success probabilities. She was not prescient, but she had a bad feeling about working with Denise Andersen. The woman was a huge character on the world stage. Her problems were bound to be huge too, much more complicated than any that Wong had previously tackled.

"It sounds dangerous. These people are vicious animals." Both Bai and Andersen nodded and waited while Wong mulled it over. "All right, I'll do it. Hopefully I don't have to act alone?"

"You can work with my security lead, Peter Bradford. Down in the trenches, you will need more help. I'm working on that."

"I'll work with him," said Wong, "but I have a veto. OK?"

Both Bai and Andersen nodded.

***

Wong didn't experience the hot sun. The visor of the radiation suit mitigated its glare and the suit's cooling system its heat.

She stepped carefully through the cemetery. It was old and run down, but here and there, she noticed a well-tended grave.

One range of the Andes loomed in front of her, the cemetery and its shadows a reminder that men's lives were but flashes in time compared to geological eons. In spite of the nearby radiation, the mountains were green and alive, contrasting with the death and devastation below.

Behind her in the distance was another chain of the Andes. Its peaks looked more mysterious since storm clouds were gathering there.

Here, if anything grew, it was often mutated and stunted. It was amazing that whoever took care of the well tended graves had been successful in finding some green plants and flowers. The cemetery was dry, dusty, and generally barren. It looked more like a film representation of Dodge City's Boot Hill than a cemetery that received lots of rainfall during the year due to its location only degrees from the equator. She imagined that during the rains it was mostly mud.

*Not much I can do about that*, she thought. *We often can't choose our last resting place.*

She was on the savanna of Bogota, that vast plain ravaged by the nuclear attack from Venezuela in 2078. She was sixty-three kilometers from the old city's center, ground zero for that attack. Millions of people had died. There was intel to suggest that a mistake initiated the crisis and that trigger-happy people on both sides continued the attack until it reached its horrible conclusion.

Nuclear non-proliferation was no longer part of the lexicon of international diplomacy. Though generally smaller now with the balkanization that was taking place during the Chaos, countries still had nuclear weapons if they could afford them. They had a sobering effect on most international saber rattling.

Wong assumed that it was only a matter of time until something like the Colombian-Venezuelan War or the second Indian-Pakistani War would happen again as Downy countries vied for influence and power. Maybe the smallness of the countries would keep the conflagrations localized.

*Hiroshima and Nagasaki were not enough. Will we ever learn?*

She found the grave, dropped her tools, and began to clean the debris away. She ended by brushing the dirt from the headstone, revealing the writing:

"Here lie Quon and Jing-Wci Wong, victims of the insanity of 2078. May they rest in peace."

It was in Spanish. She considered herself lucky. Others did not have any remains to bury.

When she finished she stood and said aloud a bit of Confucius philosophy that she remembered. That would please her grandparents.

His parents had disowned her father when he left for Mars for two reasons: He was disobeying them and he had impregnated a young girl that was Filipino and not Chinese. Wong discovered the whole story when she visited the old family farm near Vancouver. On a memory stick in an old desk in the condemned main house, she found the many video-mails from her father, received right up to the time her grandparents immigrated to Colombia to take part in its version of fascist capitalism pioneered by China Inc.

*My father didn't even know how his parents died. My personal world will be different. I will let all my descendants know who I am and what I stand for.*

She turned and headed back towards the jeep. She would soon be flying to New York and a new adventure.

# Chapter Nine

Upon arrival in the city, their captors left the car alone with some others on a lonely siding just across the East River from Manhattan. They passed a cold night there and were glad to see the weak sun filtering through the slats. It was not long before their captors came for them.

These men were others that had taken the place of Bryce's team. His rational mind told Zeb that this was a well-organized but evil operation. His emotions made him want to lash out and kill some of them.

*Good Lord, help me be strong!*

He felt like Samson, his strength sapped by the city, which had become his conniving Delilah. The journey had left him weak, hungry, and defeated. He could only imagine how the others were reacting.

The men loaded them onto a truck. Streets filled with stench and potholes brought them to a warehouse that had seen much better days. In the distance, Zeb could see the crumbling ruins of a huge stadium. Part of a huge sign was gone—he could only make out the letters Y-A-N-K followed by a huge gap and then the letters I-U-M. He supposed it was for city-sized rodeos.

The men herded them inside the warehouse. It had a concrete floor and several drains. They turned fire hoses on their captives again after ordering them to strip.

The stream of water hit Zeb and drove him back against the wall. Caught between it and the bricks, this time he stood and took the pummeling. He clenched his teeth—this time it hurt.

An additional contrast to the simple boxcar bath: men came up to him with long brushes and scrubbed him down with soapy water. Minutes later, they told him to turn around. By the time they finished bathing him, his skin was stinging and beet red.

They threw him a worn but clean towel.

"Get dry and put on the overalls that have your name sewn on the back."

Zeb found the overalls and put them on, still seething from the treatment. Some of the women were crying, as much from pain, he thought, as from shame and embarrassment. Others were stoic, if not numb. This time no one had drowned.

"OK, let's go."

They were herded into a huge area that reminded Zeb of the auction corral where he and his father had purchased Jefferson. There was even an auctioneer, but he wasn't very good.

*Out west, an auctioneer has talent and skills for his job. He enjoys it. This man is mean and incompetent to boot.*

He auctioned off the women first. They were required to shed their overalls and stand in line. They turned when the auctioneer asked them to turn. Like the livestock auction, there were large overhead screens that showed the bidders every square inch of their naked bodies. They sold Bev and the others quickly, but not Sandra. Bev was stone-faced and so was Luke.

"Too old for whores," the older man whispered. "They'll harvest the good body parts and sell them on the black market."

Zeb clenched his fists.

"That can't happen. I won't let it."

Luke restrained him.

"Don't do it, bro. You'll be bringing a heap o' trouble down on yourself."

They chose Luke to join the body parts group too. Zeb watched in numb shock while they herded the group of older men and women away.

Sandra went next. There was a lively bidding until a pimp bought her. When he led her away, she smiled back at Zeb.

"See you in hell, big boy."

The pimp jerked on her leash to silence her.

It was now Zeb's turn. The auctioneer came up to him.

"I'm going to say it only once, boy, and you'd better do what I say." He brandished a taser. "Out of your overalls and stand with your hands on your hips."

"Make me."

The taser waved close to his chest.

"This could stop your heart, you know. It's old, and I don't know the exact setting. Shall we try?"

Zeb unzipped the overalls and let them drop to his feet.

"Now here," said the auctioneer into the mike, "is a fine stallion that needs taming by a sturdy gentleman or a strong woman not afraid of a package this size." He pointed to Zeb's genitals. "Still a virgin, as far as we know, and ready to be mounted." He smacked Zeb in the gut. "Hard like a rock, this boy is too good to be used for body parts. He belongs in your own personal stable. Bidding starts at 5000."

While many participated at first, the bidding finally reduced to a duel between a tall woman that smiled frequently at Zeb, licking her lips occasionally, and a much older man who spent his time glowering. When it reached 17,700, the young woman folded.

"Put your overalls back on," the auctioneer whispered to Zeb. "You now belong to Mr. Maxwell Holland." He put a collar around Zeb's neck and cinched it down, led Zeb over to his new owner, and handed him the leash. "Your purchase, Mr. Holland. Pay at the desk on your way out."

Holland's head barely came to Zeb's shoulder. He patted Zeb on the arm after taking the leash.

"We'll be just fine," Holland said unctuously. "Come, we need to find you some new clothes."

***

At first, life with Holland wasn't bad. The older man let Zeb become accustomed to his new home, a large three-level penthouse at the top of one of Manhattan's skyscrapers. It was an old building, but stately and in fine condition.

Security guarded the building lobby. Even Holland had to identify himself. Zeb watched closely when his owner let the sensor read the imprint of his index finger. The man also bent down to receive the retinal scan.

"Shall we register your guest?" asked the security guard with a leer.

"No. My friend will be staying upstairs with me for a while. He's recovering from a strenuous journey from the Midwest."

The guard winked at his colleague. "Well, if he needs to go out alone, please remember to register him."

Upstairs Holland introduced Zeb to his staff—a butler, three maids, and a cook. Zeb learned about them during the days that followed.

The butler, Arthur, was nearly as wide as he was tall and never smiled. All three maids, Roberta, Jena, and Tracy, were youthful and pleasant women in both appearance and bearing. The cook, Rene, was a tall, thin fellow who smiled a lot, especially when one of the maids pulled one over on Arthur.

The three maids were day workers. Arthur, Rene, and now Zeb, were live-ins. Zeb had a small cot in Rene's quarters and an upside-down wooden box that he used for a nightstand.

At first Zeb applied himself to get on everyone's good side, not because he liked anyone particularly, but because he was a guest in Holland's house. He used his strength or size to make their jobs easier. He was never one to be lazy.

***

Zeb also looked for any possible means of escape.

It was not going to be easy. When Holland was not at home, Arthur chained him to a rung in the kitchen floor and made him help Rene. Most of the time that reduced to chatting with the Canadian. Rene taught him some French; Zeb corrected his English. They became friends.

Zeb had no use for Arthur. He fawned over Holland when he was in the penthouse. During those times, Arthur locked Zeb in Rene's quarters.

Arthur also locked up the youngest of the maids, Jena and Tracy, when he caught them looking through a keyhole at Zeb in the shower. After calling them sluts and berating them for their lusty thoughts, they laughed at him, which made the man even angrier. Zeb counted all three maids as his friends, but his thoughts about them were not lusty.

For the time being, it wasn't a bad life. Much better than the old boxcar.

He watched and waited.

# Chapter Ten

Wong took the hypersonic from Villa de Leyva to Singapore and then on to New York. Many of the teeming billions of Downies made less in a year than what the ticket cost, but U.N.S.A. would not even blink at the price.

The plane followed a porpoise-like trajectory at the edges of the upper atmosphere, skipping in and out of it after initially jetting out to a height of about 60 kilometers. With an average speed of Mach 10, it was the fastest way to complete a journey.

The Singapore origin gave her the cover of an Asian businessperson. She looked the part and was, for the rest of the world, Dr. Jenny Wong, Director of Marketing for one of Denise Andersen's Asian subsidiaries. It allowed her easy access to the Andersen enclave.

It was not particularly convenient, however, for developing her alter ego as an unscrupulous merchant of death. Anyone that knew Andersen could imagine that the tycoon could surround herself with such people. It was hard to imagine, though, that Andersen would allow a competing beauty crawl her way up the corporate ladder.

Five weeks later Wong knew she was ready to start the job she had come to do.

***

The East Side docks had changed a lot over the years but the area was still seedy. Customers found the whorehouses in the best shape since they still were doing a brisk business in spite of the fact that there was little ship traffic. Airfreight pilots that landed in the enlarged La Guardia Airport replaced the sailors.

Some neighborhood residents lived in nearby towers that stretched many stories above and below ground level. Others were homeless and eked out a living prowling the streets and sleeping where they could.

She walked slowly along the pathway just inside the towering dike they had constructed years ago to keep the rising waters of global warming out of Manhattan. Its role was no longer so essential, but it was easier to leave it up than spend money to tear it down. It remained a monument to both man's ingenuity and his foolishness.

The pathway, now overgrown with weeds and littered with garbage, was once part of a green park and walkway for lovers, children, and the elderly, when they enjoyed the sights and sounds of vendors hawking their wares on a summer night. Now, with the moon lost behind the dike, it was dark and foreboding.

Between one step and another, five men and three women surrounded her. One of the men, dressed in black, was facing her directly. Bald with bushy eyebrows and a goatee, he looked like a medieval portrayal of the devil.

"Jason Schwartz?" asked Wong.

"Who's asking?"

The circle closed tighter.

"Jenny Wong."

Schwartz waved his hand and the group relaxed.

"Come with me."

***

At 54<sup>th</sup> Street, they headed into Manhattan. After a few blocks, the group stopped in front of a warehouse.

"Check it out," growled Schwartz.

One of the men gave a kick to the door above the knob. The hasp's screws jumped out of the rotting wood and the rusty lock fell to the ground. With another kick, the door flew open. The kicker and one of the women went inside.

In moments, they returned.

"All clear," said the woman.

"After you, Jenny Wong," said Schwartz.

They found some candles and barrels and the members of the tawdry group made themselves comfortable.

"So," said Schwartz, taking out a knife that he used to clean his nails, "if your deal sounds as good as you look, we can do business. You weren't very specific, though."

"I want thirty per cent," said Wong.

"Depends on how risky it is."

46

"I can give you precise information on shipments coming into New York City from LEO via the various spaceports. Shipments that will bring you a lot of money on the black market."

"What about Colombia? A lot of the good stuff comes in through that new spaceport now. You have that info too?" Wong nodded. "So, Jenny Wong, I have a question. Our connections to the black market have recently been severed." Schwartz put the knife away. "Why don't you just get the drugs and sell them yourself?"

Wong smiled. She had worked hard to sever those connections. The gang was hungry. Moreover, it made the plan more palatable if they had to steal the WorldNet shipments and then sell them right back to WorldNet. Andersen would have to pay the difference between wholesale and black market price, but at least the drugs would still find their way to needy patients.

"I don't have anyone to steal the drugs. I do have the black market connections, though. A little scramjet company based at La Guardia. They're quite competent."

"Sounds easy. Make it twenty-five and it's a deal. I presume you're keeping part of the black market profits, so that seems fair."

Wong nodded.

"I'll even go down to twenty, but with one small condition."

"Ah, always the caveats. I don't like them."

Wong saw that even with that comment, Schwartz realized that she was making him an enticing offer.

"I don't give a fuck what you like. Do you know how many gangs I can go to?"

"Not if you want to leave here."

It was not an idle threat and Wong knew it. She looked around the group.

"While I'm fairly certain I could take all of you—" She was amused as all the thugs bristled. "—I'm too smart to come here without insurance."

She opened her fist, showing a vial.

"And what's that?" asked Schwartz.

"You might call it a designer drug. It's artificial but modeled after a neurotoxin assassins used to harvest from small tropical octopi. If I break this vial, you will all be dead in seconds."

"Ah, mass suicide. So romantic."

47

"I said it was a designer drug. There is a bioengineered antidote and I've already taken it." She looked around the group. "Care to hear my condition?" Schwartz shrugged, still looking at the vial. "I want part of the action. Five per cent on everything you do. Robberies, smuggling, prostitution, protection—the works."

"You should have taken over the Sharks. Five per cent is easy. You're asking for very little."

She tossed him the vial, which he caught.

"I don't want to take over. I'm not a leader. You're the leader. I just want a piece of the action."

He held up the vial, studying it in the candle light. He smiled.

"This is probably just water, right?"

"You'll never know until you break it."

***

When she returned to her hotel, Wong called room service and celebrated with a real bottle of 2031 merlot and a medium well steak. She knew she was lucky to be alive. Although she was calm, she remembered the apprehension she had experienced in Director Bai's office.

*Jenny, old girl, this case may be too big for you.*

## Chapter Eleven

"Has he buggered you yet?" Rene asked late one night.

Zeb helped him put away some crystal brandy sniffers on the top shelf of the bar's storage unit.

"Buggered?" he asked. The word was new for him. Rene spoke a peculiar form of English with a heavy French Canadian accent.

"*Mon ami*, do you know why you're here?" continued Rene.

"I have some idea. Mr. Holland keeps referring to me as his stallion. I don't know how things work in New York City, but am I going to be used for Roberta, Jena, and Tracy's pleasure?"

"Don't they wish! *Mon dieu*, you're an unsuspecting lout. Didn't you folks out in the hinterlands ever screw around?"

"Yes, if you're asking if we have sex. How do you think we have children?"

Rene handed Zeb the last of the crystal.

"Let me educate you to the ways of the wicked world, at least to the culture here in New York and every other big city as well, I imagine." Rene invited Zeb to sit with him at the kitchen table while the Canadian pushed away some provisions that he had already purchased for the next day. He plunged a carving knife into the old tabletop, making the cowboy jump, and perched on a stool, which put him at the same height as Zeb. "Max Holland owns all of us, *lache infame*. We're part of the underground slave trade going on here, but no one talks about it since, in general, it's not a bad deal." Zeb watched while Rene withdrew the knife from the wood and tested its edge. "In your case, however, it's a complete disaster."

"What do you mean?"

"*Monsieur* Holland, upstanding member of New York's City Council, which likes to think it has some say in the anarchy that's city government here, Mr. Holland is the most despicable faggot you can imagine. His only desire is to bugger and be buggered by a beautiful man-mountain like you. In other words, have sex with you, my friend."

"Sex with me? That isn't possible. I hardly have the right plumbing."

Rene broke into laughter that ended up in a coughing fit. He was not a well man.

"Oh, you have the plumbing, all right," the cook finally said, "exactly the kind he likes. Until he ruins you like his previous sex toy." Rene stood and bent over, pointing to his ass. "Right there in the old bunghole, Zeb. He ripped the guy apart. The only thing they could do afterwards was sell him for body parts."

"How does that work, the body parts thing?" asked Zeb, thinking of his old friends from the train.

Rene shrugged, sat again, and made a grimace.

"They harvest what's working for the rich people when their organs fail, then euthanize you, if you're not dead already, and grind you up for pig food. You see, the cloners can't keep up with the demand."

"Good lord! My friends!"

"Pig food. All of them. Hardly anyone can afford transplants anymore, only the rich." He contorted his face into a sneer. "And only they can afford to eat real meat." Zeb turned a light shade of green. "Hey, I don't make the rules," said Rene, noting his friend's discomfort. "At least we're alive."

"It sounds like there are no rules. Enlighten me."

So Rene told Zeb about the Chaos, how tribalism had broken down old political units like France, Italy, and the United States into much smaller ones limited in most cases to those individuals that shared the same world view, be it religious, racist, or some other cultural glue. Those individuals, in general, did not tolerate diversity within their unit.

Zeb thought of all the different sects and creeds in the center of the country and how the marauders used their lack of organization and limited demographics to rob and plunder at will. He told Rene what had happened to his family.

"Sorry about that, *mon fils*. It's not as bad here. Lots of gangs and other shit going on, but the big corporations have the firepower to keep the situation somewhat in control. After all, they need markets for their products."

Late one evening when Rene had the night free, stoic Arthur came to Rene's quarters. Zeb was stretched out on the cot reading a book from the library, a pass-time he preferred to the mindless material on the internet feeds. It was beyond him how these people could have such wonderful technology and use it in such a mindless and unproductive fashion.

"Put these on," Arthur said, tossing Zeb some silk pajamas.

Zeb held up the pajamas. They were black and had a shine to them. He rubbed the material. He had never touched anything so wonderful.

"Why?" he asked.

"It's time for you to earn your keep," announced the butler. "You're sleeping with Mr. Holland tonight."

"No, I won't do that," said Zeb, recalling the chat with Rene. "I can't."

"I had a hunch you wouldn't."

Before Zeb could react, Arthur reached over and stunned him with a taser. Paralyzed and twitching, Zeb could do nothing when the fat man undressed him and put the pajamas on. He slung Zeb over one massive shoulder and carried him away.

***

The architect had dedicated the entire third floor of Holland's penthouse to the master bedroom suite, dressing closets, and master bath. The Councilman was in the tub.

"I left him in the bed, sir. I have sedated him slightly. Enjoy."

Holland was moving one of his toy battleships within range of the other while he played in the water, its temperature kept constant as long as he cared to bathe. He soon tired of the battleships and stood to look at his dripping body in the wall mirror across from the tub.

The pills he had taken and the injection placed at the base of his penis were already producing a satisfactory erection. He had been looking forward to this evening ever since he had purchased Zeb.

He dabbed *eau de cologne* at several key spots on his obese body. He combed his gray hair, parting it down the middle just so, and studied the results. Putting on a fluffy white bathrobe, he patted down his thick eyebrows, firm in the belief that he was ready for his stallion.

Arthur had left the lights just right—dim, but bright enough to see the hunk that was waiting for him. He ached with anticipation.

He rolled Zeb over. He was a small and wiry man, but strong. He dropped Zeb's legs over the edge of the bed and lowered the black pajamas. Spreading the cheeks apart, he prepared to enter the drugged giant.

He figured that once Zeb was used to it, they could become quite the twosome. Or not. It was immaterial to him. Zeb was only property, something you used until you wore it out.

\*\*\*

At the first touch from Holland's penis, Zeb repressed a shudder. When the man attempted entry, Zeb reached back and grabbed with his left hand. Twisting around, Holland fell to the floor and Zeb was on Holland, his swollen member in hand. The right hand came down in a sweeping arc.

Zeb knew that Holland saw the flash of steel. He wanted the Councilman to know. It was too late for him to do anything. Zeb had found the scissors Holland used to trim his dapper little goatee.

"I hope there's a special place in hell for you, Mr. Holland," Zeb gasped as he buried the scissors into the man's chest.

Even in the dark, Zeb could see the surprise etched for eternity on the man's face. He grimaced, pulled up his pajamas, and raced out the door.

His plan had troubled him. He had never killed another human being and thought he would be condemned to eternal damnation. However, he decided to risk it, remembering Luke and the others.

Men like Holland were supporting the skin trade. He guessed that being a faggot was not wrong by itself, although he couldn't remember the preacher back home ever discussing gays or the skin trade. For him, moral outrage had trumped moral ambiguity: Holland was an exploiter, a cancer feeding on the body politic.

*Sometimes the Old Testament God is better than the New. I could never forgive Max Holland. I hope that God forgives me for usurping his vengeance.*

\*\*\*

Arthur was listening to the opening strains of Tchaikovsky's Sixth in the large library when Zeb entered the room. He reached for the taser but was too late. Zeb took it out of his hand and the big man shrunk away. His eyes were focused on the blood covering the pajama top.

"What have you done?"

"God help me, what should have been done long ago, I think. Now, since Rene is not here, you have to perform some surgery." Zeb tossed the scissors to Arthur, who turned white at the touch of the tacky blood. "As you probably guessed, Mr. Holland is dead. If you don't want to follow him into hell, you will take the homing device out of my shoulder." Zeb pointed to the scar. "It's buried there."

Arthur backed away.

"I can't do that. I hate the sight of blood."

Zeb threatened him with the taser.

"It will be easier with one of Rene's sharp paring knives. Can I trust you? You have no choice, you know, if you want to live."

Zeb grabbed the man by the collar and dragged him, sputtering and gasping for breath, to Rene's kitchen. He made his selection and handed Arthur a small knife.

The device was not deep and was buried in muscle. He took the pain in stride, mentally savoring it like a spiritual cleanser, a partial punishment for taking the life of another human being. He doused the wound, which didn't bleed all that much, with some of Rene's fine cooking wine. He tied Arthur's hands and feet with cords that he jerked out of several electrical appliances.

When he was finished, he held a much larger carving knife under the butler's chin.

"Why did you help him, Arthur?"

"Fear. He was a monster. A monster in upscale packaging. I went with the flow."

Zeb nodded.

"Which is why I won't kill you. Good luck, Arthur." He slammed the knife into the kitchen table with such force that the handle cracked. He hoped Rene would see the message and start a new life.

Zeb returned to the third level and rummaged around for something suitable to wear. He was surprised there were clothes his size and shoes that fit.

*One of Holland's previous victims must have been close to my size,* he thought. He shuddered to think of their fates. *What kind of world is this? How am I going to live in it?*

The penthouse had its own elevator on the third level. Zeb figured out how the buttons worked and was soon out of the building, a criminal on the run in a city he didn't, and couldn't, understand—at least not yet. Survival required that he learn very soon.

# Chapter Twelve

Peter Bradford and Jenny Wong were VR participants in a meeting between them and Denise Andersen when Wong reported on a future robbery that the Sharks would carry out. Its purpose was to give the gang confidence in Wong while the U.N.S.A. agent continued to map out the dark corners of the underworld where the gang's tentacles reached.

Wong's VR image flickered often since the unit she used was a portable one she carried, passing it off as being keen on some VR games. Together with sex and drugs, the VR games were an addiction gang members often had while they lived the high life off their spoils. Thus, the VR also served as part of her cover.

"Can we protect our guards in all this?" asked Andersen.

Wong held up a grenade.

"The Sharks will be told it is nerve gas. I will convince them it's much more effective than guns and knives. We need Peter to make sure the guards can play dead."

"What if they test for pulses?"

"Unlikely," said Bradford. "Some of the leaders are smart, but generally the gang members are dumb, uneducated bullies. The play acting should be enough."

Wong studied Bradford, a nagging worry tugging at her thoughts. *How can he be so sure?*

"OK, let's go with it. But be careful."

***

The gang members waited while Jason Schwartz tested the door. He shook his head so Wong picked the old 20<sup>th</sup> century lock. She pushed the door open slightly.

"A woman of many talents," he whispered.

"And you'll only see a small sample." She winked at the other gang members and some snickered. She pulled down her mask and everyone followed suit.

Schwartz started a countdown with his hand. At three, they burst into the warehouse. The leading gang members threw the grenades. They exploded in silence, filling the building with a thick, dense fog.

They found the first guard immediately.

"Looks dead," said Schwartz. He looked at Wong. "But let's make sure." He put a gun to the man's head.

"Wait!" hissed Wong. "There may be security alarms that go off with loud noises."

"Good thinking." Before she could stop him, Schwartz took out a knife and buried it into the man's chest. Blood spurted bright red and flowed onto the dirty cement floor where it turned a dark maroon. "Well, I'll be damned! Looks like he wasn't dead after all."

***

Wong had little time to feel bad for the victim as the Sharks began to circle her.

"Looks like your grenades just don't do the trick," said Schwartz, removing his gas mask. "I wonder why?"

"How did you know? Peter Bradford?"

"At your service," Bradford said, stepping into the circle of light from their flashlights. He smiled at Wong. "Duplicity can work both ways." He nodded at Schwartz. "I killed the other guards. Kill her and let's get what we came for."

Wong, who was standing close to Schwartz, tossed grenades at Bradford and then head-butted the gang leader in the stomach. She grabbed his gun and disappeared into the dark of the fog.

"Shoot the bitch," yelled Bradford, wiping the stinging mist from his eyes.

None of them had counted on her speed. She was safe for the moment though the gang fanned out to look for her.

However, Schwartz was inventive. He ran to the power box. Soon all the warehouse lights with functioning bulbs were blazing, dispelling both the darkness and fog.

The firefight that ensued was over quickly. Wong knew she was outnumbered. She was also bleeding profusely from a shoulder wound and many tiny cuts and scratches from the splinters scattered by bullets hitting old wooden crates. They offered little protection against the gang's firepower.

As she went from crate to crate, taking a shot here and a shot there, she knew she would soon be too tired from loss of blood to run anymore. She then saw a door. It was worth a try.

She shot off the lock and stumbled into darkness. She was in an old alleyway filled with refuse. Several times she fell to her knees while she searched for a main thoroughfare.

The alley was dark—a delivery van that was unloading produce for a restaurant blocked the entrance. She squeezed by the van and found herself on a dimly lit street filled with run-down restaurants, bars, porn shops, and other establishments that served the city's less desirable late night residents. She crashed into a couple that were making out under an old street light that came to life sporadically.

"Hey!" objected the man. "Watch where you're going, bitch."

"Shut up, Randy. Can't you see she's bleeding?"

Wong looked up at them and smiled.

"I'd appreciate it if you called some EMTs," she said.

The man hesitated but the prostitute was helpful. Wong gave her a number she had memorized.

*Pessimistic premonitions about future failure are always good for something.*

# Chapter Thirteen

.

"Have anything to drink?"

Zeb looked up and to the side, towards the voice. He was sitting between two trash bins on the three-century-old cobblestones of an alleyway, his back against the wall of a condemned eight-story apartment building. A mix of old neon and modern 3D laser advertising out in the street painted him with randomly varying harsh colors, its rapid intermittency enough to make any weak-minded person epileptic. Across the way, a broken pipe spewed raw sewage that added to the odiferous stew that was the oppressive night air.

The rising moon was behind the woman, its wane light nearly vanquished by man's creations. He couldn't make out her features, but she had a nice voice. He offered her the plastic bottle he had filled with water.

She drank and then spit it out.

"You bastard! This isn't whiskey."

"Sorry. I thought you wanted water."

She continued to curse as she sat down beside him. He looked sideways at her, the moon now blocked by one of the bins. She looked older than he was, but it was hard to tell. Her matted hair, dirty face, bare feet and torn clothes reminded him where he was. He cleaned his hands off on his pants, rubbed the sleep from his eyes, and offered a hand.

"Zeb, Zeb Lane. Last night I became a new resident of New York's underground. I think that's what it's called."

She put a finger to her lips and looked up and down the alley.

"Never admit to that. There are vultures here that will pick your bones while you're still alive if they think you don't know the ropes." She shook his hand. "Maria Elena Hakim. I ran away from my foster family."

"You left a family? Are you crazy?"

He yearned for the simpler times with his family when his main worry was doing the chores and trapping enough to pay for the few luxuries in his life. Too many years ago.

"No, because my foster father started raping me when I was twelve. I've been on the street nine years." She brushed at her dirty shirt as if her aspect embarrassed her. "By now I know how to survive. How about making a pact?"

"What kind of pact?"

"I'll give you ball-busting sex if you keep a certain vicious pimp away from me."

Zeb laughed.

"I understand the first part but not the second. Can you translate?"

"You're kidding. Where were you born? On Mars?"

"Wyoming. A long way from here."

She considered that.

"All the same to me. Wyoming, Mars—they're sounds without meaning. Nevertheless, I'll take your word for it that it's far. It must be if you don't know what a pimp is." She crossed her legs, which he could see were muscular under the grease and caked dirt. "This pimp, he has a stable of women that he owns. They have to go out on the street looking for johns—" She saw his puzzlement. "—customers or clients to you, and bring back money they receive for having sex."

"Prostitutes," said Zeb, "you're prostitutes."

She looked offended.

"Not me, bush man from unknown lands, and I don't want to ever become one. This guy, Rafael, he treats his whores really bad, always beating up on them, especially if they don't bring back enough money."

"It's almost biblical," said Zeb. "Such women were shunned way back then, but Christ showed them the error of their ways and brought them redemption."

"Oh, shit, I have a religious nut here. I suppose you can't and won't fight for me at all. So just turn the other check when they stick the knife into you. You're going to last maybe a day on these mean streets. I'm sorry. Nice knowing you."

She stood. He pulled her down.

"I once was religious, but never crazy. Now I only believe that God has forsaken this world, letting it go to the forces of evil. And I myself have become evil."

"You're so full of shit!" She punched him playfully in the chest. "So, will you fight for me? Be my insurance policy?"

"Before I agree," he said with a smile, "tell me what that means."

"I'm damn good at running and hiding, but if Rafael ever finds us, will you stand up to him?"

"Oh, that, sure. I don't have much to live for."

"I'm not asking you to die for me, idiot." She smacked her right fist in her left palm for emphasis. "I'm asking you to kill Rafael."

"If I can, I will. He sounds like someone that should be killed. I have experience with such people."

She took out pieces of bread and slices of cheese from inside her shirt, giving Zeb a peek at her breasts. He decided the loose shirt did not do them justice. She broke off the moldy parts and tossed them away before sharing the rest with him.

"We'll scrounge up some real food tonight when the restaurants start taking out the garbage. But now, tell me about yourself, Mr. Zeb Lane."

***

He told her, starting with the marauders and how they killed his family, the helicopter people, the trip to New York City, the auction, and Max Holland's perversion. She squeezed his hand at the end.

"Brother, you've had a tough time. I'm a New Yorker through and through, but you must feel completely lost. Don't worry, though." She gave him a peck on the cheeks. "I'll show you the ropes." She brushed away the bread and cheese crumbs and sat in a lotus position. "Do you know where you are now?"

"New York City."

"Zeb, New York City is so big that we divide it up into parts. You're on the island of Manhattan, the part called the West Side. Max Holland probably lived close by, though it's not the posh area it once was." Zeb saw the dark eyes scanning the alley when she spoke. "When the Chaos started, there were lots of riots, fires were set by accident or on purpose, looting occurred, and some buildings became burned out shells. But we still consider it good real estate, especially if you can find a building that has security guards. I'm here because Rafael's girls work more to the south and on the East Side, across 5$^{th}$." She looked off into the distance and sniffed. Zeb thought he saw a tear. "In between us and them are gangs. Rafael's a damn coward and doesn't want to tangle with them, but I do. My sister was mutilated by them."

"Your sister?"

"She and I were in the same foster family, but she was only nine when my foster father started fucking me at night. I knew when she was twelve he'd be fucking her, so we had to get away." Again, the nervous scanning. "One night a gang chased us. Silvia couldn't run as fast as I could. They took her, gang-raped her, and mutilated her. They were like a pack of wolves."

Zeb shuddered. He took her hand.

"We have something in common, then. Maybe I should look for this gang. It would be therapeutic to destroy them since I couldn't destroy the marauders."

She studied his strong face, scared of the hateful timbre of his baritone.

"I think you need to learn more about self defense, friend. Did you hear me say they're like wolves?"

"I used to trap and kill wolves," muttered Zeb.

"Not this kind. These have human cunning. Soulless creatures of the night, but they still have human cunning." She shook her head. "Don't misunderstand me, like I said, I'm all for avenging Silvia. But we have to do it proper. Do you know anything about guns?"

"Plenty."

"Good. We'll find some guns and you can teach me how to shoot. I'll then teach you how to street fight. With your strength, you should be able to kill a man with a well placed blow to his chest that stops his heart." She stretched out on her back. "Now, I'm going to take a nap. You should too. We've been running all night." She winked at him. "And when I wake up, maybe we'll see about that ball-busting sex."

"That's not necessary," he said, embarrassed by the fact that he hardly knew the woman, although she already seemed like an old friend.

"Don't speak for me, asshole."

Maria Elena turned on her side and was soon asleep.

# Chapter Fourteen

"You're not bailing out on me, are you?"

Denise Andersen could see that her smile annoyed Jenny Wong the moment she stepped into the office. The CEO of WorldNet stood and looked out at the gray city, not pleased at the vision of death and decay. The smile disappeared.

*I know your kind, Jenny Wong. Ever so practical, yet the world can still slap you in the face. Your nobility is something to behold.*

"No, but you and I have to rethink how to handle this. My plan wasn't successful. Moreover, thanks to Bradford, my cover is blown. Have any ideas?"

Andersen sat down again, fed up with the wickedness of the city.

"I'm working on it. Take some days off and get some R&R." She opened a drawer, rummaged around, and then tossed Wong a travel kit. "A ticket and directions to my chalet in Switzerland. Very close to the Martinez chalet, by the way, if that amuses you. I'd like to smash that bastard. He uses the gangs, you know."

"Anything that makes him money is fair game," agreed Wong. Andersen felt uncomfortable as Wong's eyes bore into her. "I guess greediness is relative."

"Oh, I know what you're thinking, but I'm not greedy. For me, it's just a power trip. I have more than enough money to satisfy my needs." She licked her lips suggestively. "I can swing either way, you know."

"Not my type."

"Why not?"

"Because I can imagine that even that is a power trip for you."

Andersen thought a moment.

"You may be right. But I can try to change."

"Yes, you can. But I'm not in the business of being your therapist. Or dominatrix. "

"You may live to regret it."

"In this business I may not live long and my life moves at such a pace that I don't have time for regrets."

Andersen stood and squeezed her arm.

"Enjoy the chalet. Come see me when you return."

"If I come back."

"You will. You don't have a rep for taking defeat lightly."

Andersen watched in good humor when Wong did a little about-face and left the office.

\*\*\*

Jenny Wong wasn't timid about her skiing. It had snowed and a new layer of powder provided perfect slopes for the sport. The sun was out. It wasn't even that cold.

She zoomed down the mountain, enjoying the thrill as much as any Downy skier, even with the tightness in her shoulder.

*Gravity can be useful.*

Coming down even faster on her left was a tall and slender man. He passed her as if she were standing still but gave her a quick wave with the ski pole.

"Show-off!" she yelled at him.

Truth be told, she had trouble adjusting to the gravity. The hospital stay had given her back her Mars legs but not her Earth legs. Skiing on the sand dunes of the Red Planet was too similar. She slowed down, not willing to risk a broken leg or ankle.

The wind had also picked up. By the time she finished her run, she was tired and cold and much in need of hot refreshment. She checked her skis and headed into the lodge.

"I haven't seen you around here before," a man said when she ordered a coffee with a dash of Jameson's at the bar. "That sounds like a terrible pick-up line, but I'm curious."

She turned to study the stranger and then shook the offered hand.

"Brent Mueller," he said. "On vacation."

"Jenny Wong," she said. "In recuperation."

"Mental or physical?"

"Both, but I don't want to bore you with details."

63

"Just an observation: You're tall. You could derive more speed if you leaned into the slope."

"Ah, you're the crazy man that flew past me in reckless abandon."

"Like I said, I'm on vacation. I like to have fun when I'm on vacation. If you have money, you can have lots of fun with the Downies." He threw down some bills. "I don't have a lot of money, but I'll apologize for showing you up by paying for your drink. Waiter, make mine the same."

Jenny watched while the robot bartender prepared another coffee like hers.

"Downies? I take it you don't spend most of your time on Earth."

"Only on some vacations. Are you staying in the lodge?"

"No. A friend gave me the keys to her modest chalet."

"Nice friend. That saves a heap of cash."

"It wasn't for that reason. It's part of the recuperation."

"And what do you do for a living?"

Wong stared into her coffee for a moment. *Do I let this go to where this stud wants it to go?*

"I'm a security agent for U.N.S.A.," she finally said.

"No, come on, what do you really do?"

"Tell me first what you do."

"Fair enough. I do long hauls on big rigs that leave LEO for the outer planets. My next trip is out to Saturn."

His story was as farfetched as hers, but she was a good judge of facial expressions. The man was telling the truth. That decided her. Brent Mueller was not looking for any personal commitments here, far from it. This was a modern sailor on shore leave looking for fun.

*Any port in a storm.*

"Well, your job is as strange as mine. I truly am a U.N.S.A. agent. I report to the Director, Isha Bai."

Mueller was impressed.

"I'll be damned. I'm surprised you can ski as well as you do. I'd have terrible problems if I hadn't grown up in Austria."

\*\*\*

"I thought I heard the word modest when you mentioned this chalet." Brent Mueller looked up and down and across the front entrance to Denise Andersen's Swiss hideaway while Jenny Wong stared into the retina scanner and pressed her thumb to the fingerprint pad. She opened the door.

"Welcome home, Jenny Wong," said the house AI. "My name is Bentley. I see you have brought a friend with you. Shall I add another place at the dinner table? Let me list the menu items." The AI started going down the list, from appetizers to desserts.

"Just surprise us," she said. "This is Brent Mueller. And yes, he's a friend. Treat him as such."

"Impressive," said Mueller as he followed her inside. "Someone really wants you to recuperate."

"Guilt feelings, most likely. I have them for failing on my recent mission, so Isha and company better have them too. Bentley, turn the fireplace on, please."

The living room became cozy and warm with its roaring fireplace.

"Considering what I'm paying for my room at the lodge, I can imagine what this place rents for."

"Most of the time it's vacant." She turned and brought Mueller's face close to hers. She kissed him. "I'm not hungry yet, so how about some mental and physical therapy."

They made love once in front of the fireplace and again in the main bedroom. She was pleased that he said nothing about the wound in her shoulder that was still healing. She fell asleep with her head on his chest.

She awoke to the wonderful smells of dinner.

"I hope you don't mind, I tweaked the AI's recipes a little. My grandmother made a mean *wiener schnitzel*."

Wong padded to the kitchen and put her arms around Mueller's naked waist.

"I don't mind at all, as long as there's dessert."

\*\*\*

There was no more skiing during the next two days of Jenny Wong's stay after which both she and Brent Mueller had to leave. They caught a helitaxi that took them into Zurich. Mueller was taking a scramjet to Villa de Leyva; she was returning to New York.

"It's been a lot of fun," said Brent. "Will I see you again?"

"Probably not. Saturn's too far away. I can't see Isha Bai sending me out there."

"Then I guess it's good-bye and good luck," said Brent.

The long kiss seemed still to hold a lot of promise for both of them.

*Moreover, it's been excellent therapy. I nearly forgot about my failure with the New York gang.*

# Chapter Fifteen


"Run it up his ass!"

From the shadows, Zeb and Maria Elena watched while two men held a third doubled over at the waist, his pants down at the ankles. A heavyset man approached the struggling victim with a broom handle.

"I'm going to run this right up to your fucking mouth, you damn bastard. Your kind has caused all the world's problems."

Before Maria Elena could stop him, Zeb ran up and throttled the attacker. He dropped the pole and struggled for air. The other two pushed their victim to the ground and turned on Zeb.

"Knives!" yelled Maria Elena.

Zeb used the fat man like a shield. One of his accomplices, trying to stab at Zeb, buried his knife in the fat man's gut instead. Zeb released his throat hold, grabbed the arm just above the wrist, and pulled the knife man forward, sealing the fat man's fate. He floored the accomplice with a vicious blow that sent teeth flying. The third attacker dropped his knife and ran.

Maria Elena took the victim in her arms and rocked him while Zeb rubbed his knuckles. He checked the fat man for a pulse, shaking his head at Maria Elena. Finding some old electrical wiring, he tied up the unconscious man.

*Let the police sort it out. We don't need to become involved with them.*

He studied the victim. The man was crying. Maria Elena helped him pull up his pants. He was only a boy, not a man.

"Why were they attacking you?" Zeb asked, rubbing the bloody knuckles once again.

"That should be obvious," said Maria Elena. "They thought they were going to have some fun shoving a pole up his butt."

"I know that. But why?"

"Because I'm a foreigner," said the victim.

Zeb noticed the swarthy skin, not unlike Maria Elena's. With his build, he could probably take Zeb in a fair fight. With three assailants, he hadn't had a chance.

Zeb offered a hand.

"I don't give a shit who you are. There's right and there's wrong. My name's Zeb, short for Zebediah."

"And my name's Pasqual, short for—"

The multiple names that followed left Zeb confused. Maria Elena laughed. "We'll just call you Pasqual."

\*\*\*

Their new friend proved to be useful. Zeb was still a rookie in the ways of the city and there were places where Maria Elena could not go alone. She and Pasqual scouted out the territory, finding food and water, and helping them search.

Maria Elena always reminded them that the mission was to find the gang that killed her sister.

"Your mission is very dangerous," Pasqual observed one night while they fed on leftover fried chicken pulled from a dumpster. "We may be killed."

"Are you scared?" asked Maria Elena.

"My life was meaningless until I met you two," said Pasqual. "At least I now have a goal."

"It's my goal," said Maria Elena. "You don't need to walk our dangerous path."

"Pasqual thinks he owes us something," Zeb observed.

He studied the boy-man who was only eighteen, feeling rotten that his coming of age was taking place in the dark streets and back alleys of an indifferent city.

*On the other hand, am I just glorifying my own background? Maybe Pasqual would be bored in Wyoming.*

"Only my life, but that's not the point." He tossed the remains of a chicken leg to a couple of rats nearby. "You are the only friends I've ever had. How could I not stay with you and help you on your quest, as fruitless and dangerous as it may be. We are like the characters of Dumas."

"Dumas?" asked Zeb. "He sounds foreign too."

"He is," said Maria Elena. "Pasqual is referring to the old novel *The Three Musketeers*. It was written by Alexandre Dumas."

"We're like Athos, Porthos and Aramis," said Pasqual. "All for one, one for all."

"Perhaps you are more like D'Artagnan," said Maria Elena, wiping grease from her full lips.

"You've lost me," said Zeb. "I suppose this is all something you learn in schools."

"Some schools," muttered Maria Elena. "The streets of New York City teach you other things."

\*\*\*

Pasqual shoved the shotgun into the man's mouth, pulled the trigger, and then whipped around to blow away another gang member attacking Zeb. He saw out of the corner of his eye that Maria Elena was doing well with the gang leader. He reloaded.

Zeb had loaded up too. He was using a fine firearm they called a Glock, a miracle of technology with a cartridge holding nineteen soft-nosed bullets. Such weapons didn't exist in Wyoming.

The two of them fanned out, hunting gang members. They showed no mercy. At the end, Pasqual only had a grazing shoulder wound. His shotgun barrel was hot to the touch.

They hurried back the way they had come to where Maria Elena was last seen dueling the gang leader. Now she was sitting on his chest, blood all over her.

"Are you OK?" Zeb asked, worried that the blood might be hers.

"Never felt better." She held up something that looked like a flaccid sausage in the dim light of the old warehouse. "Cut it off right in front of his eyes."

"He was your sister's murderer. Is he dead?"

"Only once. I wish I could have killed him multiple times." She tossed to one side what was left of the man's penis, knowing the rats would feast on it. "I need a bath."

Pasqual stooped down and rifled the man's pants. They were down to his knees due to Maria Elena's impromptu surgery. He pulled out a wad of money.

"Lotta drug money here, friends. What say we stay in a hotel tonight, have a proper bath, and eat some real food?"

Zeb shrugged. He was emotionally drained.

"I would just like a real bed."

They all laughed.

*** 

They chose interconnecting rooms. The one with the double bed was Pascual's. Zeb and Maria Elena took the king-size.

While Maria Elena took a luxurious bath, Zeb watched Pascual search both of the hotel rooms.

"What are you looking for?"

"The bar. These fancy rooms often have a little fridge with snacks and liquor. I could use a drink."

"I guess you're thrilled with killing about as much as I am."

"Probably less. It drains me, like my life force is fading away."

"And the alcohol will put it back?"

"Yeah, I know—demon rum. Well, if you had parents that spent their time coming up with new ideas on how to abuse you, you'd need to drink too."

"Were they drunks?"

"No. Wouldn't touch the stuff. They belonged to a church that taught that children had to have the devil beat out of them." Pascual was in briefs. He turned so Zeb could see his back. Old scars crisscrossed it. "That's just the physical part. I had to memorize scripture and if I got it wrong, they would beat me for that. I was always living in fear that I'd make a mistake."

"I'm sorry. A God-fearing upbringing has many positive aspects when your parents treat you with love and understanding."

Zeb saw the tears streaming down the man's face. He went to him and gave him a hug. Pasqual buried his face in Zeb's furry chest.

The hug turned into something more when Pasqual kissed him. Zeb pushed his friend away.

"What's wrong with you?"

"Sorry, I'm sorry," said Pasqual. "I thought maybe you'd go both ways. Moreover, your relationship with Maria Elena seemed ambivalent. Do you fuck her?"

"She gives me ball-busting sex," Zeb said, with a smile. "I'm sorry too. I don't go both ways, as you call it."

"So, am I still your friend?"

Zeb looked at Pasqual, his brow wrinkled. *I have come a long ways in what I accept. He is a good man.* "Yeah, as long as you don't come on to me."

Pasqual laughed in his deep baritone that nearly matched Zeb's. He flexed his abs and posed a little.

"You're not really my type."

"When we met you for the first time, those three were after you for that," Zeb observed.

"Yes, but also for being a foreigner. White homosexuals seem to be tolerated more."

Zeb knew that same sex relationships and foreigners were even less tolerated back home. Yet there he had never thought through the issues involved. *New York City, as crude as it is, makes one think about life. And tolerance.*

\*\*\*

Zeb saw that Pasqual was waiting for Zeb's comment but feared saying anything more that might offend his friend.

Maria Elena, naked and still toweling herself off from the bath, had been watching while Zeb confronted his homophobia.

"Oh, good Lord, either of you would die for the other. Let's focus. We're one hell of a gun slinging, knife wielding, jaw busting trio." She fluffed her hair with the towel. Zeb admired the ringlets of damp hair as they fell over her shoulders and breasts. "I think we should create a vigilante group. I have a name for it."

"What's a vigilante group?" asked Zeb. The distraction of her body was making all thought of guns and knives seem obscene.

"What we pulled off today is not approved by the authorities," said Pasqual. "We acted like vigilantes. We took the law into our own hands and punished those gang members."

Zeb nodded that he understood. *Not that it makes any difference. They deserved what they got.*

"So my name is Angels of Justice. It translates well into other languages too. Our mission will be to clean up New York City."

Zeb sat down on the edge of the bed and studied his two friends.

*Is she becoming unrealistic? Has her search for revenge fried her brain?*

"We're only three people. We need an army."

"So, we build an army," said Maria Elena. "I think both Pasqual and I know people that would love to participate. Zeb, you can screen them and make sure they meet your moral standards."

He considered that statement. "I'm not sure I have any left. We just wiped out an entire gang. I have blood on my hands. I have become the Devil's tool."

"More like the tool of an avenging God," said Pasqual. "You ought to read the Old Testament."

"I have. Often, in fact. You may be right. But I still have problems with what we did."

"They didn't have to fight," said Maria Elena. "And that gang leader deserved to die. Besides, maybe others will think twice before taking us on."

"They'll keep up their dirty work and just avoid us," said Pasqual. "That's why we need more people."

"Being vigilantes means the N.Y.P.D. will not approve," said Zeb, trying to prove he was more realistic about their chances.

"Who the fuck cares? Remember that the N.Y.P.D. is mostly corrupt. Those cops that aren't will probably want to moonlight with us." Maria Elena spit on her hands and rubbed them together. The towel dropped to her feet. "I can't wait."

"OK, OK, we'll try it. But I'm only in until I find this Fabio Martinez. I'll then find my way back to the Midwest."

Pasqual frowned at that.

"Don't worry, Pasqual," said Maria Elena. "I'll work on him so that he'll be so much into me that he wouldn't think of leaving."

They all laughed at that.

*I'm afraid she might be right,* thought Zeb, handing her the towel.

***

Patty Blish was the first one to join the three founders of the Angels of Justice. She was a terrific asset—strong, muscular, with two years of medical school and full training as an RN. She worked regular shifts in the old Bellevue ER, but was willing to do a lot of moonlighting. A good friend of Maria Elena, Patty's husband, a cop, had been murdered by one of the many New York gangs.

Very soon, three cops, old friends of Patty's husband, also came on board.

Word of mouth became a powerful recruiting tool as the Angels had minor successes. As the number of combatants grew, so did the number of informants and sympathizers. They even recruited a Catholic priest and two Rabbis.

\*\*\*

Their first major confrontation occurred in a Latino ghetto where a Honduran gang was extorting a Guatemalan couple that ran a *groceria*. The Guatemalans had decided to fight back. While the husband was already dead, the wife was still holding off the gang when the N.Y.P.D. bulletin went out. One Angel, who monitored N.Y.P.D. communications, phoned it into Zeb.

"This is it!" said Zeb. "Let's move."

Not all Angels were active all the time. Some seventeen showed up at 106<sup>th</sup> and Lexington and moved in on the rear of *Los Malditos*, the Honduran gang. Pasqual had the bullhorn.

"We are the Angels of Justice. Put down your weapons or die."

It was three in the morning. His voice reverberated off the walls of the surrounding buildings, sounding like the voice of God. Some of the *Malditos* dropped their weapons but their leader shot them and then emptied both his guns in the direction of the Angels.

"Let them have it," said Zeb.

It was not elegant. Both groups had a mix of small firearms, rifles, and shotguns. Maria Elena's knife throw from a distance of ten meters dispatched the last *Maldito*.

Zeb shook his head sadly. He hated the killing.

"Go comfort that poor woman," he told Maria Elena.

Maria Elena motioned Patty to accompany her. While they were attending to the Guatemalan woman, they heard the sirens.

"Time for us to go," Patty said, patting the woman on the arm. Her only physical wound was a scratch on her cheek produced by flying glass. Her mental wounds would last forever.

"Who are you?" the woman asked in Spanish.

"*Amigos,*" said Patty. "*Somos los Angeles de la Justicia.* Tell others about us. You won't have to fight the gangs alone any longer."

"*Gracias, gracias*," the woman said, watching the two fade into the night along with Zeb and the others.

# Chapter Sixteen

"You think I'm evil?" Zebediah Lane asked Jenny Wong. She shifted uneasily in the diner's booth but then smiled. "What is evil nowadays? New York City is a battleground. I'll let my U.N.S.A. bosses decide whether you're evil. I need to know more about you so I can portray you honestly."

"So, ask me your questions. I'll stop you when you start to bore me."

"Fair enough. What kind of name is Zeb?"

"It's short for Zebediah. A biblical name. My parents were religious."

"I take it you're not."

"From what I've learned, religion has caused a lot of the Chaos."

"What do you mean?" She knew the answer, of course, but this interview was really a test of this cowboy and his vigilantes.

"As I understand it, the U.S. broke apart due to regional differences caused in part by different religious beliefs."

"Not only the U.S. and not just religion." Wong realized that Lane was as much a neophyte to Downy politics as most Spacers. "It's a new era of tribalism," she explained. "Your gang, the Angels of Justice, is nothing more than a tribe, a small cohesive unit designed to defend like-minded individuals from the onslaught of competing tribes."

"I understand that. Governments throughout the world lost control. It's the good guys against the bad."

"If you can tell who's good and who's bad. It's not all that easy. However, it's more than that. Since there is very little government power, we have anarchy. The tribes can do pretty much what they want. In addition, you have the multinational corporations that wield enormous financial power but need stability to prosper. So they'll pay people like you to keep anarchy under control."

"You make it sound like a bad thing, what I do, I mean."

"I'm just saying it is what it is. I'm in the same business, since U.N.S.A. depends on the corporations."

"Well, from my point of view, religion or not, the whole center of the country turned into a savage land. Marauders killed the rest of my family and others kidnapped me, bringing me here to be a rich man's toy."

She nodded. It was a common story.

"So, how did you escape?"

"I killed the bastard. Does that shock you?"

"There's not much that shocks me anymore. Tell me about your family."

They talked for an hour. Lane then introduced Wong to Pasqual and Maria Elena, his lieutenants. Wong liked both of them. She noticed that Lane and Maria Elena had a special relationship. The woman adored her friend from the Midwest. Pasqual adored them both.

They talked some more. Wong then had to leave.

"I assume that we'll be hearing from you," said Lane.

"Maybe, but don't count on it. Any of us could be dead soon. We're all moving in very dangerous circles." She handed him a slip of paper. "I shouldn't be doing this, but you may find the information useful."

Lane looked at the Westside address. It wasn't far from his old home, if Max Holland's penthouse deserved that name.

"What's this?"

"Fabio Martinez' New York City address."

In an instant, she was gone into the night before Lane could thank her.

***

"Do we trust her?" asked Pasqual.

Zeb waved the scrap of paper. "If this works, I'll trust her."

"Fine," said Maria Elena, "but she's basically a cop. An international cop. I'd like to be sure about her agenda."

Zeb frowned while Pasqual swirled the remains of his beer. Both his friends drank too much. He sipped his coffee.

*I think I'm evil, independent of what this Jenny Wong thinks. But it takes evil to combat evil.*

"Well," said Pasqual, "we're not going to know her real agenda by sitting here in our mutual admiration society. We have a responsibility to the Angels."

"You and Maria Elena follow her," said Zeb. "See where she goes, what she does, who she goes to bed with, and so forth. I will continue to work with Arturo and find out more about her background."

"You don't really trust her either," observed Maria Elena.

Again, he waved the scrap of paper. "I have a good feeling about this, but it doesn't hurt to be cautious. There's too much at stake."

"Yeah, our lives," said Pasqual.

***

Arturo was what earlier generations would call a hacker. He knew how to break into databases. There wasn't much information on Jenny Wong. They already had all that was available without alerting authorities like U.N.S.A. Security.

"We only know that she travels a lot," said Zeb in a lunch meeting with Arturo, Pasqual and Maria Elena. "And a birth certificate."

"That can be doctored," observed Pasqual.

"I don't think so," said Arturo. "Who would change their birth certificate to show they were Martian? I think she really was born there."

"What did you learn by tailing her?" Zeb asked Maria Elena and Pasqual.

"She seems to be in a waiting mode," said Pasqual. "Lots of night life and gym workouts during the day. She's had many opportunities but she seems to be shunning male companionship. Maybe she's a lesbian."

"I don't think so," said Maria Elena. "As for the waiting, she may want to see what you're going to do with the info she gave you, Zeb."

Zeb nodded. "Yes. It may be a test. I don't know which outcome she wants in order to give me a passing grade, but I don't care." He threw bills down on the table to pay for their lunches. "We'll wait and see about Jenny Wong. Let's move on the information she gave me."

77

## Chapter Seventeen

Fabio Martinez was not a happy man. First, Isha Bai's agent had thwarted his scheme for obtaining details on the experiment at Farside. She then wiped out one of the New York gangs he had paid to pester Denise Andersen. Now his lazy, mooching son was back from Switzerland, this time with a broken leg.

"Nice to see you too," said Rudolfo Martinez when Martinez *pere* glowered upon seeing him in the study of the New York penthouse. He raised a glass to his father. "I'd ask for a hug, but it's difficult for me to get up."

***

Rudolfo Martinez looked nothing like his father. He was of average build but lean and mean. His mother once caught him torturing a cat. His dark skin and black hair barely hinted at his mother's beauty, but his permanent scowl and moody disposition embarrassed even his father, whom everyone knew was irascible.

"Can't you learn to ski?"

"Accidents happen, old man." Rudolfo swirled his drink, enjoying the clinking of the ice cubes. "Don't worry. I won't bother you. This place is big enough for an army. The two of us should be just fine."

"Why don't you go home to Argentina?"

"I'd rather bother you."

The father plopped down in a chair.

"You're succeeding. I'm busy right now, so stay out of my way."

"Any cute pussies you want me to entertain?"

"My current love interests are none of your business."

"Love. A curious word when used by a sociopath."

"So, now you've gone all European on me and learned a little elementary psychology." The expression on his father's face was colder than Rudolfo's drink. "Well, Mr. Freud, I'll have you know that I'm just an over-achiever. Time-Online said so."

"Oh, give me a break. I'm off to the guest room. I need a nap." Rudolfo stood and grabbed at his crutches. "Shall we do dinner?"

"I suppose I can arrange it. 6 p.m. sharp."

\*\*\*

Martinez watched his son clump off, the thick carpet muting somewhat the sound of the crutches.

"Idiot," he said in a low voice so his son wouldn't hear.

He went to his desk and joined a board meeting for his company using the VR equipment. His mind wasn't on the meeting, though, but on how to eliminate Denise Andersen, or, at least, her company's competition. The world wasn't big enough for the two of them.

When the meeting ended, he popped back to reality and began studying all the information his AI had gathered on the Angels of Justice.

*Did this group destroy the Sharks? Zebediah Lane? Where have I heard that name before?*

He put the question to the AI and it came up with two references. One was to a news item already several months old. Maxwell Holland, a business acquaintance and New York City Council member, was dead. The suspected murderer was a boyfriend named Zebediah Lane. The news item didn't say boyfriend but Martinez knew about Holland's proclivities.

The other reference was to a shipping list Bryce had forwarded even further back. His man put Zebediah Lane on a list of captives he wanted to auction.

*Such a person, if motivated by revenge, can become lethal. If lethal, he might be useful. Maybe I can turn him against Denise Andersen.*

Martinez smiled. His talent was in using people to further his own ends. His son was right. He only cared about someone else to the extent that they could be useful to him.

A call from his security staff interrupted him. A guard's face came on the screen.

"Mr. Martinez, warn—" Martinez jumped out of his chair when a blade appeared, slashed across the man's throat, and left it gushing blood.

\*\*\*

Fabio Martinez had never experienced fear before. He ran to arm the perimeter but an explosion threw him to the ground. He could hear boots pounding the floor at the front entrance to the penthouse that could only be accessed via elevator. His secure penthouse had become an African waterhole with hyenas, jackals, lions and leopards on the shore and crocs in the water—and he was the thirsty antelope waiting for a drink.

He rose and staggered to his desk. Pulling open a drawer, he found his gun. He swiveled and aimed when Rudolfo entered the room. His son put his hands up.

"What the hell is going on, old man?" asked his son.

Martinez pointed to the security screen.

"We're under attack!"

"Oh, shit. Do you have another gun?"

"Stay here. You—"

A tall man with his own gun appeared at the door.

\*\*\*

"I've come for you," said Zeb.

Lane didn't wait for comment. In a better time and place, he might have waited for Martinez to go for his gun. However, the images of their captors herding away Bev, Luke, Sandra and the others were red-hot pokers smoldering in his head, burning away the synapses of reason and leaving only ones of hate.

His shot hit Martinez in the forehead and the older man staggered back, already dead. He crumpled to the floor like a sack of wheat from Jesse Lane's barn. Blood pooled on the rich white carpet.

Zeb lowered the gun. Rudolfo Martinez looked at his father's corpse and then at Lane.

"Are you going to kill me too?"

Zeb hadn't even noticed the man on crutches. He stuffed his pistol into the waist of his pants. There was a curious smile on his face.

"I have no quarrel with you," he said. "Not yet. Sorry about the mess. And the rug. Good day."

He turned and left the study.

# Chapter Eighteen

Denise Andersen looked Lane over. From top to bottom, her eyes ran over him, as if they were doing a bone density analysis. When she was finished, she smiled.

"I thought Midwesterners were malnourished and fragile. You look like you could take four of my boys."

Lane looked sideways at one of the burly men restraining him and winked at Denise.

"My Ma could have taken all of them."

They restrained him more tightly.

"Let him go," she ordered.

They did so, but stood nearby, four wolves ready to pounce. Lane rubbed his wrists.

*I know you*, he thought. *You were the losing bidder. But you weren't able to bring yourself to spend all that money. You really didn't want this horse.*

"It's your move." He looked at his watch and then punched a button on its side. "You have ten minutes before the Angels storm this place. You, these four, and anyone else here will be dead in fifteen. So talk."

\*\*\*

Andersen wasn't used to receiving orders. Lane's audacity surprised her. She turned in her chair and looked out over the East River. She subvocalized a question to Wong.

"Any sign of Lane's troops?"

"Plenty. They have your place surrounded."

"What about N.Y.P.D.?"

Wong snickered. "You have to be kidding. They wouldn't be caught up in this gig. They know something serious is going down and don't want to be around."

Denise sighed. Lane was a formidable opponent.

*But isn't that what I want?* She swung in her chair again to face Lane. *He looked much better naked and after a bath. A little scruffy, Zeb, my darling. But maybe you can serve me better now.* "JoJo, find Mr. Lane a chair."

\*\*\*

After Lane made himself comfortable, she stood and went face-to-face, bending down so the tassels adorning her nipples nearly caressed his cheek. She was tall and her body seemed sculpted by the Devil himself. In spite of his loathing, he experienced the familiar stirring in his loins.

"Do you know who I am, Mr. Lane?"

"You can call me Zeb, and yes, I know who you are. Why you brought me here is beyond me. We have nothing in common."

"Oh, but we do, we do." She whipped around and punched buttons on her desk. A huge display screen descended behind her and a still picture filled it, a picture of three slight mounds with white crosses on them. Zeb frowned. "You have dedicated your life to stopping violence and have no qualms about using violence to do so. I need your Angels of Justice to clean up New York City."

Lane sucked in his breath.

"That's impossible. I'm trying, but I don't have enough people."

"That can be remedied. N.Y.P.D. can't do it obviously, or it would have done so. The Mid-Atlantic Union doesn't have the balls to do anything about it either. They're perpetually whining to the U.N. to step in, but the U.N. only acts now by handing out a contract."

"A mercenary contract," observed Lane.

"Call it what you will." She arched one eyebrow slyly, an expression that Lane liked. "I run a business, you know."

"A large one, or many, depending on one's point of view" agreed Lane.

"OK. All the same, I need the Chaos stopped in New York City. It's not good for business. It gets in the way of business. So, if I create a mercenary army and sell its services to the U.N., everybody wins."

"Except those that make money off the Chaos."

Another picture flashed on the screen, a police photo of a dead Fabio Martinez, blood and brain matter still oozing from the bullet hole in his forehead. Lane shifted uncomfortably.

"You have no idea what that man did," he said.

"Oh, I do. Did you ever catch up with the marauders that took out your family?"

"No. Unfortunately, someone beat me to the punch."

Denise's fist slammed down onto the desk.

"I'm as ruthless as the next and you will find I share none of your bible-toting philosophy, but I will not live in anarchy." She handed Lane a list of some twenty names. "Do you know these people?" He looked briefly at the list and nodded. "I want them dead!"

"Although these people are pure evil, I'm not a judge, jury, and executioner. Besides, we've been looking for them. They've gone underground."

"I know." Another picture flashed on the screen, this one of a young prostitute setting up a tryst with a john. Lane recognized the crossing streets. They were not far from St. Patrick's Cathedral and Rockefeller Center. He had gone inside the old church a few times, gone past the crumbling stone walls and bullet pocked doors, to sit down and pray in the coolness and quiet. The girl on the screen reminded him of his sister. He grimaced. "Thirteen, Lane. You think Martinez was scum, this girl's pimp runs a couple hundred underage girls, most kidnapped from the Midwest. And her pimp is not even on the list!" Denise smiled at Lane. "I want you and your troops to do what N.Y.P.D. can't do. Go underground, bribe, and threaten— anything to ferret out these rats."

"A tall order. Why should we do your bidding? You are asking for a major escalation. What's in it for me and my troops?"

"Lots of money and some respectability. Oh, there will be bleeding hearts that say you're as bad as the people you're going after. I think you have a thick enough skin to ignore what others say. Maybe not when you first came to this stinking city, but now, after you have seen what true evil can be. Are you with me?"

"I will check with the other Angels. We will want absolute veto power on any new recruits. For example, JoJo here wouldn't work at all."

"Why not?" growled the burly man.

"You like teenage boys too much."

84

JoJo pulled Lane to his feet and a fist like a hammer headed for his midsection. Lane caught it in midair and twisted it behind his back. JoJo grimaced in pain.

"Call him off or so help me God I'll break his arm!"

"So, you picked up on our little JoJo's hobby," said Denise with a laugh. "I assure you, his subjects are willing. This is a strange town, Lane. And these are strange times."

He let the man go. JoJo said nothing but glowered at Lane.

"Go," said Andersen. "Talk to your men. Come back with your demands. I'm a hard-assed business woman, but I'm not completely unreasonable."

"Believe it or not, there are women too. Will that bother you?"

"I don't care if they're elves from the Black Forest as long as they do the job."

***

Some time after Lane left, Wong entered with a smile on her face.

"What do you think?"

"He's the one, no doubt about it. Good work. Are you still going to return to Villa de Leyva?"

"My cover is blown with the gangs, but maybe not with other criminal elements. However, Lane and his crew are capable. I'm not sure I can condone their methods, so it's better that I go. I don't feel defeat and have no allegiance to you." She walked over and gave Andersen a kiss on the cheek. "You're not a bad woman, Denise. Let the good shine through."

Andersen, embarrassed, gave a little chuckle.

"Have a good life, Wong, and stay healthy."

"Likewise," said the U.N.S.A. agent, already thinking about which flight she would take to Colombia.

# Part II

## Jon Silent Eagle

*You shall know the truth, and the truth shall make you mad.*

– Aldous Huxley

# Chapter Nineteen

"I have him!" Lewis' voice, almost lost in the bubbling noise of his oxygen supply, was followed by a series of grunts. "What's wrong with Tanglevsky?" came the logical question from the team's junior member back in the shuttle. The senior member already knew the answer and mouthed Lewis' next words. "He's dead."

\*\*\*

Responsibility can sometimes play a timid second violin in an orchestra where the brass section is blaring out the strains of a midlife crisis. Jon Silent Eagle Lewis was having a hard time hearing that violin.

Middle age at the end of the 20$^{th}$ century meant fifty, plus or minus five. In 2132, you could stretch it past eighty by a combination of drugs and injections containing your own stem cells. This biogenetic cocktail produced telomeric extension when the body created new cells. The shift of the defining age didn't change Lewis' problem; from his perspective, middle age still meant that there was a lot less to be happy about.

Ever practical and prone to making lists, Lewis always believed that there were three basic joys in life: good food and drink (he lumped those two together), a good night's sleep, and good companionship. This hedonistic trinity had served him well during his best years. When he missed one leg of this psychological stool his mind liked to sit on, he experienced a mental vertigo that was a lot harder to overcome than the physical one.

*Like right now, pulling myself by one hand along this tether line. Why did hard-ass Moravcsik have to send novices like Tanglevsky and Montero on this mission? Everything would have been fine if Moravcsik had let Gus and I come alone.*

Both Gus Hanson and he had been wary of Tanglevsky and Montero tagging along, not because they were from a different

89

generation, but because the two were unknowns in an emergency. And this was an emergency, since very soon he was going to run out of steam and let Tanglevsky slip away.

Although he was floating weightlessly, the weight of his years seemed to be more than he could bear. Space had always been a young person's domain, no matter what anyone said,

John Glenn went back into space in his late seventies at the end of the 20th century. The media and N.A.S.A. had made a big deal about it, although Glenn didn't do much. Still, Glenn was one of Lewis' heroes. He didn't know a lot about the man but had idolized the astronaut since his days in the reservation schoolhouse.

Now Lewis was working in space in his eighties and no one thought it strange. Once they had fixes for the bone calcium problem and the early Alzheimer's, scientists found that Spacers lived longer on the average than Downies. Spacers' telomeres didn't go to hell as fast.

The average Spacer life span without accidents was about 160. The average Downy life span without accidents was about 140.

*Nevertheless, when Spacers have accidents, we often die.*

It was more than the weight of his years that he carried, all because their project head had decided that this particular mission needed four pairs of hands, instead of the usual two. Lewis, Hanson, Montero and Tanglevsky. He was struggling with the last man's body.

***

"Push him away and get back in here," said Hanson. "The SOB's not worth a funeral. Let Saturn be his grave."

"Gus, be responsible. I'll bring him in."

Back to those three joys of life. Lewis had developed a reasonable relationship with Susan Ito until young Tanglevsky came along. At least it was a good approximation to good companionship. Spacers are a squirrelly lot and loners by nature, so relationships were difficult. However, the sex was good when all systems functioned, both hers and his.

Tanglevsky, the new recruit, didn't require any drugs to please the women, being fifty years Lewis' junior. He was also a lot more energetic, outgoing and charming than Lewis, whom people considered too serious for his own damn good—he supposed they were right. It was one of Susan's standard complaints. She had replaced Lewis with Tanglevsky.

In the confines of cramped Spacer living quarters, events like that were common, so it didn't bother Lewis all that much until he drew the brash young man for the mission. That led to this uncomfortable situation of having to decide whether to haul Tanglevsky's body back inside or not. It also was enough to make him dredge up past regrets.

*Responsibility, responsibility. Responsibility to Susan. Responsibility to my project. Responsibility is what gives these years weight. It's not hard to imagine being carefree without all this damn responsibility.*

\*\*\*

"Your BP and pulse have unhealthy readouts, partner."

"Stuff it! I'm nearly there."

Bodies are weightless in space but not inertialess. Whereas his many years were a psychological mass that seemed to resist forward motion, Tanglevsky's body only needed to start in motion or stop. The problem was doing just that.

$F = ma$ was still a good approximation in spite of all the physics that had gone on since Newton. Tanglevsky's m was large and Lewis' one-armed F was small. Lewis swore while he swung the body around again, trying to obtain a better grip with his left arm as he worked along the tether with his right. The swinging involved the rotational version, $\tau = I\alpha$ —it was as hard to start or stop the rotation with Tanglevsky's bloodless but still flopping arms increasing the I. Lewis wasn't about to wait for *rigor mortis*.

In his basic prep and refresher courses through the years, both in virtual reality sims and real practice runs, he was well trained in what he had to do. That didn't make it any easier.

\*\*\*

His helmet visor started to fog on the inside as his old suit tried to keep up with his exertions. Other Spacers might be tempted to push the kid out of orbit in towards the rings and forget about him since he had stolen Susan, but Lewis was enough of a slave to appearances that he figured it might start people talking. Or make them angry. He tended to avoid confrontations.

He wouldn't know how to face Susan, either. She would want to give her young lover a fitting Catholic ceremony. He also felt guilty that the young recruit had bought it instead of an old fart like himself, what the psych boys called "survivor's syndrome," All of this kept Lewis struggling.

And cursing. He grunted machine gun bursts of Chinese, Spanish and English expletives while he hauled the body along, struggling with the burden of his own years and another man's religion.

*Why do I do this? The longer I stay out here, the more chance that I'll be hit by another piece of crap that goes through one of my vital organs. Am I insane?*

***

"Slow down. You have plenty of air."

"Grandma, I know how to do this. Get the hell off my back."

"Maybe you should say that to Tanglevsky."

Lewis often would stop a moment and enjoy the view before he went back inside. Saturn filled the sky in golden, ringed glory while they orbited Helene, one of its smaller moons. Saturn's beauty seemed to be more menacing now, though.

He had the reputation of being the scientist *par excellence*. Although he was there as part of an engineering and construction team, his principal occupation as a Spacer was not bending metal or hauling dead bodies. He was an astrophysicist that specialized in RF emissions from planetary atmospheres. However, his contract said that before he could start collecting data he must help build his laboratory.

They called their program Project Saturn Watch. The program's first research station was already nearing completion on Dione, a much bigger moon than Helene was. It would handle everything optical and would have an impressive array of microwave antennas to monitor the lower energy part of the atmosphere's electromagnetic spectrum.

Helene, at one of Dione's Trojan points (more specifically, the L4 leading Lagrange point), and Polydeuces, at the other (the L5 trailing Lagrange point) would only have a smaller array of antennas that could be used in conjunction with the Dione antenna array to associate radio phenomena with precise locations on the planet via interferometry. That was Lewis' specialty. He had participated in a similar project at Jupiter and was now leader of that part of Project Saturn Watch.

For him this project would be the culmination of a long career. First, there had been Mars, then the asteroid belt, and finally Jupiter. The Martian colonists had been lucky to exploit the subterranean water at the poles, more than they ever found on Earth's moon. They also found water on three of Jupiter's moons, Europa, Callisto, and Ganymede, although it was again subterranean. Saturn was collaborating in its own way. Water, necessary for all life, became a non-issue for the colonization of the solar system's outer planets. However, the precious liquid was just as much a part of the mining operations as rare Earth metals.

A thin pink fog still came from the tiny hole in Tanglevsky's suit where the bit of space matter had perforated it. There was a lot of junk in orbit around Saturn. They worked in the shadow of their shuttle's scoops that gulped up 99.99% of the harmful junk, but if the other 0.01% hit you with a good delta V, you'd better have a plug handy. A suit wasn't much protection, even if it was one of the newer models, like Roger's, which had some auto-repair capabilities consisting of an inner microscopic sheath of pasty glop and nanomachines that worked with it like good little masons.

In spite of his youth, Tanglevsky's only mistake had been to forget to carry the regulation patch kit in his suit pouch to cover those cases when the nanomachine layer couldn't plug the hole fast enough. With the help of the nanos, he might have sealed most of the leak by applying pressure from a gloved finger until he put the patch on.

That mistake was one small victory for the older Lewis if he ever decided to crow about it. Nevertheless, he guessed it wouldn't be worthwhile to point out the kid's mistakes. In all likelihood, neither nanomachines nor patches would have done any good. From the position of entry on the man's chest and the quantity of blood, Lewis surmised that the bit of space junk had gone straight through his heart.

*SOL. Snake eyes. The Queen of Spades. It's a deadly environment out here. Not as bad as the Village in New York City, but you need to be ready for anything. And then Lady Luck can still smack you. You're just playing against the odds.*

***

.

Susan Ito would have some comfort in knowing the younger man had died almost instantly and not from the decreasing pressure produced by a suit perforation for which he had no patch. Not that that would make her handle it any better.

Lewis had known the nanoengineer for years, long before their romantic involvement. She was a strong woman and would soon dominate her grief. There had been a lot of talk when she had sent him packing and married Tanglevsky, many years her junior. Marriage was not common among Spacers unless they were terribly old fashioned. Ito was. Gus Hanson had made more than one lewd joke about it, but Lewis had simply wished her happiness. Ito knew that he was envious of Tanglevsky yet had the decency to go beyond it.

*Would she blame him? How could she? Well, you're in charge here. Doesn't the buck stop with the person in charge? And what the hell does that mean? Great-grandfather would say it sometimes when he wasn't dreaming about his ancestors. The old man knew a lot, though....*

***

He ended his struggles by forcing the larger man into the airlock and then squeezing in behind the corpse. The shuttle was nothing more than steerable scoops on one end and rocket motors on the other. Space for the crew was an afterthought. After cycling the lock, he pushed the body down the flexible tube ahead of him until he arrived at the cramped living quarters. Hanson and Mikey Montero helped him remove Tanglevsky's suit.

"Not a pretty sight," muttered Montero, the junior member of the team.

With two doctorates by the time she was twenty, she was the smartest of the three present. She was also by far the youngest and most inexperienced, even younger than Tanglevsky. None of her education could prepare her to handle the situation or even provide her with the appropriate words as she stared at what hard space vacuum did to a corpse. She was a raven-haired woman with chiseled features that became even more like stone in this situation.

Lewis was sorry for her. He remembered the first time he had seen a decompressed corpse.

"I'll switch from local net to project net in order to let Susan know," said Hanson.

Like Lewis, Hanson was a veteran of the Jupiter missions. The academic training they received many years earlier (Hanson in computer science and Lewis in astrophysics) was far outweighed by their combined experience of 110 years in space. Lewis trusted Hanson and Hanson trusted Lewis.

Hanson made his report subvocally to Dione via the wi-fi device plugged in behind his ear, a device that hooked him into the ship's com, which in turn was now hooked into the Dione project net. Hanson had already shut off the video feed the shuttle would normally transmit back to Dione. Someone on Dione mercifully turned off the project net connection when Susan Ito began to cry. It was bad enough to be the bearer of bad news.

*Responsibility. I have the responsibility of comforting the woman. More than a lover, Susan has always been my friend. A friend has the responsibility of making his friend's pain more bearable. A kind word. A hug. What the hell can I do from so far away? Should I get on the com? Set up a virtual reality session? Will a VR hug be as comforting as a real one?*

He decided to wait until he arrived back at Dione with Tanglevsky's body. The funeral service would be a more appropriate place to comfort her.

*Not that I like all that mumbo-jumbo. I don't see much difference between a priest and a shaman. Not out here. God, Allah, or whatever you call Her, is much too close, peering over your shoulder all the time. We've invaded Her territory.*

"Well, he freed up the antenna," Montero observed. "Do we push on?"

The decision was Lewis', as mission commander, but the circumstances made him think that a democratic vote was in order. Everyone avoided the inconvenient truth that this was yet another accident that would not please the sponsor. However, the sponsor's approval was not much of a concern this far from Earth. The three of them had loftier ideals and Tanglevsky's death only brought them sharply back into focus.

It was unanimous. They would go on with the mission.

*It will take my mind off the midlife crisis. And my responsibilities, for now.*

"Mikey, get suited up. You and Gus are going out to spread the solar panels. I've had my exercise for today."

.

# Chapter Twenty

Juanito was the gazelle running from the lion, the penguin trying to escape the leopard seal, the rabbit dashing to avoid the talons of the hawk. The men behind him—or were they in front?—these men were predators. He was their prey.

He understood all this at a fundamental level. His only consolation was that the voices had stopped with all the adrenalin pumping. His salvation might be that he could run fast and for long distances. He had the build of a runner. The problem was fuel—a lack of food was a constant in his miserable life.

Neither his father nor mother had possessed any visible deformities. Juanito's was a shriveled left arm that was useless and no left ear. His legs were strong, though, and now he was stretching their strength and speed to the max. The words "socorro" and "ayudame," Spanish for "help" and "help me," were formed silently by his parched lips while his frantic mind focused only on escape.

***

Bogota had once been a teeming capitalistic metropolis that overgrew its original borders, its demographic tentacles reaching from one chain of the Andes to another across what was once a prehistoric inlet of the ocean that had existed before the mountains were born. Now it was a slagheap, a grim reminder of the destruction even a few nuclear warheads could bring, creating death where there was once life. The Venezuelan warheads that rained down on the Colombian capital had possessed the same Chinese model number as the Colombian ones that rained down on Caracas. Such were the ironies of history.

Juanito's home, if it could be called that, was in a region halfway between ground zero of the nuclear bursts of 2078 and the new spaceport. Amidst the square kilometers of ruins in the savanna of Bogota and the surrounding hills, shantytowns of sorts had grown up where descendants of the survivors of that nuclear holocaust tried to scratch out a living by farming in the radioactive soil or by herding radioactive sheep and goats.

Generally forgotten by an indifferent world, the local Human population provided an example of Darwinian evolution run amok since the mutation rate here was the highest on Earth, with the possible exception of Caracas and Maracaibo. More often than not, the children born to these nomads were deformed and dead. Once surviving birth, life expectancy was not high, since many died an early death from cancer.

Juanito Morales was one of the lucky ones—physically. He was just deformed. But mentally he was more crippled. Voices would speak to him all the time, confusing him, making him pound his head with his fist. Sometimes he would chew the wild leaves that made him crazy in order to shut off the voices and find some peace.

He couldn't think very well either. In fact, most of the time he barely functioned.

*** 

Juanito's father died in a brawl when he was three and his mother, after leading a life of prostitution for seven more years, succumbed to a brain tumor. Juan didn't know that, of course; he thought she died from headaches.

He had known hunger all his life. Hunger had led him around a brushy hill peppered with large regular granite stones left over from some suburban cathedral; the stones were arranged along lines that pointed to the old heart of the city, radiating along the direction of a bomb's shock wave that had come this far.

Among the stones, a cracked bell lying on its side gave mute testimony that God had forsaken this land and the apocalypse had come, bringing death and destruction to millions of innocents that once lived in the vast urban area. Ravaged by the guerrilla on one hand, which was financed by the illicit drug trade, and paramilitary groups on the other, right-wing groups that killed many innocents in their haste to kill guerrilla members, all these were now finally at peace.

Not so the ones that remained among the living.

Juanito had sensed there was something special about this place. Yet he had no idea what the bell was used for. He was not religious. He didn't even know what religion was.

His life was all about survival; he wasn't capable of thinking about an afterlife. This was a new place to him, so he thought maybe there would be something edible here. He hadn't eaten in two days.

He was a wild animal, as wild as the goats that sometimes came down from the mountains. Nevertheless, in his own way, he was also very intelligent. And curious.

His curiosity won out over caution when he saw the men and the truck. They were dressed in radiation suits, directing the stubby vehicle into a tunnel that burrowed into a hill.

He had seen men in radiation suits before, but these were acting strangely. He crept closer. It was too close since one of the men saw him.

So, here he was, hungry, wasting energy running from the men in radiation suits, and damning his curiosity.

*Big deal! So I saw them take a truck into a tunnel. Perros asquerosos! Mad dogs! Why can't they leave me alone?*

He would have been fine, except he became lost, and then realized that he was running in circles. He ran into the outstretched arms of one of the men that wrestled him to the ground and held him down.

The others joined them and one helped the first tie him up. Juanito winced when they bound his shriveled arm.

*What does he think I'm going to do with my useless arm? Fly away? Rip out his throat?*

\*\*\*

They carried him back to the hill and took him inside the tunnel. The entrance to the tunnel would have been spacious if it was not for the trucks and bulldozers. Juanito figured that they used most of them to excavate the tunnel.

Farther into the tunnel, there was a huge metal wall with a door. One of the men punched some buttons and the door opened with a whoosh! They all entered and the door closed behind them.

The room was large enough to hold some twenty men on each half. The half farthest from them had shower nozzles in the ceiling. They carried Juanito through. He was drenched and started to shiver.

They removed the bulky suits and hung them up. They were then through another door into a large room with tunnels leading off from it. There were rows and rows of machines.

*Computers. They must be computers.*

Not a whole lot of blinking lights like those that he had always imagined. There were graphics terminals and some keyboards for data entry, along with some helmets that had electronic baubles all over them. He wanted one of those. It looked like something a pilot might wear.

Some of the screens were lit and people were sitting and staring intently at them. Most of them had helmets on and spoke softly. Everybody wore heavy clothes. There was a steady breeze and the air was cold.

*Much colder than outside.*

Juanito shivered—the water soaking his clothes was evaporating in the breeze.

He tried to make out what the men were saying. It sounded foreign, so he supposed it was English. He knew some English words like "help me" and "I'm hungry" since he begged from the scientists that came to take radioactivity measurements, but he didn't understand enough to make out what these tunnel people were saying.

"*Habla ingles?*" one of the men asked him, as if he were a mind reader. He had changed to a heavy sweatshirt with a hood, although the latter was not in use. He was solidly built with black hair streaked with gray and reminded Juanito of his father.

"*No, senor hijo de puta,*" replied Juanito.

The tinkling sound of a woman's laughter filled the air. She came into view.

"Blake, he just called you Mr. SOB." She bent over and jerked him up by his collar, tearing some of the seam of his old shirt that was weakened by dirt and sweat. Speaking to him in Spanish, she said, "Listen to me, you little piece of shit. Hell, you even smell like it!" She shook him. "I'll give you only one chance to answer this question: does anyone know you're here besides us?"

Juanito looked around wide-eyed, first at the man, then at the woman. They didn't look too happy to have him as a visitor.

That was not strange. Most of the *gringos* didn't like beggars, especially radioactive ones.

\*\*\*

The man was George Blake, a high-ranking officer in the corporate security apparatus of GenCorp. An Englishman, during the years of the Chaos he had drifted from the English army, through various mercenary groups, and finally up the ranks of one of the remaining efficient security organizations, more powerful than any government's.

Efficient did not mean ethical—especially not in GenCorp. That was why there were also places in the organization for people like Amanda Chu. She played a double role. As an expert in computer security, she knew more about breaking and entering protected computer systems than any one of her colleagues. Her other expertise, more of a passionate hobby, was torture.

\*\*\*

Nominally the boss in the operation, Blake was nonetheless afraid of Amanda, and decided to let her handle the situation with the boy. In this case, Juanito's answer sealed his fate.

"No one knows I'm here," he said. Since she was a woman and she spoke his language, he felt safe telling her the truth. He figured that these people, like the other scientists, would have pity on him, give him some food, and send him on his way.

The woman's evil sneer told him how wrong he was. She turned to Blake, drawing a finger across her throat.

"Get rid of him," she said.

Blake nodded and gestured to one of the burly men that had chased Juanito.

"Take Yacob and dispose of this garbage. There's a pond about half a kilometer due south. Weight him down with something, throw him in, and make sure he doesn't come up."

All this time Juanito was screaming obscenities. Chu cut that short when she stuffed an old rag that smelled like oil or kerosene in his mouth and slapped duct tape over it.

"You'll receive your reward for being a little snoop."

The other man collected Yacob, who was even bigger than the first. He hoisted Juanito over one shoulder like a sack of flour. While the two men put on their radiation suits, Juanito wriggled quietly, doing the best he could to loosen his bonds. He nearly had the wrist of his good arm free when Yacob picked him up again.

They went outside.

***

The two men took turns carrying Juanito during the walk to the pond, which was much more than a half kilometer away if you counted the excursions around shale and rockslides. He worked at the ropes all the time.

At the edge of the pond, the first man tied a heavy rock to Juanito's feet. They both picked him up and tossed him far out into the water without another thought.

*The water's cold.* He fought panic while he struggled with the ropes. *I can't stay in here for long or I'll freeze to death.*

The shock of the cold water matched the shock to his mind. The haunting voices came back, along with visions.

"Juanito, *para mi*—for me, you must survive," his mother said. "Do not give in!"

"*Mamita! Salvame!*" He reached for her but she was lost in the silt and bubbles.

***

First, he freed his hand, then his feet. He swam the best he could to the surface, gulping air with as little noise as possible. His lungs were aching, but he knew he had only been down two or three minutes.

Fortunately, Yacob and the other ogre were already heading back, convinced that their murderous chore was done.

Juan dog paddled into the reeds by the shore and waited until he could no longer hear their footsteps. Next, he crawled onto a ledge of rock that was in the sun and, ignoring the voices and his headache, fell asleep.

# Chapter Twenty-One

Henry Posada's eyes moved rapidly as if he were in REM sleep. He looked like a patient tended to by an invisible psychiatrist while he lay on the comfortable, contoured couch. If someone could observe the rapid firing of his synapses, he might conclude that the patient was psychotic and under drugs. Nevertheless, he was just data mining.

The data rushed in and out of the computer's wireless data link jacked into the side of his head. He and the computer were essentially one while they played off each other, breaking into databases supposedly protected, looking for that unusual datum that would end his quest.

An IV drip hung by the couch, its plastic tube needling into his left arm above the elbow. He was on that evening's third cup of synthetic coffee—he couldn't afford the real stuff. Although the 2078 attack on Bogota hadn't had much affect on the Colombian coffee industry, anything real was hard to come by these days.

\*\*\*

"Take another look at that South China Republic issue," Isha Bai had suggested. "My other people can't figure it out."

Sometimes Bai would send him off on a fool's errand, but more often than not, she had an uncanny ability for finding something that was the devil to figure out.

*How does she have time to do it all?* he would ask himself.

To the outside world Henry Posada was a meek computer scientist based at MIT in the New England Commonwealth. Many professors now lived elsewhere, even in other countries—in his case, New York City in the Mid-Atlantic Union.

An expert on number theory and quantum encryption, to U.N.S.A. he was Mr. Computer Security. He and some eight hundred others worked hard to maintain data integrity and to keep vital data necessary to take informed decisions flowing into the

U.N.S.A. bureaucracy. He moonlighted while most of the others didn't.

He was well known in scientific circles as the inventor of the newest encryption codes, undecipherable even by the nearly sentient bioengineered quantum computers, the latest rage among security specialists. It was only natural that U.N.S.A. decided to adopt his techniques, but the transition was only partial, The Agency still had many installations on Earth and in space based on traditional server technology.

***

At Bai's request, Posada was trying to find out who was trying to break into some of the U.N.S.A. databases that he had so lovingly protected, although he had used the old technology. It was frustrating to find the break-ins because he believed that in some months none would be possible.

He suspected one of the multinational corporations was responsible. Less likely would be any of the other U.N. agencies that fought for pieces of the funding pie, although they accomplished little.

As Bai had suggested, he had traced one set of intruders back to the S.C.R. That was unusual in itself since the S.C.R. had a violent coup only five months earlier, fell into a general state of anarchy when it became a full member of the Chaos club, and was negotiating with WorldNet, GenCorp and other companies' mercenaries to come in and establish order.

He figured it was only a matter of time before they would send one of those groups to the S.C.R. It was a common practice in a world gone insane with old, established nations breaking up into feuding ethnic or political units, almost tribes in some cases, linked only by their common thirst for the technologies fed to them by the corporations.

Remotely logged into the U.N.S.A. computer complex at the spaceport in Singapore, he used algorithms modified from those of the zookie entertainment industry. The addictive zookies provided endless electronic tales of virtual lives lived by sexy, glamorous, but virtual people.

Designer drugs and zookies provided a welcome escape from the drudgery of working long hours. Quantum computing was now making every zookie tale different, so that buying one meant buying an infinite variety from the many worlds of quantum mechanics.

In his case, zookie VR and reality had become indistinguishable. He used it like a tool for manipulating and visualizing large quantities of data, as long as he had lots of bandwidth. A programmer could mold the interface to his own preferences, establishing his own visual and audio cues as icons. To him the databases were like oceans, the data like currents, and his avatar navigated its way through them with the help of the AI programs in the computer.

The human mind was limited, of course, in speed and storage capacity, compared to any of the computers in the U.N.S.A. complex, even the older servers. However, the AI programs needed human input to increase their selectivity. A request for information on any topic might produce billions of hits if they operated on their own. There was so much information that the old search engine technologies from one hundred and fifty years earlier would be woefully inadequate. Instead, human operators had to train them in real time.

***

"We are like any multinational corporation," Isha Bai had explained, "in that our data and our ability to manipulate it are important assets."

Posada was a fan of Isha Bai. U.N.S.A. dominated the U.N. bureaucracy and was an important contributor to world progress in his opinion. Moreover, its Director was as beautiful as she was intelligent.

*It's a pleasure to work for her.*

About three in the morning Posada broke through to a site near Bogota that linked through others in Ho Chi Minh City, San Diego, Anchorage, Santiago, and finally to one of the offending sites in the S.C.R. He put down an electronic tag to it, set things on hold, and pondered his find.

As far as he knew, Bogota was radioactive slag. The brief nuclear war between Venezuela and Colombia had destroyed it. Still, that's where the entry was made.

*Worst of all, I don't know who Bogota belongs to, or even if it's legit and somebody is using it illegally.*

He decided the mystery could wait—he was through with databases for the night. Although he was tired, he lived in the city that never sleeps.

As he withdrew the large bandwidth wireless connection from the side of his head and took the IV drip out of his arm, he was thinking of a night in the Village—there would still be plenty of activity outside. Although he often ended up going home alone in spite of the money he threw around on drinks and food, being in the company of other young believers in the nightlife was exciting. It was what made his trips to Cambridge so infrequent, disappointing his graduate students to no end.

He fit in with Village life. He was an exceptional human specimen even in a world where many parents could afford at least some genetic tailoring for their children. He helped himself by working out when he could but good genes were the foundation.

He, like most people, could not understand what the big deal was when they read about the history of the ethical debates of the 21$^{st}$ century surrounding the growing use of genetic engineering by parents wanting to have the best children possible. Parents always wanted the best for their children.

*Why shouldn't they make the best of the genetic material that is available to them?*

As he walked through the Washington Square maglev station, he was just one beautiful person among many others out on the town. Women and men representing a mix of races from all over the world and many sexual persuasions went about their business, some looking at him, others ignoring him.

One very blond woman with soft oriental but blue eyes winked at him and licked her lips suggestively. A diamond stud was in her navel and little mother-of-pearl shells covered her nipples. Posada was almost tempted, but decided to find some protection first.

While the Village was a lot safer than it had been ten years earlier, it was still wild. The WorldNet mercenaries couldn't be everywhere. It was always better to have an insurance policy, so he contracted a bodyguard not long after he left the maglev station.

\*\*\*

The woman was well armed, serious, and not keen on starting a conversation.

"Do you have a name?" asked Posada.

"Serena," came the curt reply.

He nodded. He was already enjoying the way the local street thugs backed away from them when they came too close, their eyes on the tall woman. He was sure Serena could do them damage if the circumstances required it.

*Moreover, I could help her, just for the hell of it!* He connected to the internet and began scouting out the list of restaurants and nightclubs in the Village. *It should be a fun night on the town, and very secure.*

He was addicted to his data, though. As they walked, he stayed plugged into the U.N.S.A. network with his data link. It was an old habit. Some might call it multitasking. Long ago, they had declared it an illegal activity while driving. He wasn't into the data as much as he had been with the large bandwidth connection, but he already had a picture of Serena in her birthday suit together with a complete bio.

*No privacy at all,* he thought with a smile. *Bai would be pissed that I'm using her servers in this way. Too bad!*

Unfortunately, Serena was only good for protection from the common street thug. She was no match for a hired assassin. They were as uncommon in New York City as anywhere else that mercenaries kept the peace. Nevertheless, a worldwide economy meant freedom of movement for anyone that could pay for it, so it was not possible to eliminate all danger.

A man or woman pissed off at his girl friend or her boy friend could make one call and set up a hit, for example, if he or she so desired. It was a lot easier now than at most times in human history. It was also illegal and if caught, both the assassin and the person that hired the assassin would receive a lethal injection, unless there were mitigating circumstances.

However, the death penalty wasn't much of a deterrent. Never before in human history was there such material abundance and never before was such a small value put on human life, especially in the large cities suffering through the Chaos.

It didn't help that many people were armed either. The smallest argument could turn into a blood bath when tempers were lost over trivia and hotheads went for their guns. It was a trend started in the U.S. over a century ago when the Supreme Court interpreted the Second Amendment of the Constitution as a personal right to bear arms although the amendment only mentioned militias and not individual persons.

The trend to carry weapons openly had spread throughout a world uneasy about its future, especially in nations where anarchy ruled and life was cheap, nations where food and medicine were often obtained at gunpoint. When the mercenaries swarmed in their first action was to disarm the population, by force if necessary. The U.S. Constitution and its legal progeny were just relics.

However, New York City even under WorldNet occupation was still very dangerous. Posada knew that life was not this way among the Spacers. Therefore, he had often thought of becoming a Spacer. Almost immediately, the big negative would jump up and slap him in the face: he would miss his nights in his beloved Village.

***

The assassin found him in the men's room at *Tio Pedro's*, a posh new bar on Bleecker Street. Posada had stopped in for a *mojito* while he still went through the list of restaurants and nightclubs. He would often visit two or three during a night on the town.

Wild conversations drowned out *Tio Pedro's* booming sound system. Pulsing lights turned customers into psychedelic aliens. Women with proud breasts and gyrating hips and their muscular male companions endeavored to hold their partner's interest. Unattached men and women circulated in search of fresh prey.

Posada left most of his drink, which was poorly made, bent to whisper a few flirtatious words in the ear of a supple black woman at the next table, and made his way to the WC. Serena followed.

She was standing discreetly back by the sinks, waiting for Posada to finish his business at the urinal, when the assassin came in.

"Look out!" she screamed.

The man had stepped up to a urinal on the left side of Posada, who was struggling with a stubborn zipper that had lost all memory of its purpose in life. It was an old pair of pants and the MEMs didn't always function correctly.

108

He glanced towards the man and saw a vibrablade arcing towards his back. Serena stopped it in mid-arc and applied enough torque to flip the man over.

Unfortunately, the attacker didn't lose control of the knife. He simply switched hands and threw. Serena's shot went wild as the vibrating knife landed below her left breast.

"Sorry," she whimpered sadly, falling to the floor, gushing blood from the knife wound starting to cover her torso. She dropped the gun on the way down.

Posada backed away from the assassin. Although he knew that someone outside in the bar had probably heard the shot, he also knew that no one would dare investigate. Not in the Village.

*But why me? Why is a pro coming after me? Who have I pissed off enough for this to happen?*

The man picked up the gun, fired three rounds in a tight cluster into Posada's chest, tossed the gun down on the dying woman, and hurried out of the men's room. Already on the cold tiles, Posada watched the feet of the man disappear.

The data kept coming. *My data.* He touched it with his mind, caressing it, feeling its information content. *Entropy. Shannon's theorem. So much to know, so little time. I need to smack Shannon around a little. He didn't know quantum encryption. I do. Too many worlds of data.*

And then all turned black.

# Chapter Twenty-Two

Lewis was surprised to see Moravcsik's avatar at the funeral. Spacers' funerals are private, even in VR land—simple affairs that are respectful to the grieving next-of-kin and close friends. Tanglevsky had few friends so most members of the small group visiting Susan Ito's place in cyber space were there to support her.

*Consequently,* thought Lewis, *either she invited Moravcsik to join them, highly unlikely, or the brass-balled SOB is violating Spacer conventions and hacked into her VR space.*

Mikey saw him too, and dug her virtual elbow into Lewis' side. Her real body was stretched out on a cot in her quarters, in REM sleep, but her avatar was tireless.

"*Que pelotas tiene,*" she murmured, knowing that Lewis knew enough Spanish to understand her meaning. Since her words agreed with what he was thinking, that Moravcsik was very ballsy, he only nodded.

Moravcsik's avatar was standing next to Hazel Zuckerman's, Dione's unofficial chaplain. Moravcsik was a small, wiry man who smiled rarely except when he believed he had pulled something over on someone. His skin was almost translucent and the slant of the eyes and high cheekbones made him look like a ghoul.

*A space ghoul,* thought Lewis.

Zuckerman, a plump and pleasant person, served as Guide to the Way, a new religion taking hold among the Spacers, but she was also an authorized representative of a number of other religions. Spacer society allowed that. It would be unheard of back on Earth, except on the battlefield.

Zuckerman did an appropriate job of comforting Susan Ito; said the minimum number of words of the Catholic ceremony that would let Tanglevsky's soul go to wherever it was destined to go as a consequence of the good or bad deeds done in his Catholic life; and watched as Tanglevsky's avatar faded from their virtual world in a glow of shimmering blue light. The real body had already gone into the Dione recycling system a day earlier.

The ceremony was over.

***

Lewis immediately went over to Moravcsik.

"I didn't expect to see you here."

"Jon, in spite of popular opinion, I do have feelings for the people that work for me. As head of this project, I felt it was my duty to be here. Pay respects and all that. He was too young to die."

"We all are," said Mikey, coming over to stand beside Lewis. "But he shouldn't have been there. Neither should I. We weren't really needed."

Moravcsik blushed at that direct criticism of his command decisions. Even the Dione science station's old computers were that good. They could detect all the nuances of facial expression and play them back on the avatar, unless the avatar's owner broke the rules of VR social intercourse.

*But then you would know it,* thought Lewis. *The body language would be all wrong.* Lewis now respected the spunky Argentine more, even though she was only standing up to Moravcsik in cyberspace, which didn't count for much, especially in a court of law. *But then, you can't kill an avatar.*

"We needed to run with that part of the project," Moravcsik said. "Let's just say that it's barely off the starting line, so more people can help it along."

The bureaucratic bricklayer philosophy that twice the people did work twice as fast was a criticism of Lewis' leadership, which both he and Moravcsik knew was unjust. Mikey gave him a sideways look that settled him down, though, so he didn't strike back.

"At any rate, he's dead," said Lewis, "and maybe we should all go away and let Susan be alone with Hazel for a while."

"Perhaps you should leave cyberspace and comfort the real Susan," observed Moravcsik with a lewd wink.

Lewis nearly lost it at that point, but Mikey's expression warned him that this wasn't the time or the place. *I'll add another item to your IOU list,* Lewis mentally told the man. *I'll make them come due all at once, and when I do....*

"But then, that would be a distraction from your work," continued Moravcsik, oblivious to how near he was coming to a verbal thrashing. "You all do it so well that the whole project should march along smoothly. The only problem is, the rest of Project Saturn Watch, like your little piece of it, keeps falling farther and farther behind the schedule originally submitted to Isha Bai, which she in turn negotiated with our sponsor. So our sponsor is not very happy."

"To hell with the sponsor," said Lewis, immediately regretting it. Nevertheless, he decided to plow on. "It's high time that Earth-bound bureaucrats stop trying to put scientific research programs on a schedule. They've almost killed every project I've worked on because some artificial milestone wasn't met when they thought it should be."

"Maybe that says something about you," commented Moravcsik. "All you scientists are so engrossed in your work that you become stuck in the quicksand of details and lose the big picture. The sponsor, on the other hand, has the big picture, and I share that vision."

"Which is to maximize profit in the minimum amount of time, of course," said Lewis with a smile. "I always knew this mix of scientists and profit-hungry corporations wasn't a good one. I don't know why Isha Bai ever allowed it."

"Careful, Lewis. If you keep talking like this, you will succeed in pissing off every one of your backers. You might have to go back then to your reservation and herd sheep."

Moravcsik did a smart military about-face and strode out of the cyber room.

*** 

"What did he mean by that?" asked Mikey.

"I'm part Navajo, born and raised in New Mexico. An anachronism, at least from Moravcsik's point of view. Believe it or not, some of my relatives still herd real sheep, forever resisting the ways of the modern world."

"Why, the bigoted SOB!" said Mikey. "I thought racism like that was a thing of the past."

"Don't believe it. Although most people cannot claim to be pure anything anymore, you'll still find pricks like Moravcsik. Moreover, he's probably not even racist. He knew that that would be a good cyberslap in the face at me. And it was. He earned a whole bunch of negative points today. And I won't forget them."

"Well, table it for now. I think we should say something to Susan."

Lewis did so, mumbling something comforting and giving her a cyberhug. She wasn't crying. At least her avatar wasn't. People would forgive her if she were cheating a little, considering the circumstances.

*A strong woman. Most Spacer women are strong. Or dead.*

\*\*\*

"Buy you another one?"

Lewis looked up from his equations. Hanson was holding a pint of beer in a plastic sippy bottle and was pointing at Lewis' empty one. They were deep into the sleep cycle, but Lewis couldn't sleep.

"You know, there was nothing you could have done. Most people would push him planetwards."

The robot server plopped the beer down and scurried off to take care of another scientist or technician.

"Let's not talk about it."

"Well, I'm certainly not in the mood to talk about your damn equations." He took a long gulp and winked at Lewis. "Let's talk about Montero then. She's very limber, I bet. Have any intentions there, old man?"

"Not me. I've sworn off women. Go for it."

Hanson had a rep as a ladies' man. Lewis knew that his first and only attempt at a long commitment had gone up in flames when the woman married someone else.

"Do you think she'd go for an old fellow like me?"

"I wouldn't if I was her, but that's just me. You're not cute anymore."

"I was never cute, not even as a baby. It's my effervescent personality that women are attracted to." Hanson guzzled some more beer.

"From the beer bubbles, I suppose."

\*\*\*

113

In her cabin, Montero waved her hand to shut down her terminal. The 3D representation of an extensive dataset faded from view. She didn't even keep it in her mind's eye. Instead, the visual memory of Tanglevsky's body made her shake her head and shiver.

*It is not revenge when you see a dead body. What a waste!*

She didn't dwell on that bad memory. Her thoughts soon turned to Lewis. She had learned something new about him. He was a scientist with moral scruples, a man tied to his responsibilities. Also a little inscrutable. A real nice mystery man.

*Am I attracted to him? He could be my grandfather. However, Tanglevsky turned out to be a cad.* In Spacer society, differences in age didn't matter so much, but those differences often correlated well with choices in life styles. *I'll have to learn more about Jon Silent Eagle Lewis.*

# Chapter Twenty-Three

"Cold for a swim, isn't it?"

Juanito opened one sleepy eye and squinted into the fading sun. Some twenty meters down the shoreline stood a dwarf dressed in denim and animal skins. He stood beside a burro that had no ears and patches of hair missing.

"Leave me alone," moaned Juanito.

"Can't. I saw what those normals did to you."

"Normals?"

"Yep. You, me, Pedro here, we're mutants. Me, I can see the future. Just sometimes, 'course, in my dreams. Name's Horacio, and what I see is you going on a journey with me."

Horacio walked along the bank bringing Pedro and him closer to Juanito.

"Go away." Juanito was still enjoying the warm sun but his stomach ached with hunger. "I don't care what you see."

"No one else does either, but I do. I figure if I see it, I must act correspondingly." He curled a finger at Juanito, beckoning him to come. "I know you don't like the idea about swimming in that icy water again, but Pedro here wants to make a new friend."

Juanito studied the dwarf. The tiny gnats that swarmed around him accented his slovenly appearance. A scraggly beard fell down his barreled chest to the rope at his waist that served as a belt. An old baseball cap covered a thick mane of hair.

Juanito shrugged, left the stone, and waded through the water to where Horacio was standing.

"Take off your pants. I have a blanket."

They pitched camp right by the lake. Juanito helped the old man gather wood for a fire and then helped him eat a roasted rabbit with only three legs. After dinner, he curled up in the blanket and fell asleep.

\*\*\*

"Where're we going?" asked Juanito.

He was perched on top of his new friend Pedro and was just becoming used to the swaying gait of the burro. Horacio walked ahead, eyes focused on the horizon, looking for game as well as two-legged enemies.

"Northeast, I'd say. I dreamed that I'd leave you by that new spaceport."

"Why?"

"If I knew answers to questions like that, I could predict the future. I'd find my way to those casinos in Cartagena or Santa Marta and gamble my butt off." He coughed and spit blood and sputum into the tall reeds. "The dreams come and go. I can't explain it."

"But why the spaceport?"

"If I knew answers—"

Juanito stopped the old man's repetition. "Oh, shut up. You know what my question means. What am I going to do at the spaceport? Just watch?"

"My dream stops when I leave you there. You'll have to figure it out."

"There are too many people there. Either they'll catch me or I'll starve. Not that I wouldn't mind seeing it before I die."

"There you go. You'll see it. Then you can die."

Juanito threw a peach pit at the gnome. It bounced off his backpack.

*The peach was shriveled and bitter. At least I got some good out of it.*

"When you're up to it, change places with me," said Horacio, ignoring Juanito's anger. "We'll make better time trading off that way."

\*\*\*

The trek took them less than a month. They joined up and followed the main highway between Bogota and Tunja. It was first a cracked ribbon filled with many potholes caused by winters of disuse. As they continued, though, the surface improved. They saw more and more people, fewer mutants and more normals.

A gang of mean kids threw garbage at them in Tunja and chased them out of town. Otherwise, the *campesinos*, the

Colombian farmers, took pity on them and their burro. The two lived on their handouts and the small game they hunted.

Horacio had a pleasant voice and sang *bambucos* and the *bunda tolimense*, keeping on pitch without any accompaniment. Soon Juanito was able to join him.

*Must be in my blood*, he thought. He had never heard music before.

Horacio was also a good storyteller. One night he told Juanito all the names of the brightest stars. Another night he told the story of how the despot, Rojas Pinilla, had declared Villa de Leyva a national monument. He was a progressive force in Colombia a long time ago, bringing to end a bloody civil war, but a coalition of politicians swept him aside. He was, after all, a dictator.

"Did you know him?" asked Juanito.

Horacio would laugh at questions like that. Even Colombia was ancient history.

\*\*\*

Posada awoke. It seemed that he had been sleeping for a long time. He wanted to stretch but there was nothing and nowhere to stretch. There were threads of light that he could see but he had no eyes. Moreover, when he willed his hands to grasp the threads, there were no hands.

He seemed to be on a data mining expedition again. However, before there was always a remaining sensation of a peripheral body—now there was none. Instead of moving through vast terabytes of information, he was intertwined with their currents, nearly drowning in them. He was cold yet experienced prickly heat and the buzzing of mosquitoes.

*Where am I?*

The void didn't answer his question. He had memories, many of them. There was that first explosion of pubescent orgasm when he came with Martina, the high school chess champion. There was even the death of his dog Shucks when he was only two. He remembered further back in time swimming in the womb, sensing the comforting throb of his mother's heart.

He was giddy with the overload produced by the memories. It was a strange sensation, this wraith-like existence among the terabytes. His emotions were like a flood speeding down an arroyo, carrying him along while they drowned him.

117

Yet all the memories were tagged and ordered, streams and streams of data, all completely logical. He could sample one, then the other, as if they were files in some vast computer architecture.

He then found the last memories before the flood started. Serena dying. Henry dying.

*Better question: What am I?*

⊪ ⊪ ⊪

His new environment gradually conditioned Posada.

*Or am I changing it, molding it to my needs?*

It was an interesting question. Whatever it was, it was like moving through a viscous fluid. It resisted. It sapped his mental energy to push against it. Nevertheless, he was in no hurry and appeared to have all the time in the world.

Input and output were the hardest. He had to conquer these serial processes step-by-step. It was like learning to walk but much more difficult. The pointing finger became a laser writing on the paper of a color printer. Thoughts became words that became voltages sent to a speaker assembly.

After a perceived long time but what really amounted to only six days, he looked out into a darkened room with people busy at terminals.

*Where am I? What am I?*

***

Juanito always heard a steady murmur of voices in his head. Sometimes they seemed loud but most of the time they formed a noise background that he could tolerate, although it gave him headaches.

He nearly jumped off the burro when a new voice was added to the choir, strong and resilient.

*"Hola Juanito, como estas, mi amigo?"*

He studied Horacio up ahead but the little man was oblivious to the new voice. Horacio had been telling Juanito about religion, about God, Jesus, and the Virgin Mary, along with the other saints.

"Are you God?" he asked the voice inside his head.

118

A chuckle echoed back and forth in his skull. "Not likely. My name is Henry. I'm dead."

Juanito began to worry. "How is it then that I'm speaking to you?" He was afraid to know the answer.

"I wish I knew, and why. You are much more receptive than Horacio."

"You talk to Horacio?"

"No, but I can influence him a little. His dreams about the spaceport come from me."

"Then he can't see the future?"

"That he can but I can help with the details. I'd call it bringing the image into focus, but you don't know what that means. I don't know how I'm doing it, though. Can I ride with you?"

"Since I can't reach in and tear you out of my head, I guess I don't have any choice."

"Good. Let me teach you some things."

***

In Tunja, they turned west. For Juanito the trip took an eternity, but he enjoyed it. Except for the voice that was trying to teach him. He was not a fast learner.

They eventually found themselves close enough to the spaceport to hear the roar of the shuttles as they raced towards the clouds above the Andes. Horacio would point to the sky and Juanito would see a ball of fire ascending.

"Why don't they burn up?"

It was an innocent question originating from fear. The dwarf's answer was quick and was loaded with awe and admiration.

"They're in a bottle-like enclosure, riding on top of the fireball. You'll soon see what they look like on the ground."

***

The day came when Horacio left Juanito.

"What am I supposed to do now?" he asked the little gnome, tears in his eyes. By then he was fond of him and for once knew what it was like to say goodbye to someone you care for.

Horacio twirled his moustache a moment, deep in thought.

119

"I still got nothin', *amigo* Juan. I just know I'm heading for the coast and you're no longer with me. I think I only see your future when it overlaps with mine, but I don't even see all of mine."

"What will happen to you on the coast? And what is a coast?"

Horacio answered the second question first. He scowled then and looked at the clouds, obviously avoiding the first question.

"*E bien?*"

"If you must know, I think I'm going to die. Or be killed. Effectively the same outcome, I suppose."

"So, if you stay here, that won't happen."

"I always go where my dreams lead me."

Juanito wondered if his friend Henry would continue to affect those dreams. "Well, make an exception this time."

"I'd need an answer to your first question then: if I stay, what will I do?"

"So you leave me pondering that question and you take off with Pedro?"

"No, no, Pedro stays with you. I go alone." He approached Juanito slowly. They hugged. "Good luck, Juanito. Hopefully, you won't need it."

Juanito wiped away the sting of the tears in his eyes, leaving a streak of mud on his face. Horacio blotted it away.

The boy waved to the dwarf as long as he could. He then mounted Pedro and rode towards the spaceport.

# Chapter Twenty-Four

Moravcsik's office in the Dione science station was small but comfortable. It was also the most luxurious, but to a Spacer luxury didn't mean the same as it did to a Downy.

He sipped a glass of Beaujolais (he had always preferred red since he was a boy) while he keyed in the passwords that would allow him to contact Earth. Audio only, no video. He also keyed in the code that would tell the computer and communications console to transmit directly from the data link device behind his ear. It was the most secure way to handle the communication.

The computer would take his subvocalized commands, encrypt them using the quantum key, and send them on their way to Earth, thus leaving as the only place for interception to occur the half-meter distance from the terminal to his head. Even that was a directional beam with an encrypted signal.

He really didn't have to worry much about security on his end since none of the scientists and engineers working with him would invade his privacy. Spacers were notorious for respecting the privacy of individuals. Ted Moravcsik knew, however, the man on the receiving end was very paranoid about secrecy and didn't understand Spacer culture at all.

"This is Moravcsik. Transmission for Martinez."

A direct conversation with Earth was impossible, of course. The one-way trip back to Earth took more than one and a quarter hours, the exact duration mostly depending on how far Saturn was from the Sun, since the Earth-to-Sun distance was negligible compared to the Saturn-to-Sun distance. It was just another brick to add to the wall of isolation between Spacers and Downies.

"There are no significant problems to report. We lost a man. Tanglevsky. He was married to Susan Ito. She's taking it as well as anyone can expect. Lewis is on my case about it since I forced him to take along Tanglevsky and another newcomer, Mikey Montero, to help him with his Helene project." Moravcsik swallowed when the bitter memory stirred up his acid reflux.

*Scientists are a hard bunch to handle.* "Tanglevsky had the additional job of giving me dirt on Lewis. I'd like to get rid of Lewis. He makes my job difficult since he's actually busting his ass to do his work well. However, eliminating him is not so easy here as there. There's no dangerous Village around. End contact."

***

Two hours later Martinez' sent his reply.

"I do hope you keep that information to yourself. I think I overstepped my own security rules when I told you. I'm proud of it, but you really have no need to know."

There was a pregnant pause. Moravcsik imagined that Martinez was gathering his thoughts.

*Let's hope this thug has no surprises for me.*

"And, by the way, I don't have time for your petty local politics. We have bigger fish to fry here. I've just come up with the *coup de grace* in some plans that I've had sitting around, waiting for the right moment. Again, no need to know, but I like to brag."

"The Man is going to speak in Philadelphia on July 4. Being a Spacer, you may not realize that the date has some importance for the Mid-Atlantic Union and some of the other North American countries, since it's the day the old United States of America declared its independence from England. President Ruffini will be speaking and I think he's trying to line up some of the other heads of state from North America."

There was now an audible chuckle.

"I think it's only become a day to watch fireworks and get drunk. Ruffini's good at the latter. Besides, I have plans for my own fireworks show. You don't have to worry about a thing. Just sit back and enjoy it. Keep up the good work there. We want to make Denise look as bad as possible. End contact."

Moravcsik didn't really want to hear any more. Obviously, Martinez was planning something big for July 4, 2132, but he didn't want to know any details. The mother planet and its messy politics were not his top priority.

He turned on some classical country music, which made him think of his Dora. She was a classical music lover and was always amused that her ex, with ancestors from the land that produced composers like Smetana, Dvorak and Janacek, was more

122

a fan of the old U.S. country and western style music that she called Texas noise. His grandfather and father's taste in music were the same, though, so Moravcsik resented her joke. He had no idea where the family predilection for country music came from. He had been born on Mars. Such music just fit in there. It was a frontier planet.

"You run your business there, whatever it is," he muttered as if Martinez were sitting in front of him. "I want to ensure a safe and comfortable retirement on Mars where I can watch my grandkids and think about the mysteries of existence. End contact."

***

On the next trip out after Tanglevsky's funeral, it took two days to finish installation of the antenna mounting system and lower the assembled structure down to Helene, another two to set up the com hut. Another ship and team that would start the construction of a base camp then relieved them. The new team also included Susan Ito and her nanoengineers, who would program their little friends to stitch together a habitat for any research team members who happened to be stationed on Helene.

"It'll be nice to remove some of this grime and grit," said Mikey, as the three afterwards shed their spacesuits at the base camp on Dione.

"My smell is part of my charm," Hanson said. "Want to go out on the town?"

"Not much of a town, and not right now. Look me up after I've slept for about forty hours."

"I can think of less boring things to do between the sheets," Hanson said.

"I said to look me up in forty hours." She sauntered off on her own, heading for the small cubicle that she shared with five other unattached women.

"She's a firecracker," Hanson observed.

"Talks a good line anyway," said Lewis. "I'm not sure you could handle her, old man."

"Who you calling old? *Compadre*, you're three years older than me. You're a founding father of the geriatrics club."

Lewis chuckled. "What say we clean up and go find some action in the lounge?"

"Think there's a game on?"

"There's always a game on."

\*\*\*

Four technical staff members were already into a heated mixed live-VR poker game when Hanson and Lewis joined them. Two were from the medical department and the other two from the team that would relieve the workers on Helene the third shift. One man, three women, and it looked like the women were winning.

They continued to win after Hanson and Lewis joined the game, so after two hours Lewis folded. He found himself a vodka and tonic squeeze bottle in the refrigerator and sat down to suck on it while he looked at a news program that was on the lounge news feed.

There was no sound, since the news feed was piped into a general intranet channel that he could tap into via his implant. With subvocalized commands, he could instruct the network servers to record specific news items, or even images, for future reference. However, nothing caught his attention.

Fighting was going on near Vienna and the whole region was in chaos. WNN showed GenCorp mercenaries strung up and crucified on crosses along one road leading into Grado. In Norway, the Swedes were almost ready to make their move on Oslo but fighting was still intense behind their most forward lines. In the U.N. High Assembly, threats were being made against the Norwegians, promising disbarment from the world body if they made good on their threat to use nukes on Stockholm. Patsy Rose, the hottest new singing sensation, just had her/his second sex change operation, was once again Pat Rose, and was going to marry Helen Clark, the president of the Trans Canadian Federation.

After Pat Rose, Lewis lost interest. It was hard for him to relate to any of it, since a lot of it didn't make much sense to him.

"Can't compare with out here."

Lewis looked away from the video screen. Mikey Montero stood next to him.

"You mean space?"

\*\*\*

The mere word had a lot of emotional baggage for Lewis. He figured he could have done any job as long as it was in space. He was happy with what he was doing, most of the time, but ever since he was a kid looking through a telescope, he knew his future was beyond Earth, even beyond LEO.

He also knew he was very lucky. Only the vagaries of politics affecting space exploration delayed it long enough so that he could do what he had done in his lifetime. If he had been alive in 1969 and extrapolated to the future, he would have concluded that something similar to Project Saturn Watch would take place about 100 years ago. Space exploration was the rage in 1969 when man first walked on the moon.

By 1980, it was passé. Like a drunken pendulum, the world periodically lost its motivation. Lucky for him, he decided, but not lucky for those poor bastards in the last century and a half who didn't lose their wonder but were caught in the down cycles.

*Shit happens,* he thought. *Just ask the Neanderthals.*

She sat down beside him. "Yeah, space, I can't get enough of it. Even with what happened to Tanglevsky, I'm hooked on it. Oh, I respect it and know it can kill me, but I'm hooked. Is it the same for you?"

Lewis thought about it some more. At the risk of being preachy, he decided to offer some advice to the young.

"Most of the time. When I was your age, maybe more so, but then I was also more afraid. Out here a respectful fear is healthy."

She nodded.

"You know I'm new at this and I know you still don't have complete confidence in me." When Lewis politely started to object, she waved the objection aside. "I want you to know that if I'm ever making a major screw-up, you should tell me."

"Won't be necessary." He smiled at the questioning rise of her dark eyebrows. "If you have a major screw-up, you'll probably be dead."

"Well, aren't you cheery? Have I had any minor screw-ups?"

"Only one. I'm old enough to be your father."

"That obvious, huh? In fact, you're probably old enough to be my grandfather or great-grandfather. You and Hanson swing the other way?"

"Hell no. Gus is an incurable woman chaser, whose perpetual horniness might be of use to you right now, but he's incapable of making a commitment. Still, if it's a quickie you want, maybe you should approach him."

"I don't know what I want right now. Men always have that commitment problem and often mistakenly think that all women want it. Evolution at work, I guess." She winked at him. "What about you? Are you into commitments?"

"Never found the right woman. Once, I thought it might be Susan Ito, but that didn't work out." Lewis was becoming uncomfortable with her teasing smile and mischievous eyes. "I'm not sure where you want to go with this. If you don't mind, I'd prefer not to talk about my unsuccessful attempts to establish a meaningful relationship with a woman."

"I'm with you there," she said, knocking her squeeze bottle together with his in a toast. "About the relationships, that is. However, don't give me crap about your age. I've caught you and Hanson both with that look on your sweaty faces that tells me you're mentally undressing me. Men are pigs." She laughed. "Necessary, at times, but pigs nonetheless. It's evolution, I think. You complain about women being emotional, but you're also slaves to your testosterone. And when you find a woman who's smart, you become intimidated all to hell."

"That's a little heavy for out here, and especially for me. I like smart women. Besides, we work so closely that everyone has to respect everyone else, independently of plumbing or age. In general, that's the way it has to be, or you shouldn't be expecting any help in a tough situation."

"OK, points for you. I was actually speaking of Downies, and, in particular, my birthplace. Latin America still has a ways to go in men treating women like equals."

"They've had their ups and downs like anywhere else, I guess. Where do you come from?"

"Argentina. Cordoba, to be specific, but I haven't been there in years. Back to the meaningful relationships. If I'm willing to forget the meaningful part for now, do you ever screw just for the pleasure of doing it?" Little crow's feet around the corners of her eyes were pointing now at the sparkle within them.

"That happens a lot out here too, you know." He decided to go the academic, safe route. "It's called recreational sex by our

126

psychologists, who consider it a healthy way to relieve stress, which we seem to have a lot of."

"I know all that touchy-feely 'it's good for you' crap. Why don't they come out already and just say it's fun? Everybody psychoanalyzes everything to death."

"You're preaching to the choir, *tavarisch*," Lewis said, trying to keep his smile from becoming lecherous when he finally realized that her attentions were genuine. He said something in Spanish. His accent wasn't particularly good, but she blushed.

"The flower is ready for the bee, Romeo. Lead on. I need to take my mind off Roger."

\*\*\*

It was only some time later while they were resting from their first exertions that she provided details about her affair with Roger. It meant more to her than Roger, so she was hurt. She was looking for that commitment but Roger was only using her for extracurricular activity while he shacked up with Susan Ito.

*Respect for the dead be damned*, thought Lewis. Now he disliked the bastard even more.

She wanted to kill him when he broke off the relationship and then he did die. Lewis tried to comfort her with more sex but it had been an unplanned encounter for which he wasn't chemically prepared. She didn't seem to mind and fell asleep in his arms.

# Chapter Twenty-Five

President Craig Ruffini watched the newsnet report on the riots with some interest while toweling himself off. GenCorp mercenaries from the Northern Italian Union were trying to stop the looting and violence near Vienna's famed Schonbrunn palace, but he knew their heart wasn't in it. The mercenaries were on loan to the Holy European Empire, consisting of parts of the old Czechoslovakia, Austria, and Hungary. Milan, the mercenaries' home, had to seem far away to them.

Many pundits in the international media figured that if Vienna had something worth saving, the belligerent theocrats in charge there should save it themselves. Her Highness, the Alternate Pope, had fled to Budapest during the fifth week of her fasting protest and was reported to be on her deathbed. Most of the troops believed her death would restore some sanity to her country.

Ruffini's interest was more than historical. Many centuries ago, his ancestors had left Milan to come to America. Genealogy was a hobby for him that was not as questionable as some of his others.

As President of the Mid-Atlantic Union, he had been one of the first to make a pact with the multinational corporations. Their mercenaries were an effective albeit expensive police force, so he had plenty of time for his hobbies. They had brokered an uneasy truce in both New York City and Philadelphia, so things were quiet and he was still in control.

Of course, there were other prices to pay for stability. One was associated with the first visitor on his official morning schedule. It made him uneasy that his most important campaign financier had asked for an appointment for his personal avatar.

\*\*\*

Ruffini was neither a handsome nor a healthy man. His parents, subscribing to a minimal health plan, had not been able to afford gene therapy for their three children. Consequently, he was short, overweight, with both high cholesterol and type II diabetes. This together with the stress of his position and a long life of excesses with sex, drugs, food, and drink, most of them financed by taxpayers, left medical science very little to work with in spite of the fact that he could now afford full medical coverage.

His ego was very healthy, though, since he never doubted whether his official actions were beneficial to his country or not. While he dressed for his appointment, he admired the sleeping and angelic little slum girl who had been the target of his affections the night before.

*A night of pleasure compared to a day from hell. What does the man want?* He shivered.

***

The object of his dread was striking even as a holographic avatar. It was the first time he communicated with him via his personal avatar, previously depending on his minions and their encrypted messages to receive his orders. In a world where international corporations were more powerful than any government, his daily quota of admiring sycophants visiting in the flesh was smaller than a CEO's. This fact saved on bodyguard bills for both of them.

"It's a pleasure to meet you in person," Ruffini said, standing. He realized his error when the man scowled. VR was the next best thing but it wasn't "in person."

"I see you dabble in current events," Martinez said, indicating the screen, now muted. "Do you realize how much those stinking riots cost me?"

Ruffini realized it was a rhetorical question. He offered his unwelcome guest a chair. Senator Rudolfo Martinez was a good five centimeters taller than he was. His avatar pretended to sit.

"I assume you're here for some other reason. I can't imagine what can be so special about our conversation that you can't contact me as you have before. But I'm at your service."

His guest waved a hand at the screen again. "None of your obsequious drivel. And turn off the news feed. I don't want distractions." Ruffini did so. "Do you know about Project Saturn Watch?"

Using his data link implant, Ruffini consulted various databases.

"Low cost research project sponsored by WorldNet. It's behind schedule, plagued with accidents, many screw-ups. So what?"

"A lot of that I organized." He smiled at Ruffini's rising eyebrows, but his deeds seemed to startle the President more than his admission of guilt. "I'm calling in a favor here. One of my best computer people has found out that U.N.S.A. Security is about to send one of its best troubleshooters out to Saturn. Your ex-sister-in-law is captain of the big rig the trouble shooter's going to be catching up with."

"Cecilia? You want her to do you a favor?"

"No, the favor comes from you in convincing her. Pressure her a little with her daughter, who works at LEO—whatever is needed. I want this agent out of my way. First, I have a little family score to settle. Moreover, that way, by the time the U.N. can send out another trouble-shooter, my people in Project Saturn Watch will have brought it to a screeching halt."

Ruffini twitched at the words "score to settle." Rather than attack something that sounded like a mafioso's revenge threat, he attacked on a different front.

"Why don't you take over the project by offering more supporting funds than Denise Andersen? You could easily do that."

"Yes, and I could buy the Mid-Atlantic Union, too, but it's much cheaper to buy you. Then I own the Union as well." The avatar smiled and Ruffini grimaced. "There's no real discussion here. Do as I say and you will have your third and final term in office. If you don't, I can make your life much more miserable and worthless than it is now. Understood?" Ruffini nodded. "This is, of course, between you and me. Your dear ex-sister-in-law is to know nothing about who is calling in this favor."

"She'll figure it out."

"But, with you as middle man, I have deniability." He stood, so Ruffini stood.

"One other item," said Martinez. "We are going to have a world-wide readiness exercise. Don't become upset when you hear there are a bunch of mercenaries stationed in Harrisburg." The smile was pleasant now. "We'll have them all over the world. For example, down near Bogota."

"Readiness for what?"

"To protect the things we don't want to lose." The avatar flickered as Martinez seemed to move closer. "Only 60% of the world is under the control of the corporation mercenaries. Some of that 60% and most of the 40% still suffers from the disease we call the Chaos. We have momentum. I don't want to lose it. Momentum for bringing order out of the Chaos. It's a vision many of us have."

Ruffini nodded. *Was the man insane?*

"But enough. Do like I've asked and you will be rewarded."

Ruffini watched the fading avatar, imagining that it left sulfurous smoke and sparks trailing behind it. He had heard about the Catholic version of Hell from his grandmother. Martinez could be the Devil's chief agent if not Satan himself. He even looked the part. He had never met a man like him. He was not sure that he wanted to repeat the experience, although it was only with an avatar.

With regret and after some hours of soul searching, Craig Ruffini turned to do the Devil's bidding and contacted his ex-sister-in-law. He knew he was too weak to stand up to Martinez. To assuage his guilt, he contacted Isha Bai to tell her about the readiness exercise. He had a gut feeling that Martinez was up to more than revenge in that case. If anyone could stand up to him, the Director of U.N.S.A. could.

# Chapter Twenty-Six

It was 1985. They confined car races back then to the ground. The autos in this race were dusty, oil-covered, gas hogs that tore around the circuit in dangerous bunches moving at incredible speeds. Rabid fans cheered on their favorite drivers. At random moments their chariots would joust against each other or bounce off barriers and the crowds would cheer at the smell of new blood.

Her car was something called a Pontiac, although she knew that no car sold at that time had much in common with what she was driving, in real life or virtual reality. It was a fiery red and bore the name "Demon Beast."

She turned into another curve, nearly slamming into one of the neighboring racers. She was three cars behind first and was intent on making some of it up in the curve. The other drivers would not be generous.

"Jenny, are you there?"

Jenny Wong reluctantly unplugged herself from the VR set. *NASCAR 1985* was a new zookie. Henry Posada gave the game to her the year before on her birthday. She used it and other games for fun but also to keep her U.N. troubleshooter skills sharp. Racecar driving required quick mental and physical reactions.

She missed Posada. She had rarely seen the young genius, knowing him more in the VR world of avatars in U.N.S.A. Security meetings, but she had liked him. In their own way, they both shared a thirst for life that took them from the mundane levels of existence to a higher plane. She had asked Isha Bai to let her work on solving the crime but the U.N.S.A. Director refused, saying that it was a New York City crime and that Denise Andersen's mercenaries were capable.

That she doubted. As much as she appreciated Zeb Lane's many skills, he was not a detective. Of course, neither was she.

Most of U.N.S.A. Security's responsibility split in two branches, protecting the U.N.S.A. Director from would-be assassins and gathering information she could use from areas not under the U.N. umbrella. Wong was her agent-at-large, which meant simply that she did many things for the Director. Isha Bai was very creative about sending her on challenging assignments.

"I thought I had some more time off. And where are you?"

"No more time since we have a Rich Uncle crisis. And I'm in Australia."

"Rich Uncle crisis" was code for some rich patron of the space program becoming disenchanted with how they were spending his money. Considering past events, Wong imagined that it was Denise Andersen, about as demanding as they come.

"Why does Rich Uncle need my personal pampering?"

"You're her favorite. A little sojourn to Saturn is required. I'll give you four days to put your affairs in order. When you're ready, you can take a shuttle to LEO out of any U.N.S.A. spaceport. I'll start a download of the relevant info now."

Wong smiled, thinking of the days she had spent with Brent Mueller. The Farside work and the previous work with Denise Andersen had been draining. The time spent in Switzerland had been good therapy but not nearly long enough.

*Fate and Denise will bring Brent and me together again.*

\*\*\*

Wong knew the Saturn trip would be long, even the way Bai planned it. She barely had time to arrange for real estate agencies to rent her tiny apartments in New York City and Singapore and put her meager belongings in long-term storage.

By the time she was on the way to the shuttle launch area at the port in Singapore, she had already learned enough about her next case to realize that she could be an unpopular person again. Spacers disliked the confining bonds of U.N.S.A. more than those of the multinational corporations.

They were refurbishing a large part of the spaceport, so there were minor inconveniences in moving from the residential area to the space shuttle terminal. She was a little bit late even, but the shuttle *Hercules* didn't dare leave without her. Isha Bai had made it clear that they had to wait for her agent.

Wong slid into a seat beside a silver-haired scientist as they closed the doors.

"Cutting it a little close," the man said, visibly annoyed by the fact that she was the reason for the delay.

It briefly startled her since she was downloading additional info about Project Saturn Watch. It didn't require her conscious attention since her data link device would store the information and play it back for her at her leisure, but she was already on her way to formulating a plan of action. She left the device on automatic with some subvocalized commands and turned to the man.

"Sorry. I often have to travel this way. Lots of running around down here, then boring months in space."

The man hesitated, reconsidered his opinion, and held out a hand. "I know what you mean. Name's Davis, Hal Davis."

More subvocalized commands to access a U.N.S.A. database. "The astrophysicist. The Terrestrial Planet Imager Project." She shook the hand. "Exciting stuff, TPI."

"Not nearly as exciting as the results from TPLF. Those were real breakthroughs."

Wong nodded. Terrestrial Planet and Life Finder was a project consisting of fifteen 25-meter telescopes that orbited around the Sun between Earth and Mars. Using precise laser ranging and thrusters, the scientists maintained their positions in an interferometric array spaced 1 kilometer apart to a precision of 1 micron. Already U.N.S.A. scientists had not only extended the long list of E-type planets orbiting other stars but also, using high-resolution spectra, they had discovered that the major constituents of some of the atmospheres of those planets were very Earth-like, namely water vapor, $CO_2$, nitrogen, and oxygen.

The first case was a public relations coup that had given new impetus to TPI. For weeks, the news was on the nets and in the global talk shows, both on Earth and throughout the solar system: the nearby star Tau Ceti, very nearly a twin to the Sun, had a terrestrial size planet in an orbit that put it in that star's habitable zone and that planet had an Earth-like atmosphere.

As often happens, public interest waned somewhat with further discoveries. The TPI project was the next step forward where scientists hoped to image oceans and continents on a twin Earth.

Wong already knew where Hal Davis was going, whom he would be working with, and what they hoped to accomplish, in more detail than the scientist could imagine. The clearances she possessed were only one notch below those of the U.N.S.A. Director.

Nevertheless, she was impressed. Smart people always impressed her.

"I wish you luck at Waypoint, and please say hi to Jules Bilodeau," said Wong. "I've not seen him in years. I went to school with him."

Davis only had time enough to realize that Wong was familiar with the ins and outs of TPI when the acceleration slammed them into their cushions. To Davis it was an agonizing few minutes, but Wong turned back to analyzing her downloads.

\*\*\*

One of the operators in Singapore's command and control room slammed down his tuna sandwich and started cursing.

"I just lost contact with *Hercules!*"

Others leapt into action and confirmed that the shuttle, bound for LEO, was off the grid. It didn't make sense since they were already past burnout.

"LEO, do you have contact with *Hercules?*"

"Sure do. Right on schedule."

"Then you'll have to guide her in. Somehow, we've unlinked."

Loss of communication with a shuttle happened often enough that the C&C group soon put the incident out of their minds. In particular, the first operator decided he hated syntho tuna.

\*\*\*

The acceleration stopped and Davis turned green. This was the worst part for him, the zero gravity environment. He was not in any condition to do any more talking until they were approaching LEO.

He smothered a burp with his fist and tried to think happy thoughts.

\*\*\*

Posada peered into the control room of *Hercules* and understood. He transferred to LEO and watched for a time until they guided the ship into a docking area near the space station.

*Piece of cake*, he thought. *I can do that.*

He had discovered what he was. He was not sure that he liked it.

* * *

Wong sprightly crawled through the docking tube, leaving Davis far behind. She figured she would just have time to pee.

Sure enough, the small robot-flitter was already checking out instrumentation as she squeezed into one of the four acceleration berths. A technician gave her an injection. Another threaded feeding and breathing tubes down her throat. Still others made other necessary connections to collect her bodily wastes. The first technician shut the plastic door. The berth filled with a green, gelatinous material. She was ready.

The flitter was a variant of standard emergency crafts found on the big rigs that cruised out to Mars, the asteroids, Jupiter, and beyond. They were designed to save lives and often did.

She would make half the trip with a 5 g push and the other half with a 5 g deceleration. It was the fastest way to travel from point A to point B when A was in the Earth-Moon system and B was beyond.

In this case, B was the *Valiant*, a big rig that was currently beyond Jupiter on its way to Saturn. It was not the best way to hitchhike, but there was no danger involved. Wong would have thought nothing of it, but, at that moment, conscious thought was gone.

She dreamed.

# Chapter Twenty-Seven

The phone rang. Clinton Bridges decided not to answer. He didn't like or use a lot of the new technology. In particular, he didn't have a place to plug in a wi-fi device surgically implanted behind his right ear.

Most friends thought of one of two reasons for his choice: either he's tight with his money or he's scared of the surgery. The real reason was that, in an age where communications toys invaded all aspects of life, he considered his privacy too valuable a commodity—even at the risk of missing a real emergency.

He was in the bedroom and the old-style cell phone was in the study off the living room in the heap of clothes they had left behind. He therefore ignored it. Moreover, it would be impolite. The young woman mounted on top of him was half his age and hell bent on coming again.

As a Cornell astrophysicist and full professor about to become emeritus, he knew better than to fool around with students, but Ursula Schmidt was a visiting biochemist from Hamburg whom he had met several weeks before down at one of Ithaca's better hangouts. Now she had shed her meek demeanor along with her clothes to become a wild woman.

*Uncle Raul was right. I'm a predator. I prey on young academics looking for a little spice in their lonely find-the-next-grant existence. It's easy hunting.*

Since he was also enjoying himself, he let his personal computer take the message. Sometime later, while she stroked his great handlebar moustache with one hand and his limp member with another, he remembered that he had received a call.

His apartment was not as modest as those of many of his academic friends. Clinton Bridges had been born into wealth. His father had been the more active partner of Bridges and Stern, one of the early pioneers in micro-g pharmaceuticals. The energetic and dedicated chemist turned entrepreneur had little time to spend on his son, so Clinton's earliest male role model was his mother's half-brother Raul.

Uncle Raul was a soccer star for the Chicago Hellions before the Chaos and always considered life an extension of the game he played. He played hard, too, and taught Clinton to do the same until the boy was seventeen when Uncle Raul died in the first New York City riots.

On the other hand, his mother, a dark-haired beauty from Santiago, had been a successful biochemist. She still held the record for patents in micro-g pharmaceuticals. Unfortunately, Clinton's father also neglected her. The Bridges' divorce made international news due to the size of the settlement. Clinton's mother was spiritually crushed. Alcoholism and drugs ended her life, leaving Clinton very rich but also very much alone.

Uncle Raul had taught him never to consider himself a victim, though, so he embarked on a scientific career along with an active social life that was the envy of his less gregarious colleagues. He enjoyed life to its fullest, from the mysteries he studied in the cosmos with his vast computer models, to the women that filled his life.

With respect to the latter, though, there was only one woman in his life that would make him ever consider signing a nuptial contract. The message was from her.

\*\*\*

Bridges sat down in an overstuffed chair, scratched around his mohawk, and logged onto his home workstation to hear what his caller had to say. The diminutive woman on the screen looked tired but around her was an aura of authority.

The black eyes were bright and sparkling, though, and the raven hair silky and short, just as he remembered. She had on a brightly colored housecoat with a high-necked collar, so the rest of her was covered, but Clinton knew every inch of what was underneath.

"Clinton, my dear, I hope you are having more fun than I am. At least, I bet your sex life is better." The screen barely captured her blush. "You know about my grandiose plans for the agency. Well, I think I may have become a victim of my own success." There was a pause while she rummaged through some papers. "I think we're going to have to swing the pendulum the other way for a while. I've been thinking about this for some time, but the Man has too, so now let's say it's almost an official order from the boss. I need your help in planning how to do this. Can you come and meet with me here?" She blew him a kiss. "Let me know your travel plans."

In a sense, it wasn't a question, but a command. As Director of U.N.S.A., Isha Bai was now used to commanding people to do her bidding by asking questions like that.

But Bridges was a citizen of a country where no treaty had yet been signed with the new U.N. (the Great Lakes Confederation was a little backward that way—even with its big cities Chicago, Cleveland, Detroit and Toronto driving its economy). He could thumb his nose at her and she couldn't do a thing.

Once he crossed over to New England or Mid-Atlantic, though, the U.N.S.A. security apparatus could take over and haul him down to Villa de Leyva, the new spaceport and new U.N.S.A. HQ, whether he liked it or not.

*Of course, she won't have to do that, since I'll go to Villa de Leyva on my own accord.*

While Ursula was a wonderful woman, she couldn't compare to Isha. Besides, Ursula was going home soon. Moreover, Isha sounded like she needed help. The Latin *zorro* in him couldn't pass up the opportunity. Maybe he could be in her good graces again.

*And her pants.*

Nevertheless, his citizenship did pose a travel problem, since U.N. affiliated nations gave travel priority to their own citizens. He wondered how long it would take him to travel to Villa de Leyva.

*Should I go through New York or through Boston?*

Both choices involved crossing country borders. He went to join Ursula in the shower, still mulling over the problems of international travel.

In a sense, it was a hassle he didn't need in his active but ordered life. Nevertheless, it would be an adventure. He hadn't been to Latin America in a while, not since his last trip to Cerro Tololo.

\*\*\*

Isha Bai turned away from the big screen on the wall facing her desk, opened the blinds, and stared at the Andes in the distance, always green, always silent. Shrouded in clouds that announced a pending thunderstorm, they looked down at the human beings who had progressed from savages that believed in magic to space-faring sophisticates who created their own magic.

There were now at least twenty flights per day to LEO from the Villa de Leyva spaceport alone. An average of one big rig per day docked up in LEO to unload its ores and micro-g products mined and developed in the out-world Spacer laboratories.

*Have the huge corporations that control Earth and beyond decided that U.N.S.A.'s piece of the action was no longer necessary, not even for political correctness?* she wondered.

It was a complicated question and one where she needed help. That was why Clinton Bridges was in Villa de Leyva.

She had gone hiking with Clinton only three days earlier. He tried to renew his relationship with her and was upset when he couldn't. Now, sitting across from her, stroking his great moustache, she regretted that. He was more than a friend but she didn't have time to renew personal relationships right now.

There was too much going on that she didn't understand. The Project Saturn snafus, now summarized by Ted Moravcsik, began to take a back seat to political problems within and without the U.N. organization. Ruffini's call hadn't helped. She started to feel overwhelmed by it all.

"So, I'm not sure why I'm here." The astrophysicist's heavy eyebrows danced. "Moravcsik's sleaze. We both know that. He knows a lot more shit than what he's saying in those reports. But so what? Do you think it relates at all to the problem the Man asked you to look at?"

"So you think Moravcsik's keeping information from me? Both GenCorp and WorldNet are heavy investors in the U.N. space program and, as I said, they'll resist my swinging the pendulum the other way. I don't trust Moravcsik and suspect he may be working for both of them."

Clinton Bridges chuckled.

"Yeah, Moravcsik would do that."

Bridges had said that he once met the man on Mars and knew right away that he would never be one of his favorite people. Still, he didn't have a bad rep as a project manager. That was a skill they both knew Bridges did not possess.

"Let me handle the Man's problem. He's right to worry about it and I have ideas about how to go about swinging that pendulum. Denise Andersen and Rudolfo Martinez and the rest of their ilk may not like them but I don't give a shit. Anything else, love?"

"I asked you to stop calling me that. Not at the office."

"This office is secure. We once had a good thing, you know."

"Youthful indiscretions. You're Dr. Bridges here and I'm Dr. Bai."

"No hope, huh?"

"Maybe with time." He stood as if to go. "But there's something else to talk about."

"I'm all ears, as they say."

\*\*\*

She told him about her conversation with President Ruffini and the strange request that Martinez had made to move his mercenary troops into the Harrisburg region. Other troops were stationed not far from Villa de Leyva.

"I've checked around. Security confirms that this is going around all over the world, so I called General Marshall."

"Why not Martinez himself? Horse's mouth and all that."

"I never understood that expression. Your speech is often an anachronism. I'm just more comfortable with Judith Marshall."

"Because she's a woman?"

"Partly. I trust her more than Martinez, although I could be mistaken. The Man liked the way she handled the events in Northern Italy and then in Scandinavia, so that's another point in her favor. She confirmed most of what Ruffini said and added that it was indeed all part of a readiness exercise."

"Readiness for what?"

"Martinez is afraid that the progress made to end the Chaos will have setbacks. He doesn't know where or when but wants to be prepared to save lives if possible."

"And you believe General Marshall's story?"

"I don't know what to believe. Denise Andersen knew nothing about it but she is paranoid about Martinez. Aren't we all? The world is a complex place. We have thousands of small countries playing around with nukes. Moreover, we still have extra

141

billions of people, many of them poor, starving, and angry. Holding it all together is a tenuous spider's web of multinational corporations motivated by greed. It's amazing that we've survived so far."

"I hate to say it but in my opinion those multinationals have helped a lot. Once we were past our Frankenstein complexes and went heavy into genetically improving our food production and spreading nanomachines around, the process of living has become a little less painful for most. The population topped out forty years ago and is in steady decline, even discounting all the Downies that have migrated into space. We have a chance to fix old Gaia up too."

"Ever the optimist. While you carry on your principal task, keep your eyes and ears open for anything that might perturb that vision you have of Nirvana on Earth. I believe in balances. But right now, the political winds are blowing every which way. Project Saturn Watch is the least of my worries. In addition, I'm not sure where this freeing up space R&D from the corporations stands either. The Man can be very idealistic some times."

"That's why people like him, love."

# Chapter Twenty-Eight

"So you're Jenny Wong."

Ceci Romero used the stump of her arm to indicate an open chair. Her only hand was holding a plastic squeeze bottle filled with coffee. Wong sensed that she had a natural distrust for bureaucrats.

Ceci, somewhat shorter and heavier than Wong, had her hair cropped short enough that the scar on her forehead, caused by the same accident that took her left hand and arm up to the elbow, glared white in the light of the rec hall aboard Valiant.

Wong had awoken aboard Valiant in one of the regular crew's quarters. Her flitter joined Valiant's other seven, lashed on to the principal axis of the big rig. After the five-day sleep on the high-g trip, she was bored.

The Valiant was also Brent Mueller's ship. After a passionate reunion, she asked him to set up a meeting with Captain Romero. He informed her that the Captain kept pretty much to herself but he would tell her.

The Valiant belonged to Denise Andersen who was having second thoughts about her investment in Project Saturn. The subprojects associated with the project were two years behind schedule on the average, so Jenny sympathized with her old friend. However, it would take her another three weeks to arrive at Saturn. Therefore, she wanted to do something useful.

"I needed to meet you face to face," began Wong. "I'm offering my services."

"Sorry. I don't swing that way. I get my jollies with the boys. I've heard that you do too, at least with Brent. Or are you looking for a ménage-a-trois?"

Wong smiled. The ship's captain was crusty, affable, perhaps a sensitive human being behind that gruff exterior. It made her job easier.

"My technical services. I'm no specialist, but I have general knowledge of what it takes to run a big rig. I shipped out on one when I finished school."

"Ah, where was that? Berkeley? Mid-Atlantic? Oxford?"

"Haven't you read through my records?"

The Valiant's captain drummed her fingers on her desk. Wong's ability to read body language and facial expressions told her that the older woman seemed to be struggling with an inner torment. Finally she spoke.

"No, I haven't. While there's probably a database somewhere that will tell me how many times you farted in 2129, and I could call it up easily enough, I figure your previous life is none of my business." She picked at a scab on her stump. "Besides, I don't have time for it. In addition to Brent Mueller and yours truly, we only have five more people in the crew. I take turns cleaning the toilets like everyone else."

"Olympus Mons," said Wong, ignoring the diatribe. "And I know how much you're overloaded for work. That's the whole point."

"OK, so you're a Martian Downy instead of an Earth Downy. That brings you up from hell to purgatory, but you're still damned as far as I'm concerned, if you'll allow me a religious metaphor that no one cares about any more. If you want real crew work, you'll have to tell me what you can do and convince me you won't kill me or my crew while doing it."

"What about killing myself?"

"I don't have a problem with that. Just one less U.N.S.A. bureaucrat, as far as I'm concerned."

"FYI: I don't consider myself a bureaucrat. In fact, I can wipe your granite face up and down this bulkhead before you even blink. So, show some respect, Captain, and I'll show you the same."

\*\*\*

Ceci Romero smiled at that. This oriental woman confused her.

Wong was dressed in standard female Spacer attire—bra, loose shorts, and slippers. She was 1.65 meters tall, large for a Spacer, but she was not fat. Well-toned muscles rippled beneath that golden skin.

144

*A tough woman*, she thought, *hides behind that demure, oriental exterior, and I like that.*

"So, what can you do for me?"

"Engineering, navigation, clean toilets—you name it. Tell me where you're short and could use some help and I'll do my best. Even better, work me into the regular rotation. I prefer it to boredom."

"All right. Good attitude, I guess, as long as you don't screw up. I need some extra hours of sleep myself. Know anything about computers?"

"I received a tech's license when I was fifteen," said Wong. "A dear friend on Earth kept me somewhat up-to-date. Although I'm not an expert, there's nothing aboard Valiant I can't handle."

"So you've noticed that she's old. Our patron doesn't believe in wasting up-to-date equipment on a ship that mostly hauls ore, even though that ore contains high-grade rare Earth metals."

\*\*\*

Wong had more than noticed Valiant's age. She experienced it. Without accessing any database, she would have guessed the ship to be at least 100 years old. In fact, she was 107 and one of the first nuclear thermal rigs constructed in Mars orbit. It was hauling twenty-two thousand metric tons of supplies for Project Saturn Watch with a constant 5 milligees of acceleration.

Among the thousands of ships making the long trips inbound to Earth or Mars and out-bound to the asteroids and Jupiter's moons, the Valiant represented a still-functional relic of a better era. She had started out life with N.A.S.A. and had progressed through a series of owners. Now even her newer company markings were mostly invisible due to the many years of fading in the harsh environment of space.

\*\*\*

"As you can see," Romero continued, "we're not rolling in luxury here. Speaking of that, the roll stabilizer is whacko. We don't have to fix it until we're closing in on Dione, but it can be one of your jobs." Wong nodded and turned to go but stopped at Romero's next question. "Why are you doing this?"

"I'm bored," she repeated.

"Not enough reason. You so far outrank me and everyone aboard this ship that you needn't bother giving us the time of day, except for Brent. So, why bother?"

"You have a jaded view of humanity, Captain."

"Ceci, it's just Ceci. Yeah, in my opinion, humanity sucks. Especially Downies. They've made one planet a shit pile and they're doing the same to Mars. My question still stands."

"Let's say that my father always taught me that it's a lot easier to make enemies than friends, but you need the latter much more than the former."

"Inscrutable oriental mysticism?"

"No. I think he heard it on one of the cartoon shows beamed to us from Earth."

***

Cecilia Romero was still smiling when she sat down at the secret com link in her cabin on which she had first received the call from Craig Ruffini. Supplied by WorldNet, she had been surprised that her ex-brother-in-law had received access to its special channels.

Now she was using it to communicate with him again. She didn't understand all the ins and outs of the politics involved, but she was doing what he asked of her.

Stashed inside a niche hidden in the wall, the transceiver fed into the main antenna pointing back towards Earth. Her message to him was short: "Contact made."

She was uncomfortable but he had been convincing. She turned out the light, stripped naked, and climbed into her bunk. Sleep did not come easily. She was thinking about her daughter back at LEO.

At sixty-five, Cecilia Romero didn't have much else to keep her going. The same accident that took her arm had taken her husband, Craig's brother, leaving her alone with a young daughter to raise.

Every time she left LEO, she knew that precious months with Silvia were being lost. Now her daughter was a grown woman, almost a stranger at times. She blamed Denise Andersen for that.

In theory, it could be very easy to transfer some of that blame over to Jenny Wong since Romero felt corporate sponsors owned U.N.S.A. She didn't know whether she could do it in practice.

# Chapter Twenty-Nine

Rudolfo Martinez looked around the virtual table at the virtual persons seated there.

*A very select group of thugs*, he thought, *these captains of world business and industry.*

It would be hard to destroy them so it was necessary to control them. Part of his plan was to offer them up to Isha and then, once she was finished, go in for the kill. The details depended on how events played out and what order they played out in, but Martinez thought he had all possibilities covered.

*Daddy would be proud.*

The group was not large, which only said that the number of people that controlled the world was small. In fact, Denise Andersen, addicted to power, was sitting there as if she owned the world.

*She practically does.*

Half a dozen others, not as rich and powerful as Denise, completed the group of magnates. They, their bankers, and other sycophants controlled about 90% of the world's wealth.

*No, not world's. Humanity's. Our reach extends out to Jupiter and beyond. We have become gods and ordinary men and women, mere mortals, are our slaves.*

It was not fun to work with them, but it was necessary for his plans. Of course, his plans were his own, while they thought he was their stooge.

*So much for intelligent people in the corporate world*, he thought.

"I've called you together so we can talk candidly. This is a shielded and doubly encrypted VR link—isn't technology wonderful?—so don't try to use your data link devices. The scrambling will give you a tremendous headache." He waited until all their avatars seemed comfortable. "Here's the problem: my informants tell me that Isha Bai is reconsidering the working relationship that she has established between the space industries and the agency."

*That much is true*, thought Martinez. From hacking her servers, he knew that Isha Bai had already received the word from the Man and ordered Jenny Wong's long trip to Saturn.

"Up to now we have been very effective in convincing her that space exploration is too expensive to be financed on the backs of taxpayers. She now believes that she has gone too far down that road and wants to balance things out a little."

He smiled at the collective groans. Their greed was the ring in the nose by which he could lead them where he wished. He, through his father, knew that it was Isha Bai who had convinced many of these same thugs that it was in their interest to finance space exploration. They had all been surprised when it turned out to be so profitable. Now they were accustomed to the profits and wanted to maintain the *status quo*.

***

It was classic Martinez family strategy: put two strong forces working against each other and go in for the kill after they had left each other bloody and battered. It had last worked with the Alternate Pope, who now languished in a cell in Turkey, still very much alive but powerless.

*Nearly a fiasco, however, so I'm tired of doing things piecemeal. July 4 looks better and better.*

"I have no time for this nonsense," said Andersen. "Project Saturn Watch has become a continuous drain for me, so I'm not even sure I care if Isha Bai takes us out of space. In fact, I have instructed Isha to do something about it, so don't mess up my plans. I hate to lose money."

"Must be bad management on the part of the corporate sponsor," commented Martinez. "If you like, I can set up things so we take it over from you. I wouldn't charge much for the favor."

"Do you think I'm making gifts to charity here? Over my dead body."

Martinez shrugged.

"Your call, my dear." His avatar looked at the rest of the group. "I believe you will all agree that everyone has benefited from the stability the mercenaries have brought to our unstable world."

There were nods. Where the mercenaries under U.N. auspices had moved in, peace was enforced. That human rights often suffered was considered necessary collateral damage.

"I'll agree that where there are mercenaries we have peace and markets for our products," said Andersen. "That's only about 60% of the world but it's the 60% that counts. What's the point?"

"We even have left the masses with the impression that they still have a say in the running of this world with the democratic elections held in those countries. Among that 40%, we have the Holy European Empire and many of those impoverished Muslim sheikdoms that have been good markets for you too. You and your minions have had a free hand in doing just about anything you please. Am I correct?"

Again nods, even from Andersen.

"However, there are two things to consider here. Number one, public opinion favors Isha Bai, therefore she is dangerous. Number two, your profits may go to hell if she moves space exploration back into the public sector, Project Saturn Watch or not. Does anyone want that to happen?"

Even Evgeny Zhukov, the Russian weapons mogul, shook his head in the negative. All his operations now were nearly legit albeit morally ambiguous, but Martinez had a large file in his database that told him that they hadn't always been that way.

"All right, then, here's my plan."

*It's easy*, thought Martinez. *They're all so stupid.*

\*\*\*

"You want us to shut down the operation? I don't understand." George Blake's voice was whiny.

"I'm not saying shut it down, you idiot. I want you and Amanda to dedicate your time to another matter related to stationing all those mercenaries down there. Give the data-mining part of the operation to some of your people who need a promotion. Besides, without Posada, it's not as dangerous." Martinez looked out his window over Central Park, his roving eye spotting a hawk circling low over the trees. *An omen?* "Your next project is so sensitive that I want you to fly back to New York to discuss it in person with me. I won't trust an internet channel. So hop to it."

"All right. We're on our way."

Martinez knew they would be in his office the next day. He had two more calls to make. The one to General Judith Marshall went well enough, as he knew it would. He then made a call to a person he didn't know, had never seen, and didn't want to ever see.

"Call Eagle Talon," he told the AI. A wait. A deep baritone voice then answered. There was no video.

"Eagle Talon here. This had better be important. I'm sort of in the middle of something."

"It's always important when I call, *tavarisch*, since it only happens when I need your special talents for a little project. Halt whatever you're doing. Again, it will be worth your while. There will be a drop made to you at the New York Hilton. Black man, tattoo on left cheek, briefcase. Tomorrow, 6 p.m."

"I'll determine the price when I've seen what it is. And it had better be worth my while, asshole."

*The wheels within wheels are in motion now*, thought Martinez. He sat down at his desk, still staring at the hawk in admiration. It was all about knowing the right people and having something on them that allowed him to own them. *Except for Eagle Talon. Money owns him.*

***

Half a world away Nicolai Karpinsky, otherwise known as Eagle Talon, threw the cell phone aside and continued his search for an orgasm mounted on his current lover, a young woman he'd picked up in the Manila slums some days before.

Not yet sixteen, she was well endowed and very skilled, parrying every thrust with one of her own. Her younger brother, deer-eyed and laughing, knew what to do: he applied the whip rhythmically to Karpinsky's butt.

The sound system drowned out all noise. It was playing Sousa's "El Capitan March." Karpinsky loved Sousa.

Like Singapore, Manila had graduated from being the center of one of the most authoritarian regimes in the Asian world to being the center of liberal enlightenment. Long years of religious strife had left the Philippine economy impoverished in both morals and wealth, but it was on its way to better things even while the Chaos was just starting in other countries.

Part of that was because the Asians, in particular, the Filipinos, had been the first to recognize that there was money to be made in exploring the vastness of the solar system. The Asian economies now drove the world. Most were fascist, like the S.C.R., but that was changing with time as their tyrannical leaders realized that there were enough riches to go around and they were in no danger. Methods used in a modern authoritarian state were so effective that revolution was practically unthinkable.

Two hours later he figured he was satiated enough to handle any job Martinez asked him to do. He closed the hotel room door silently behind him, leaving the young man and woman, each with their throats slit, staring wide-eyed at the ceiling.

*Too bad, but no one who sees my real face can live.*

He had already put on the wig and skin-coloring lotion. In his special shoes that added three centimeters to his height, he looked like he did when he came in, a businessman from Europe. His accent and travel papers indicated that he was of Italian origin, but they were as false as his hairpiece. Yet he spoke fluent Italian and four other languages besides English.

In the hotel lobby, he purchased a ticket to New York. The ATM didn't question his credit since the person he was impersonating had plenty of money in his account. In a bathroom in the terminal in New York, he would change identities again, this time to make the pick-up. Not even Martinez knew his real identity.

*He probably prefers it that way,* he thought. *All of my clients do. Deniability is a wonderful thing.*

***

Martinez studied the faces of George Blake, Amanda Chu, and General Judith Marshall. There were no avatars here. They were all physically present in Martinez' office. Each was patient, waiting for him to speak.

*There's also the smell of sweat and fear. These three are ruthless, but they're still afraid of me. I'd have it no other way.*

At the same time, in a room at the New York Hilton, many blocks away, he knew that Nicolai Karpinsky, connected via VR, would be opening the folder of documents he had found in the briefcase. His avatar was not at Martinez' conference table either. He had none. Only Martinez knew he was there.

*These are the best at what they do*, Martinez thought. *We will be the harbingers of the new world order.*

His plan still had rough edges, he knew. Nevertheless, they would polish it here and then put it into action. It was time.

He thought of his father who had found himself on the wrong side of Denise's mercenaries.

*Old man, you'd probably say I'm a fool. However, your problem was that you never thought big enough. I have the big picture and I like what I see.*

"I've gathered you here to talk about Project Firecracker. Each of you will play an all-important role in it. I'll also say up front that every one of you will become very rich. For me, that's not the important point, of course."

He touched a button on his console and an image of a world globe floated into view. "You all know the problem. Here we have the Mid-Atlantic Union where President Ruffini was the first to call for help from the corporate mercenaries. Right next to it, we have the Great Lakes Confederation that has resisted calling any of us for help, no matter how much I've tried to destabilize the country. Countries like Great Lakes keep the world from progressing. I'm tired of waiting for economic and political pressures to bring these recalcitrant fools into line."

"The Man believes in a natural evolution to a world united in peace and tranquility, although the political units are small and more homogeneous. He believes that the world will be stable now that the huge empires like China and the U.S. have been broken up. We all know he is a fool. He is the problem. We must eliminate him."

Blake turned pale but the rest nodded with a smile. Martinez often worried about Blake. He would have Chu keep him on a short leash. At the same moment, he imagined that Eagle Talon was admiring his audacity.

"You can't be serious," Blake said. "You would create more chaos than we have now. People can become desperate when something like that happens. Nukes could be unleashed."

"I, for one, think the panic is controllable," General Marshall said. "By force. I can have our mercenary troops in friendly nations like Mid-Atlantic ready to take control in places like Great Lakes. It wouldn't take many. Most people have lost their fighting instincts. They have become conditioned to fear war."

"You are correct," said Martinez. "But Mid-Atlantic is even more special."

"The independence celebration," observed Amanda Chu. "It's perfect. I know what Eagle Talon's role will be. But he'll cost you plenty."

"Let him name the price. I don't care about that. There are many details to work out. In particular, the mercenaries stationed near Villa de Leyva must be prepared to act at the same time all of this is going down." His arrogant and egotistical gaze swept like a blowtorch around the table. "Needless to say, what we have discussed here goes no further than the four of us. And Eagle Talon, of course. Let's get to work."

# Chapter Thirty

The nanoengineer Leo Rodino was a quiet fellow who kept to himself. Thus, when his string of Italian expletives came buzzing over the intranet local to Helene, Hanson and Lewis both put down their tools and rushed to the center of the crater.

Rodino was pulling Mikey out of the hole. Her Spanish expletives were now making a chorus with his Italian ones and neither of them stopped until the other two began to laugh. In this micro-g environment, there was not much danger of a serious fall, but the embarrassment was another matter.

At first, they didn't have a name for it. They thought it was a geological fault in Helene, a big empty space left over from the moon's formation billions of years ago. That opinion lasted about five minutes until Rodino discovered that the perceived floor of the vault was made from a sheet of unknown thickness comprised of a strange titanium, carbon, and aluminum alloy fused with the rock on the topside of a large cavern.

\*\*\*

Lewis suffered anguish thinking he had lost Mikey. They had become close.

It had seemed the poorest way possible to start a relationship. He was sure that nothing would come of it. Nevertheless, as time went on, the two scientists were inseparable. Those three joys of life he so valued had taken on a new meaning.

Evidence for that was the way they were able to entertain their friends playing four hands at the station's only piano and singing duets. Mikey's zest for living trumped Lewis' basic shyness.

His favorite duets with Mikey were the Argentine sambas from Mikey's childhood, rhythmic snapshots of life very different from the Brazilian pieces of the same name. The Argentine samba was not a dance. It was instead a type of folksong with a very particular beat. It sprang from Salta, the northern regions of the old country. The words sometimes did not make much sense, especially to a hardened Spacer, although he knew some Spanish. The lilting Argentine Spanish added to the music and the rhythm.

.

\*\*\*

As Gus Hanson often said, Helene was a beautiful name for an ugly piece of rock. Approximately 1200 km in diameter, Dione, their main base, was a sizable satellite. Helene, at 32 km in diameter, was not. Together with Polydeuces, they circled Saturn at a distance of 390,000 km.

Instead of leveling out a large area for the first domed living quarters, the nanoengineers had programmed the little robots to finish a job that Mother Nature had already started. A small crater about three hundred meters in diameter had a smooth bottom. The little beasties had just finished touching up the edges. The crew of four was starting the heavy work of excavating a shaft at the center for the reactor.

Hanson and Lewis were cleaning away debris from the area and Mikey was operating the plasma drill when a hole opened up. She lost control of the drill and it fell inside. The momentum of the drill, not the gravity, carried her behind it, but she caught the edge of the hole and hung on.

\*\*\*

"It's like the rock was replaced by a metal egg," observed Rodino. He was studying the metallic structure under a scanning electron microscope.

"Is it manmade?" asked Hanson. He was on the WAN com with Dione.

"I would bet not. I don't know of anyone that could make something like this, and I'm up-to-date on material science research. Besides, consider where we are."

Mikey, who had recovered from her scare, seemed ready to move ahead. "We have to float some tethers down here. In this gravity, one of us can climb to the bottom of the hole and see what's there."

"There's your so-called bottom right there," Lewis said, shining a light inside the hole. "It's only about three or four meters below the opening, flat, and angled about twenty degrees with respect to the horizontal."

"Hold on, guys," said Alice Chang at Dione. "I'm getting Ted to sign on here. Don't take any unilateral decisions."

Lewis looked at Hanson and Hanson shrugged. Considering that WorldNet paid for most of the project, it was understandable that they wanted their man on the job. However, there was also the technicality that this was Lewis' project, which meant that he could raise a stink about who had on-site command, since Moravcsik was back on Dione.

Lewis took the easy way out and decided to avoid confrontation. He nodded to the others.

"Copy that," said Mikey. "We'll start gathering equipment and wait for Ted's OK."

"You have that," came a new voice over their wi-fi devices. "Only I want two to go in so you have a backup inside. I suggest Lewis and Montero since you're the freshest. Alice, get Bill Glover on line."

Glover was their exobiologist. He didn't have many scientific duties on their missions and only provided extra muscle when he was in the field. Up to now, his had been a theoretical field, except for the microbe colonies found at the Martian poles and on Europa.

"Do you think we have an E.T.O.?" Rodino asked.

Moravcsik was non-committal about the prospects of having found an Extra-Terrestrial Object so they let that slide too. Besides, Mikey and Lewis were soon inside.

They had to use tether ropes since the surface Lewis had spotted was very smooth and provided nothing for their boots to grab on to. Their sensing devices told them that the S.E.T.O., as they began to call it (the S was for Saturn), was a very large chamber that was honeycombed with many smaller ones, most of them empty.

They began the laborious procedure of cutting through the walls of one chamber to enter the next. It took ten standard days and four more crews before anyone found anything. Both Mikey and Lewis were in the lounge when the message came through.

"We have some little green men," came Alice Chang's voice over the intranet. "A whole zoo of them. All dead, of course."

# Chapter Thirty-One

Jenny Wong loved to be in space. It was exhilarating and humbling at the same time. The stars were hard, brilliant points of light buried in an infinity of velvet blackness. Even the sun was only a bright star, somewhere on the other side of the ship, she supposed. It was as close as a human could be to God admiring His creation on His seventh day of rest—a creation of frightful purity.

She smiled while she remembered the myths of her child-hood. She had matured and, with maturity, had come new perspectives about the human condition.

*You have to know yourself and be content with your place in the universe in order to see all the real beauty buried in this vast nothingness. Otherwise, you can go mad.*

She had once visited an asylum on Mars. Most of the ex-riggers there had a blank stare and spoke gibberish, their minds ravaged by this same infinity of space. Not many were violent, but their fate was something she planned to avoid at all costs.

She also loved the slow shuffling motion of her walk as the magnetic soles of her boots kept her from floating free. She reveled in the crinkling sound of the spacesuit around her, the only thing between her and a horrible death. She didn't even mind the discomfort of the various tubes that were stuck in various parts of her anatomy, since they made the long space walk possible.

\*\*\*

The Valiant's age didn't detract from its majesty in space. She looked along its length to their destination. Newer ships were smaller, since improvements in shielding meant that the reactor and thrust chamber didn't have to be as far away from the crew quarters. Valiant was big.

This ship was nearly seven soccer fields long, the crew quarters at one end joined by girders to the propulsion unit at the other. In between was the cargo, the solid part in crates, the liquid load in tanks, and all strapped down to the girders, which formed a hexagon at their cross section.

On opposing sides and attached to two of the girders was a crude patchwork structure of smaller girders and flat sheets of metal alloy. On this was mounted a potpourri of antennas, cameras, and telescopes, the Valiant's eyes and ears for communicating with her sister behemoths and the inner solar system.

***

Wong was about a quarter of the way back to the reactor and thrust chamber from the crew quarters, a tether hooked into her waist. Romero was at the other end of the tether while they headed to repair the forward com antenna, the one that would soon allow them to communicate with Dione.

Wong had turned into the general fix-it specialist. The crew had already guessed that there was a lot more to her trip to Saturn than she would tell. They saw that she spent time studying info bulletins from the ringed planet. Nevertheless, by then the rest of the crew liked her.

Mueller was typical of the eccentric individuals that one often found in the space lanes. Her relationship with him had started with a bang in Switzerland but now it was mellowing like a fine wine.

*Is this what having a marriage contract is like?*

She had learned that he internalized many of his problems, not wishing to burden anyone else with them. He was a loner, even among Spacers. She felt a strange attraction to him, though, a mysterious prescient knowledge that some force not yet revealed bound them together.

*A Zen attraction of soul mates?*

She often smiled when she thought that, chalking it up to her oriental mysticism that had replaced her parents' and grandparents' Christianity, a mystic belief in the inevitable that Isha Bai often ridiculed. Nevertheless, with time she knew she could penetrate to Brent Mueller's core and become his friend as well as his lover. However, there probably wouldn't be time on this trip. Everyone was too busy.

Still, there was time for poker. With Mueller's urging, she had even become a regular at their games, although she lost more than she won. She came to know the eccentric crew better with each passing watch, the exception being Ceci Romero. That was not strange, since rig captains often kept to themselves. Nevertheless, Wong wanted to know the woman better.

She was surprised when the captain volunteered to go on the space walk with her.

\*\*\*

It was soon obvious that the forward com antenna was indeed a two-person job. A constant babble of raunchy barbs and pep talk came from Brent Mueller and the other five crewmembers while the two women approached the antenna. Mueller had taken over the helm while his captain was out on her space walk.

Wong responded to some of their banter, but Captain Romero was quiet. The antenna dwarfed them. They already knew what was wrong with it. A slip ring on the azimuth adjustment motor had broken, a victim of metal fatigue brought about by old age and the tremendous temperature variations of outer space.

At the antenna, they clipped their tethers into rings in the superstructure of the ship and began to work on disconnecting the antenna from the motor. While there was no weight, there was plenty of inertia, so both relaxed when the antenna floated free. They anchored it down with other tethers, since infrequent micro-course corrections would otherwise cause it to drift away.

"Watch out!"

Romero's warning came too late. One of those micro-course corrections came at the same time that Wong applied leverage to a wrench. It was only then that she realized that her own tether was loose.

She floated away from Valiant. The delta V was tiny, but it was enough. She pushed the panic down into the dark recesses of her subconscious and forced herself to think clearly. Looking back along her trajectory, she decided on a course of action.

She reeled in the whole tether. When she passed the farthest point of the antenna array on her way to being lost into space for eternity, she reached out and hooked the tether onto one of the elements, hoping that it would not come loose.

***

While this was happening, Romero stood on ship, a crooked smile hidden beneath her darkened visor. Mueller was pleading with his Captain to do something while he yelled at Wong to hook on to anything.

Just before Wong hooked the element, Romero flung an object away from her, disgusted with herself. The little microwave unit she had used to trigger the course correction would beat them to Saturn by several hours since she had thrown it with such force.

Reconsidering and cursing Rudolfo Martinez, Romero launched herself after Wong.

It was only when Wong reeled herself into the antenna assembly that Romero knew she had miscalculated both Wong's resourcefulness and her location. She also had too much delta V. When she sailed by the other woman, her tether snapped close to the end where she had connected it to the ship.

Wong reacted instinctively, launching herself from her perch on the antenna with a delta V calculated so she could grab the other woman's tether. Ceci was now the one hoping the element would hold.

***

Wong reeled the Captain in, and they both made their way ship ward along the antenna array.

"I'm going to have somebody's ass for not checking out those tethers," Romero said, panting with adrenalin and exertion. "There is no reason for one to break."

"Ship's old," said Wong. "Otherwise, you wouldn't expect the antenna to break either." She caught her breath, still fighting down the panic, this time due to the realization that they had both had a close brush with a slow and agonizing death out among the stars. "That course change was badly timed."

***

"How'd you become unhooked?"

Cecilia Romero knew the real answer, of course. She was just making conversation while her mind raced, trying to form

162

excuses that would appease GenCorp. She was nauseous, but relieved that this whole nonsense was over.

Whatever happened, she would not do any more dirty work for a Downy company.

# Chapter Thirty-Two

Martinez reviewed Moravcsik's message yet again. Here was another man he despised. Yet such men were useful. He flipped on his transmit switch.

"I've reviewed your download. We can't allow this to go public. The idiot masses and the sensationalist media would have a field day. It might even give some of them hope. We can't even let Isha Bai see it. Please advise on how you will proceed. End contact."

A little over an hour later, the reply came in.

"All of that's easy to do. I control the transmissions and the reports to U.N.S.A. HQ. They will never hear of our little green men, if that's what you want. End contact."

Martinez' reply was nearly immediate if one allowed for the transmission delay.

"Good. I want you to especially see to it that Wong's messages are never received by Bai, or, better yet, use some of that fancy speech synthesis software I sent you to make up false reports, you know, enough to sound somewhat realistic, but don't give away any critical information." He cracked his knuckles in frustration. "It turns out that my little plan to eliminate Wong failed, so it's in your hands. I don't care about my feud with Andersen any more. It's all too petty, compared to my overall plans." *Petty and trivial, except for the little green men.* "You just hold up your end there and I'll take care of everything here. You will soon be a rich man back on Mars."

Martinez had already made sure news of the discovery on Helene would not be broadcast beyond his office. While he started to change for the Secretary General's reception, he wondered if the corporations' mercenaries were enough to keep the clamps on permanently, especially in U.N.S.A. Some of those people in Project Saturn Watch had acquaintances on Earth and elsewhere with whom they communicated.

He would have to enforce secrecy on the Saturn end. It would be impossible to work it from the rest of the solar system. There were too many people to eliminate.

After changing, he joined his security contingent that walked him to the garage and then drove him from the West Side to the East Side of Manhattan.

He would be early, but the Man had wanted to see him for a bit of professional chitchat before the guests arrived. The Man was a living anachronism. He had live parties and believed in the personal touch.

***

Otto Bonafacio was the Man. A towering, gentle giant from South Africa, he was the son of a white woman and a black man that Earth's billions respected as an architect of peace.

He calculated every move for both purpose and effect. Every speech he made he wrote himself and they were always a gem. Educated at Princeton and the University of Paris, fluent in ten languages, he was one of the most intelligent men that Martinez knew.

His major weakness was innocence. He would never be able to imagine all that was going on behind the scenes with the corporations. On the other hand, maybe he did know a little and thought it was necessary to preserve world order during the years of the Chaos. A lot of the other U.N. nobility certainly knew and looked the other way.

*Politicians are usually pragmatists, although their own agendas often distract them.*

***

Bonafacio pumped Martinez' hand.

"We need to talk, old friend," said the Man. "Isha Bai is going to be here tonight."

Martinez' only answer was raised eyebrows.

"Although we have kept it from most of the multinationals, I passed on to her the idea that the pendulum has swung too far and space exploration now has become a completely commercial venture. She and Clinton Bridges have designed a plan to make it

165

swing back to a more balanced place where commercial and scientific interests weigh equally, if I'm keeping the analogy straight."

*You aren't,* thought Martinez, *but it doesn't matter. No one expects you to have a degree in physics.*

"We will have to review it in detail since I think we have to be careful and move slowly. You see, there is not a lot of love lost between Spacers and Downies, although no outright animosity—yet. The last thing I want is a Spacer attack on Earth or Mars. Earth must retain control of space, whether commercial or scientific."

Martinez nearly dropped his glass. The Man had vision. Martinez hadn't included the Spacers in his calculations. He would have to rectify that, and very soon.

# Chapter Thirty-Three

Henry Posada didn't have much respect for Amanda Chu. While he wound through cyberspace at U.N.S.A. HQ, he came across her spoor. His new existence was perhaps an unfair advantage, but he was still not impressed.

Chu was very skilled at what she did, yet she still was a mortal of flesh and blood. Moreover, she didn't have the big picture that Posada's extensive mathematical background provided him. She would call his discovery one of those unfortunate accidents that are often called luck, bad or good depending on which side the coin fell. He knew better.

A message from Amanda Chu to Nicolai Karpinsky had gone out over a GenCorp encrypted channel. However, Chu had forgotten to turn on the internal encryption. The message simply said, "Sweet Honey to Eagle Talon: Re: Philadelphia plan. Info for your target at…" and continued with a pointer to some page in a database.

Posada couldn't enter the database, though, since he had neither the passwords nor the encryption key for its content. However, he did note something unusual: the routing of the message, which he was able to track, was the same one that he had discovered that fateful early morning.

Bogota was up again.

It was easy for Posada to commandeer a print queue for a millisecond and send a message.

### ***

Clinton Bridges paced while Isha Bai read the message to him.

"I don't like that word 'target'", he said. "Either somebody's going to shoot a missile at people, or somebody's going to assassinate someone."

"'Target' could mean the object of someone's hack," suggested Bai.

"Possibly. I wish I knew whether your Bogota node is really in Bogota. Any way to check on that?"

. "Can't do it electronically. Take some of the security people out to see."

"Good idea. I'll see to it and get back to you."

***

Two days later Bridges was again in Bai's office.

"Bogota is real. It appears to be one of the nerve centers for the emergency readiness exercises that the General is planning. GenCorp security has it sealed down. We need to go through Marshall."

Bai nodded. "I've been thinking about the last line of the message. It's a sign-off from the sender. 'This Bogota link is very suspicious. P.' Who do you think P is?"

"Beats the hell out of me. I'm more worried about Philly. Marshall has troops out in the Pennsylvania countryside. I wonder if they're a target of terrorists."

Bai shrugged. "Ruffini was too obscure so it's hard to see a correlation. Keep digging and keep me informed."

***

Pedro stood still when the jeeps surrounded him. Juanito couldn't make him move. The burro only turned his head and twitched, studying the boy for a moment before facing the spaceport again.

"*Estupido! Muevete, amigo loco.*"

One of the men from the jeeps, clean-shaven and dressed in the simple white uniform of U.N.S.A. Security, approached Juanito.

"Friend, where do you think you're going?" The question was in Spanish.

"This stupid burro is lost," he explained. It was a tiny lie.

The man smiled. "And the rider?"

"No, sir, not lost. I know that's the spaceport."

"He's a mutant, Captain," said one of the other men.

168

"Probably. Think you'll be contaminated, Corporal?"

"No, sir," said the Corporal, turning red.

The Captain walked over to Juanito and held out a hand. When the boy went to shake it, the man jerked the boy off the burro.

"Hey, let go!" screamed Juanito.

The Captain let go of the hand, put his arm around the boy and began to walk him to the jeep.

"When did you eat last, son?" he asked, hoisting Juanito into the passenger's seat of the jeep.

"Three days ago. There's nothing much to eat around here."

"You have that right. How 'bout dinner, courtesy of U.N.S.A.?"

The man had a kind face and there was a smile on it.

"I could go for that."

"Fine. Corporal, tie the burro onto the back of your jeep. You'll have to go slow because the burro looks very old. We'll see you back at HQ this evening."

The rest of the men smiled. They all gunned their jeeps and rode off towards the spaceport.

***

Bridges was becoming tired of playing Sherlock Holmes. If Bai had been amenable to some rolls in the hay, he would have felt better about puttering around amidst the intrigues at U.N.S.A. He left her to attend other business and walked through a maze of corridors until he found the cafeteria. He took a burger and beer, paid, and sat down at one of the tables.

He was three bites into the cheeseburger when he felt eyes on him. He looked across the room. From about ten tables away some Hispanic kid was studying him.

"Can I help you?" asked Bridges.

"I like your mustache," said the boy in Spanish. "You look like an old bandit."

"Grab an ice cream," said Bridges, also in Spanish, "and come sit with me. I don't like to eat alone."

"Can I also have a cookie?"

Bridges nodded. Soon the boy was at his table.

"Name, rank, and serial number," Bridges said.

"My name's Juanito. I don't know about the rest."

"A joke. Never mind. What are you doing here, kid? Are you some kind of idiot savant helping Isha?"

"I don't know what that means. The Captain's taking care of me for now until he figures out what to do with me. He says even normals can't make decisions some times."

"Normals?" Bridges then saw the shriveled arm. He refrained from backing away and smiled at his Frankenstein complex. "Oh, I see. Intellectually the word doesn't mean anything."

"You talk like Henry."

Bridges had to set through the whole story about the trek on the burro. The kid had the annoying habit of arriving close to the present and then flashing back each time nearly to the point where he had begun. It took him forty minutes for his story to arrive at the cave.

*The mysterious link to Marshall's HQ. Interesting! These people are bad medicine.*

"Sr. Posada keeps telling me to tell my story, but the Captain has been too busy. Do you think you count, Sr. Bridges?"

*Posada? P?*

"You betcha, *amigo mio*. I count for a lot. I'm Isha Bai's agent-at-large."

The kid seemed to study Bridges' build and huge mustache. *He's deciding whether 'at large' is appropriate. Maybe I should lay off the burgers.*

"Oh, so Isha is a person. Sr. Posada talks about her a lot."

"Smart boy. Yes, she's in charge of this whole establishment and many similar ones spread across this planet and around the solar system. She's a very important woman. And I work directly for her." Bridges watched the boy's eyes open wide. He liked this kid. "Now, about Posada? Does he work here?"

"I don't know," said Juanito, taking a huge bite out of his cookie. The ice cream was already history. "He talks to me up here." He tapped the top of his head.

"Let me see behind your ears, boy. Each one." *No wi-fi connection. What's going on?* "Are you hearing voices inside your head?"

"All the time. But Sr. Posada is different. He keeps telling me that bad things are going to happen."

"What bad things?"

"He doesn't know yet."

"The only Posada I know is Henry Posada," said Bai. "I should say 'knew.' He's dead."

Bridges stroked his moustache and scratched his head. *This is becoming very strange.* "Maybe the kid talks to dead people? I chatted with the Captain. He says he's a great kid but very weird. He has a spooky look about him that makes you think it's possible that he has psychic powers. But I don't believe in that crap."

"What's the Captain's plan for the kid?"

"He's trying to find a nice orphanage. Not much chance that a couple would adopt a deformed little fellow like him, though."

"Well, I would like to talk to him myself. I don't believe in psychic powers either, so if he's scamming us, I'll give him the boot."

"You can't," said Bridges.

"Why not?"

"Because he'll melt your heart."

Bai stared at Bridges for a moment and then laughed. She changed the subject.

"For the sake of argument, let's assume that Henry Posada is talking to the kid and Marshall's Bogota site is the same one Henry found. The latter's probable enough, whether the kid is psychic or not, with the forensics we did after Henry's death. So, let me ask: how many troops are in the vicinity of Bogota?"

Bridges shifted uncomfortably.

"I was thinking you might ask that. There are enough to cause your local U.N.S.A. security some problems. Do you think U.N.S.A.'s in danger?"

"We're all becoming paranoid," said Bai with a laugh. "But I'm wondering what the connection to Philadelphia is? That's where the message ended up, after bouncing around through the South China Republic and so forth. The mercenaries are in Harrisburg, not Philadelphia."

"Sweet mysteries of life. Let me know if you have any answers to your own questions."

# Chapter Thirty-Four

Ted Moravcsik was nervous. He had known about the arrival of Jenny Wong for some time and also had Martinez' orders firmly in mind. However, he also knew of her reputation as a hard-nosed trouble-shooter for Isha Bai. Captain Romero's failure and Wong's arrival could only make life more complicated.

*Between Ito, Romero, and Wong, women have been giving me many problems. Payback for my divorce?*

Although many perceived that he had devoted a lot of energy to moving Project Saturn Watch forward, it kept falling behind. Morale had been going downhill since Roger Tanglevsky's death and news of the near accident on Valiant didn't help. Spacers were a suspicious lot and some were already thinking the project was jinxed.

As he waited for the flitter to dock, he mused about his career with U.N.S.A. He once was a capable scientist that had come to believe administrative promotions were the only way to move ahead. It didn't make him popular with the men and women under his authority.

Nevertheless, no one considered him a bureaucratic lackey either since he had taken their side on more than one occasion. Opposing occasionally the U.N. juggernaut and its sponsors kept him from a comfortable desk position on Mars or Earth and left him with few friends in the U.N. hierarchy or among the worker bees under his command.

"Captain Romero, Commander Wong, welcome to Dione. You've come a long way."

"Cut the formal crap, Ted," said Cecilia Romero. She had known the Czech for years, even liked him, but thought he could be too full of himself at times. "The people on the dock here tell us you've had some excitement."

"Ever my charming Ceci," said Moravcsik. "Yes, there's a lot of gossip going around. What's true is classified information that we have not released to the public. I expect you and the commander to respect the U.N. security rules, so no word of this outside secure channels. Now, if you'll both follow me, I'll show you to your quarters."

"The best accommodations this side of Jupiter?" Jenny Wong was referring to a descriptive and humorous e-brochure Moravcsik had downloaded to everyone on the Valiant before arrival. "I hope your description of the problems here won't deal with such tautologies." She waved a hand to cut him off before he protested. "But first things first. Ceci's right. Tell us about the little green men. I want to know."

Moravcsik knew that was a command. She was pulling rank.

*Not a good way to win my sympathies, but she probably doesn't give a damn.*

"None of them were green, as far as we can tell. The skeletal remains showed there were three distinct species in S.E.T.O., all alien. What amounted to DNA also showed that they were all distinct and unrelated among themselves or to human beings or anything else from Earth, for that matter."

He paused to link arms with the two women. "There was a small skeleton in one of the chambers of the vault and two other types in another. Someone made the suggestion that all the little skeletons that were mish-mashed together were food for the bigger ones."

Moravcsik stopped in front of a sealed door and pushed a switch that was recessed into the wall at the door's side. Behind them, another door hissed shut and the one in front of them then opened. "Emergency air locks can be used if any sector loses air. You have to get used to it as well as not being in zero-g."

"I spent my summers as a kid working on Deimos. Less gravity but very similar. So is this S.E.T.O. a spaceship?"

"I wish I knew," replied Moravcsik, while they continued their shuffling walk into the interior of Dione. "Most of the chambers in the vault were empty. There wasn't anything that looked like a control room, but one chamber could pass for a galley, another for a head, and a third for a library or lounge area. This last area contains thousands of small crystalline cubes scattered throughout drawers and spilled onto the floor. We think they might be some sort of information storage media."

*Am I sounding pedantic? But she seems interested.*

"In the center of the egg-shaped vault there's another chamber that resists all our attempts to enter it. Although it seems to be made of the same material as the other chambers, where torches easily slice through, the walls of this chamber only turn a slight blue at the point where the torches are applied."

They were passing through the lounge area and Moravcsik greeted several of his people on the way through. "You can get a good poker game going here most any time of the day."

Romero waved at a woman that she had known at LEO some fifteen years earlier, glad to see a familiar face. She then saw Gus Hanson.

"Excuse me a minute."

Ted Moravcsik felt lost when left alone with Jenny Wong. He was afraid the U.N. troubleshooter would want to start talking business. He wasn't mentally prepared for that.

Romero walked over to Hanson and embraced him.

"I can't believe it's old whore-face back to torture me," said Gus. The kiss was genuine, full, and promising. "I knew you captained the Valiant but I thought you'd given up your commission five years ago. How have you been?"

Romero dug him in the ribs with the stump of her arm. "You always knew how to charm the ladies, Gus. I was set to give up my commission, when I thought, maybe, just maybe, I could see you a few more times and kick your ass up between your ears."

Gus made a sign to Ted Moravcsik. "Hey, Ted, I'll show Ceci to her quarters. It will be a pleasure."

Moravcsik smiled a thin smile, shrugged, and motioned for Jenny Wong to follow him. His office was on the way to her quarters, so he stopped by there, thinking to get the inevitable out of the way. He offered her a drink but she gracefully declined.

***

"Obviously you didn't come all the way out here to talk about E.T.O.s," Moravcsik began. "We didn't make the discovery until you were already on the Valiant and, as I said, I've had it under security wraps. Let's get down to the bottom line. How much trouble am I in?"

Wong was uncomfortable. The man was direct. She decided to parry.

"Do you mean with me and the U.N., or GenCorp and WorldNet?"

Moravcsik choked a little on his sherry. "I meant the U.N., of course. What does GenCorp have to do with anything?"

"U.N.S.A. Security has discovered that you have a second salary from GenCorp in addition to your inflated one from WorldNet—boondoggle is the old word that's appropriate. Would you care to explain that?"

Moravcsik nodded and turned his glass around as if to study the mysteries of the liquid within. "They do have a small stake in this operation."

"Why then is the GenCorp salary not small?"

Moravcsik's answer was a long time coming.

"I suppose I should resign."

"I haven't asked you to do that. Yet. Are you directly reporting to Rudolfo Martinez?"

"No, not most of the time. Rudolfo, in his parody of the old-time spymasters, has set me up with a handler. On Mars. I generally communicate with him through my ex-wife."

"Your ex is on Mars and you involved her?"

"It's a strange universe." Moravcsik now looked tired. Wong began to feel sorry for him. "Call it greed. Or stupidity. We're still friends. I—or rather we—thought that we could play GenCorp and WorldNet off against each other. We don't think either one should have anything to do with scientific exploration. Especially now with S.E.T.O."

"I happen to agree with you on that. Nevertheless, it is the system. Neither GenCorp nor WorldNet will make any profit off S.E.T.O. However, WorldNet won the contract to support Project Saturn Watch. That's the way the system works. You're just as much a U.N. employee, although you nominally work for WorldNet."

"I said I will resign."

"And who will pay for your trip back to Mars? Everything costs, Moravcsik. No, I don't think we'll let you resign. We'll keep you here. For now. But we won't let you keep on sabotaging these operations."

"Cost overruns and delays aren't sabotage. Most of those I didn't have much to do with. A prod here and there to help the natural flow. You can't force scientific research to adhere to a schedule or a budget."

"I know that. I also know about bad scientists that become bureaucratic assholes. However, I am a tolerant person. I'll keep you around as long as you're useful."

She stood up. "As I said, you will continue to be the esteemed leader of this little group, at least in public, but we will be working together behind the scenes. We have three months to turn this project around." She paused at the door. "And we'll start passing false information to your sweet handler ASAP to make Martinez think events are going his way." She flashed him a smile. "Thanks for the welcome. I can find my own quarters."

"I believe I should be more hospitable, especially considering this discussion. Would you like a tour? Our Dione installation is impressive. As science stations go, of course."

Jenny considered his offer for a moment.

"All right. Give me an hour. We'll meet here."

\*\*\*

Moravcsik's tour was professional and thorough. It was clear to Jenny that the man took pride in the science station independently of his bureaucratic shenanigans.

The goal of the whole project was to study the often-turbulent atmosphere of the gas giant below them. Saturn has bands like Jupiter and huge storms the size of many Earths often propagate across its face.

Of the many projects on the drawing board, Lewis' project impressed her the most. She decided that she needed to meet the man and his colleagues, Hanson and Montero. When on-line their project would require most of the station's computer power using special algorithms developed by Hanson and Lewis.

Those thoughts made her sad when she thought of Henry Posada and his prowess as a computer scientist. The solar system had lost its foremost computer expert.

"This is command and control," announced Moravcsik when they entered a dark room. The men inside greeted their boss and were introduced to Wong. "We call it C&C. Here we control where all the antennas are pointing, what instruments are on-line, and so forth."

"Any security installations?" she asked.

"Not as many as I'd like, but this is a science station. Since we're remote to Helene and Polydeuces, catastrophic failure there or in any of the planet-bound probes are avoided by a remote self-destruct capability." He smiled at her arched eyebrow. "Official-speak for small, fast intercept missiles that can either be nuclear-tipped or used for kinetic kill. The missiles are launched from Dione. They're only a precaution."

"And if you have failures here on Dione?"

"The old C4 at strategic points. Of course, all the standard electrical fire and atmospheric failure safety devices are also in place. On Helene and Polydeuces the construction is on-going."

# Chapter Thirty-Five

Clinton Bridges was a hundred meters away from the mercenaries' tunnel near Bogota. He had taken it upon himself to obtain a closer look at Martinez' "emergency readiness" preparations. The tunnel glowed through the night-vision goggles.

His guide was not in a radiation suit. Juanito had offered to come along to identify the people who tried to kill him. The young boy would have nothing to do with the suit.

"It's like some monster put me in a cocoon to feed its monster babies."

Bridges felt sorry for the kid. He was scared of many things that go bump in the night, like many kids, but he was truly afraid of the people in the tunnel.

*I might be too if they had tried to kill me. Bastards!*

Bridges studied the boy's face through his darkened visor and saw the fear in his eyes. Nevertheless, his eyes were also bright with adventure.

*And the possible prospect of sweet revenge?*

Bridges himself was not comfortable in the anti-radiation suit. There was an annoying itch under his nose. He hadn't trimmed his mustache in weeks and it was becoming ragged. Sweat condensed on it, the residual salt causing the itch.

His mind raced back to the day before when Juanito had called for him. It was around 3 a.m. U.N.S.A. HQ time....

\*\*\*

"This had better be good," said the scientist, sitting down at the cafeteria table with a steaming hot mug of good Colombian coffee.

"Actually, it's very bad," said Juanito. "Sr. Posada has now found out some things. Old General Judith Marshall isn't the innocent woman she pretends to be. She put the Alternate Pope in a Turkish prison. Sr. Posada smells a rat, maybe lots of rats, with this emergency readiness exercise."

"How do you do this?" asked Bridges. "Why doesn't Posada talk to me?" Juanito shrugged. "Well, if you can, tell Posada I think Martinez has a good idea. We're a long ways from solving the problems that produced the Chaos, so the situation could become ugly very fast. If he can save lives by doing this readiness exercise, in particular my own life, I'd be eternally grateful."

"You must listen to Sr. Posada," insisted Juanito. "He has made contact with Sr. Zeb Lane, one of Senator Andersen's mercenaries in the City of New York. Sr. Lane provided two pieces of interesting information." The boy scratched his head, but then he smiled when he remembered the message.

*Small successes mean a lot to him now. How much radiation has he received in his lifetime? Maybe that's how he can talk to Posada. Alpha, beta, and gamma particles fried his normal brain circuits.*

"He has nothing that will stand up in court, but he told Sr. Posada that an assassin contracted by one of the corporations killed Sr. Posada, GenCorp being Sr. Lane's best guess." Bridges let out the breath he had been holding. "The second piece of info is that word is out on the street that Sr. Eagle Talon is in Philadelphia."

"What, or who, is this Eagle Talon? Are we talking about some voodoo shaman?"

"I don't know what that is. But Mr. Talon is an assassin, a good one, top of the line, that does lots of wet work for politicos, terrorist groups, and so forth. All Sr. Lane knows, from Interpol and other contacts, is that Sr. Talon is probably Caucasian. Sr. Lane says people attribute more to him than he's really done, which is usually the case, but there were eyewitnesses and their description of his build is consistent, although nothing else matches. There's only about a sixty per cent probability that these 'sightings,' as he calls them, are the same person."

"Sort of like the Loch Ness monster," commented Bridges, "or a voodoo shaman. So, this guy's in Philadelphia? Hmm. I see. Bogota to Philadelphia. And how can Sr. Lane talk to Sr. Posada?"

Juanito shrugged. "I'm only the messenger, Sr. Bridges. You should ask Sr. Posada."

"I wish I could."

Bridges watched the tunnel door open. Ten armed soldiers in blue anti-radiation suits came out of the tunnel and fanned out into a search pattern.

*In my youth, I would hang around long enough to capture one of these bozos and grill him on what he knows. Now I'm too old.*

"I think we'd better leave," suggested Juanito.

"Practical boy. They must have picked up our emissions. *Nos vamos.*"

He grabbed the boy's hand and they beat a hasty retreat.

# Chapter Thirty-Six

Rudolfo Martinez seemed angry and the President trembled. Craig Ruffini counted himself lucky that he was again only a virtual presence, not real.

"You incompetent little toad! Now I have that U.N.S.A. whore at Project Saturn to check up on Moravcsik. For all I know, he's sending me false information. I want rare earth metal rights in the rings, Ruffini, and you'd better obtain them for me. If I can't bankrupt Denise Andersen, I can at least make her hurt!"

"What do you want from me? Cecilia can't do anything to the U.N.S.A. agent there. She's due to start the return trip soon. I'm out of the loop on this one."

"As far as eliminating Jenny Wong, yes, I suppose you are. I should have known a relative of yours would be as incompetent as you are. How a turd like you ever was elected President of Mid-Atlantic, I'll never know."

"The people love me," explained Ruffini. "I have the best polling agency around. They tell me what the people want and I try to give it to them. Therefore, they love me. You should try it some time. It might help your public image."

"I don't need a public image. I could give a rat's ass about what the public thinks." The avatar made itself comfortable in one of Ruffini's overstuffed chairs, but there was a thin glistening seam where the AIs joined the scenes in each man's office. "And if your loving public ever knew how you screw orphans that receive state support, yours would take a down turn. So don't give me that shit. Figure out how you're going to obtain my mineral rights in the rings."

"That's a difficult problem."

"Work on it. But there is something more important that is worrying me." He told Ruffini about the S.E.T.O. discovery.

"Fantastic! Wait 'til that hits the news nets!"

"Idiot!" said Martinez. "It's not going to hit the news nets. We are on the cusp of important world events. The last thing I want is to distract the whole population of Earth with some ancient bones. Even worst, it might give everyone hope that they have salvation out there among the stars. I don't need that. At least, not yet, not until events are under control. Do you understand?"

"No, frankly I don't," said Ruffini. "My ex-sister-in-law's out there, playing at least some small role, and you're telling me I can't talk about it? You're out of your mind!"

"Not quite. Let me just say that if you ever breathe a word of this, you will be dead within the next 24 hours. I guarantee it."

"Shit. Why did you even tell me then?"

"Consider it a test. Instead, I told Moravcsik and you might as well know that my mineral rights are a secondary issue right now. Big events are happening. Just make sure you give your little patriotic speech on July 4."

"You didn't have to jump all over me then."

"Oh yes I did. I needed the release. It was fun."

***

General Judith Marshall listened in to Martinez' conversation with Ruffini. She contacted him after he was finished.

"Can you trust him?" she asked.

"Trust is a funny thing. I trust Ruffini since he's afraid of his own shadow and wouldn't dare cross me. But he's stupid enough to make errors."

He put his hands nearly at shoulder level as if he were testing the relative weights of two masses. "On the other hand, I don't trust Moravcsik, even though he keeps sending me information. Like I said, for all I know, this Wong woman has turned him and he's passing me false data." Martinez brought his voice down several dBs to where it was only abrasive. "Agent-at-large Wong did a real number on one of my father's ops on the Moon. Of course, she didn't realize it was his. At any rate, she is very good and may have turned Moravcsik."

He snapped his fingers. "But we don't care, *mon general*. The lag time for Spacer intervention is too long. Our little plan will be a *fait accompli* very soon. We can then worry about the Spacers."

"Well, I'm all ready. Can Amanda be trusted in Bogota? Bai brought in some astrophysicist from Cornell."

182

"What's an astrophysicist know about thwarting a *coup d'état*? Bai is unschooled in matters of world affairs. She's out of our league."

"I don't know. She runs a tight ship. Don't underestimate her."

Marshall had a small office several floors below Martinez'. When his avatar signed off, she began to check all her logistics once again.

*He doesn't realize how difficult this might become. And it's my job to make it look easy.*

***

Nicolai Karpinsky checked into the Philadelphia hotel with a false name. Among the remaining downtown hotels in the City of Brotherly Love, it was not expensive. Filled with business travelers instead of tourists, it was functional rather than glitzy, efficient rather than ostentatious.

The manager almost tempted him. She was a young and pretty black woman by the name of Beth Johnson. She had a slight Southern accent, maybe from Virginia, he guessed. She was very useful in helping him link his computer and VR peripherals into the network hookups the hotel provided in his room. By her body language, he knew that she also could be helpful in other ways. Nevertheless, he controlled himself, bid her *adieu*, and set to work.

Amanda Chu already had broken easily into the databases containing the plans for the Independence Day celebration. It was a simple manner to access them and obtain the information he wanted.

The Man would be speaking from a grandstand in the new park built across from Independence Hall. The area was a mix of new and refurbished parks and buildings, along with some derelicts that neither the Mid-Atlantic Union nor city politicos had bothered to demolish.

Five hundred meters away from the grandstand was a condemned cell phone tower. The organizers would hide its deterioration by flags and bunting, but he was sure they wouldn't allow anyone near it.

Security would be heavy, both U.N. and Mid-Atlantic, since President Ruffini would also speak live at the celebration. He had little use for Ruffini.

*Maybe I'll pop him too, just for the hell of it.*

Stretching out on the bed, he napped until 2 a.m. and then dressed. Black pants, black sweater, black boots. He took some black face paint with him too. This was not the time for security agents or civilians to see him.

The tower deserved to be condemned. Structurally it was an accident waiting to happen. Apocalyptic graffiti—he saw one dated 2012, warning of the Mayan end of the world—glowed on its rusty girders while he climbed the main stairs, avoiding those steps that were weak and could break a leg, or worse.

There were two landings on the way up where the homeless had sometimes passed a windy night. Trash was abundant and two corners smelled worse than a public restroom. Condoms and syringes littered the area. It was not pleasant, even for someone as hardened as he was.

Above the second landing, the stairs turned into a rusting metal ladder that seemed safer to climb than the stairs.

At the top, he had a commanding view of the park and the site where the grandstand was going to be.

Satisfied, he went down the ladder and the stairs. Then up again in the dark without a flashlight, this time looking at his watch to determine how long it took him.

He practiced it two more times before he was satisfied.

# Chapter Thirty-Seven

Activity had picked up with the arrival of the Valiant. For one, Lewis saw less of Gus since he seemed hell-bent on rekindling his old romance with Cecilia Romero. She was a bit crass but seemed good for Gus, so Lewis didn't mind. Moreover, Mikey was taking up more of his own time.

Moravcsik assigned a small group of scientists and engineers full time research on S.E.T.O. They were all sworn to secrecy. They were also lost to the main business of Project Saturn Watch, so a reduced staff handled running Dione and the various experiments that started to come on-line.

A still smaller group was also dedicated to the more mundane tasks of finishing the bases on Helene and Polydeuces. The existence of the S.E.T.O. meant that they had to move the Helene base to a different crater that was nearby. Although busy with his own work, Lewis was good friends with several of the people on the S.E.T.O. project, so he kept himself informed, in spite of Moravcsik's imposed secrecy.

*** 

Moravcsik was smart enough to know people would talk about S.E.T.O., so he arranged a schedule of meetings, briefings by the S.E.T.O. group where the others could chip in with ideas.

The first full staff meeting after the discovery of S.E.T.O. was acrimonious, however, since Moravcsik was giving people that had strong opinions on the origin of the vault a bad time, whether they were working on S.E.T.O. or not.

"Speculation is fine," he said, "but remember you're scientists. I'll accept all ideas as long as there is some sound scientific reasoning behind them."

He then berated them by saying he hadn't heard any of the latter.

"So, personally, what do you make of it?" Lewis asked Mikey.

Lewis was lying on a sofa in the lounge, his head on Mikey's lap. Their relaxation and small talk had been interrupted by the call to the staff meeting. Others in the lounge were playing cards while they all listened in via their avatars.

"I don't know."

It was not often that Moravcsik was perplexed. Since Lewis had little use for the man's egomania, he felt satisfaction that something could mystify the great mind.

"How the hell did it get inside all that rock?"

"Maybe it materialized there," Mikey observed.

Lewis marveled at her creative imagination. It was a workable hypothesis but so far from established scientific norms that few people could have suggested it. He told Mikey to throw it on the table.

***

Lewis was waiting for Moravcsik to scoff at Mikey's suggestion, as he had with others, some of which, Lewis admitted, were pretty far out. During the following days, Moravcsik did lead the charge but he also had plenty of company, mostly people who attacked Mikey's hypothesis in favor of theirs.

However, one by one, they abandoned the alternate hypotheses.

Nevertheless, Moravcsik never gave in. Even when Mikey's suggestion remained the only viable hypothesis, he simply marked S.E.T.O.'s origin as "Unknown."

*What an ass*, thought Lewis. *And people think scientists are so damn objective.* However, he realized Mikey's theory was hard to swallow—even she thought it was farfetched.

The S.E.T.O. researchers didn't make any progress in penetrating the central section. It was not even clear that the vault was a vehicle in the usual sense of the word. Attention turned to the skeletons and the crystalline cubes.

Moving in and about all the usual project activity and some of the S.E.T.O. talks was Jenny Wong. Lewis found her hard to read. She seemed to be everywhere, asking questions, pointing out inefficiencies, berating incompetents, and praising good work, all in her soft, lilting voice.

However, Moravcsik was concentrating on S.E.T.O. while Wong was trying to play it down.

At least that was what Lewis thought until she called him to her quarters. He was wary about talking to her in person since she could say anything she wanted to him over the Dione LAN. Or send her avatar to visit him.

She was going through one of those oriental martial arts routines when he entered her cubicle. It was impressive. Naked, with eyes closed, she seemed to be gyrating in slow motion to some silent, cosmic music. He found it erotic and was sorry it stopped when she sensed his presence.

"Do you follow the Way, Lewis?"

"No. Some of us have latched onto it, but it's more popular among the rig crews. I'm basically agnostic."

"A simple no suffices," she said, pulling on her day clothes. "I am attracted to some of the principles, but maybe I'm too attached to the stink and filth of the third planet. Brent Mueller also dabbles in it. He's better than I am at it."

*No explanation needed*, he thought. *I don't care how you and Mueller get it on.*

Lewis had only a nodding acquaintance with Romero's second in command. He knew, however, that Cecilia Romero had a high regard for the man. Presumably, Jenny Wong did too.

"Earth?" he asked.

"Of course. Is there another solar system to talk about?"

"I mean, I'm surprised you're so attached to it. You seem to be more of a Spacer than many of us."

"If you're referring to my nudity, Mars is much more an enlightened society than here. I grew up on Mars and was there when it shifted from a closed, conservative, and repressive society to an open, liberal, and hedonistic one. It's mellowed a little with the years." She dropped to the floor, flowing into a lotus position. "Come, sit with me, and tell me about S.E.T.O."

"Moravcsik is not keeping you informed?" He sat down in front of her on the floor. In the micro-gravity, it was easier than it would have been on Earth, but his old bones and muscles still protested. "I'm surprised. He seems to have succumbed to your administrative powers."

"My people skills have not yet been contaminated with bureaucratic intrigues like his have. Have you ever suspected that Moravcsik works for many masters?"

"It wouldn't surprise me. I suppose many bureaucrats do. Mostly they work to further their own agendas. It's their nature. In my own small way, I'm also guilty of it. But why tell me this?"

"Like I said, I want to know about S.E.T.O. Moravcsik is withholding information from me. He works for U.N.S.A. and WorldNet officially and GenCorp on the side. Since I know Denise Andersen well, I guessed it was Rudolfo Martinez who's pulling the puppet strings. Moravcsik confirmed that."

"That would make sense because GenCorp is WorldNet's competitor. Is Martinez doing more than just making trouble?"

"You've guessed that some of the so-called accidents weren't accidents, I take it." Lewis nodded. "Moravcsik as much admitted to that. He claims that he works through Martinez' handler on Mars. Hard to check that, since the handler is his ex. However, I suspect some more direct contact that started with S.E.T.O. A lot of info is going out that I'm not receiving."

"I can only tell you what I know from my informants in the S.E.T.O. group."

"That's all I'm expecting, Lewis. This conversation is private, by the way. You'll keep it to yourself, or I'll make you eat your own balls. Understood?"

Lewis nodded. From what he'd seen and heard, she could and would do it.

# Chapter Thirty-Eight

Clinton Bridges was in the middle of a computer game. They had programmed the zookie well. It performed its required task of relaxing him. Not as good as sex, but Isha Bai seemed remote. The escape from the mercenaries at the tunnel had left him exhausted.

*Not so that little bug, Juanito. Brave kid. We know a lot more now but still lack the big picture.*

The zookie started acting strangely. The demons and dragons in the old English countryside gave way to a beautiful lawn that sloped down to a pristine lake filled with ducks and swans. The sky was no longer an ominous gray but a piercing cyan filled with warm sunshine.

*What the hell?*

As if in response to his question, there was a disturbance in the water about a hundred meters from shore.

*Is the Lady of the Lake coming up to give me Excalibur?*

A pair of ducks announced the parting of the still waters. When Mr. and Mrs. Mallard flew off, a golden figure emerged from the water. He started to walk on the water towards shore. Bridges watched while he came through the reeds, not a drop of water or pond scum on him.

He stopped in front of the scientist.

"I always wanted to do that," said the golden man. "My name is Henry Posada."

"So Juanito is not crazy."

"Just a little different than you, Dr. Bridges."

Bridges bowed deeply. "If we're going to go academic, Dr. Posada, tell me how you did that—or how you communicate with Juanito—my scientific curiosity has peaked. You're supposed to be dead, you know."

"I wish I had time to work with you on that. For now, let me say that I don't know how it all works. However, we have more important issues to address. And then I must be off for Saturn."

"Do you mean the mercenary build-up under Marshall?"

"Issue one. I believe in earlier times they called it a *coup d'état*. This is more like a *coup du monde* or a *coup des beaucoup états*. My French is a little rusty, but the basic idea is that Mr. Rudolfo Martinez has a Hitler complex."

Posada sat down on a boulder that had conveniently appeared. Bridges could still see the lake through the glowing figure and the boulder.

*Weird, weird. Am I having a stroke?*

"Dr. Bridges, Rudolfo Martinez has a plan to kill the Secretary General and bring all the more important Downy countries under the U.N. umbrella, especially the ones not controlled by mercenaries already. Of course, his U.N. will be completely different than the old one. Finally, he plans to destroy some archaeological finds in Saturn's moon system. Knowledge of those finds would be a tremendous morale boost for the human race."

"That's quite a program for one man. How's he going to go about doing all that? And what's this archaeology business?"

"I don't know all the details. You'll find what I do know in a computer folder that I have placed in Dr. Bai's workspace. I called it 'Doomsday,' a name that's *a propos* if a bit melodramatic. It's a hidden folder, but if she, and only she, types that name after the open command, she'll have access. I'm sorry I'm being so primitive with my computer skills but even that takes some effort on my part."

"And Saturn?"

"I may not survive the transmission. Nevertheless, I'll try. It may be the most important thing I ever do."

"I wouldn't do it then. We'll find—" But the golden man vanished and the game ended.

Bridges shook his head in disbelief—and dizzy from the abrupt transition of VR world to real world.

*I'll have to hand it to Bai. She presents me some weird problems.*

***

Posada found the trip to Saturn caused him nausea.

*How can I experience nausea if I'm only a bunch of bytes? I don't have a digestive or nervous system.*

190

As the many terabytes that were his essence traveled over the spread spectrum com beam broadcast from U.N.S.A. HQ, he performed a self-diagnosis once the first part of him arrived on Saturn. There was plenty of time.

His conclusion was that he was suffering from compression. The coding scheme was lossy—very high frequency components of his being were being snipped away.

*I'll have to factor that in if I ever do this again. But how do I compensate for a lossy channel when I don't understand how this damn process works?*

Once the transmission was complete, it was easy for Posada to snoop around the Dione network.

The Spacers used very little security in the Project Saturn LAN. After bouncing around from terminal to terminal—they used old technology—he found what he was looking for.

Using the small camera hooked on the monitor, he was able to see that Jenny Wong was alert. Tired, but alert.

\*\*\*

Wong sucked in her breath when her old friend's head appeared in the state space of the old 3D terminal. There was a flicker and the color tones weren't quite correct. She first thought it was an old video clip and wondered why someone would play tricks on her.

*But he looks alive!* "Henry?"

"Yes, it's me, or some electronic facsimile. Don't ask me how." He winked at her. "You're looking as beautiful as ever. How's it going with Brent?"

In spite of herself, she blushed. "How'd you find out about that?"

"I was trying to go back through computer records to see if anyone was tailing you in Switzerland. You weren't out skiing all that much."

"Tailed?"

"There's something major going down on the Downies' side of things. Moreover, Rudolfo Martinez definitely has it in for you. But I'm here for something else."

"Here?"

"In the Project Saturn LAN, better said, in its server farm. Old-fashioned, by the way. You'd think these science types would have the latest and greatest."

"They have what the sponsors pay for. But let's focus. Why are you *here*?"

"Martinez wants to make sure the Downies never learn about the fossils they found on Helene."

"How dare he! I can't understand that. It's the greatest news since the Rosetta stone. It would be a great morale boost."

"He doesn't see it that way. Nonetheless, in case he's successful, I'd like more info. Have they been able to penetrate to the core of the spacecraft?"

"They're not even sure it's a spacecraft. It might be a research station run by some alien consortium. There seem to be three different species, or two and what was live food for them."

"We have to be careful not to anthropomorphize. I want you to try to enter that central core. I need to know what's inside."

"Understood. And what are you going to be doing?"

"Trying to ascertain whether Martinez and/or Moravcsik have specific plans for S.E.T.O."

She nodded.

***

Lewis' only revisit to S.E.T.O. occurred when Jenny Wong asked Mikey and him to show her inside. Personally. It surprised him that a U.N.S.A. rep would want to make that trip across the Helene-Dione-Polydeuces orbit when she could just look at tapes. However, from their previous conversation, he knew Jenny Wong wasn't your usual U.N. bureaucrat.

*Besides, I'm not about to pass up the chance to see it again myself.*

In fact, Wong handled herself well aboard the shuttle, acting more like a crewmember. Lewis hadn't had much to do with her since she had spent a lot of her time with Moravcsik, Mueller and other higher-ups, so it was a pleasant surprise when she turned out to be more of a Spacer than a Downy.

She also hit it off well with Mikey.

No one else was at S.E.T.O. since Moravcsik's team had a three-day break from its labors. Lewis was sure this was a factor in Wong's decision to visit it at the time and enjoyed Moravcsik's displeasure. The project director couldn't even send anyone with them from the S.E.T.O. team since no Spacer would give up a three-day rest unless it was an emergency.

"The entrance has been cleaned up," observed Mikey, while she lowered herself into the vault after Wong and Lewis.

"But it's more of a shambles inside," he said. He had been the first in and came upon the first wall they had partially dismantled. "We may not find much here. I think all of the bones and cubes are back on Dione."

"I've looked at those already," said Wong. "I want to get a feel for the size of this, its age, and so forth. Don't you think it's an incredible coincidence that it was in the same place you selected to build the Helene base?"

"The matter that was there went somewhere," said Mikey. "I'm not a geologist, but I think that could explain most of the crater. Moreover, it is the closest one to be directly facing Saturn. Remember, Helene always has one side facing the planet, like the Moon."

Wong nodded as they moved into the chambers. The ambience was surreal. Lewis wondered again how long S.E.T.O. had been there.

*How do you tell the age of a crater?*

"Where's the part we haven't been able to penetrate?" Wong asked.

"Quite a ways in," said Mikey. They were adjusting to the twenty-degree tilt of the floor. Even with Helene's very low-g environment, that tilt was a nuisance. "Not much to see there. We've scavenged this well."

"Like vultures," Lewis said. "I'll lead the way to the mystery area."

"Have they tried any dating techniques here to see how old the vault is?" asked Wong as they shuffled along.

Lewis was glad to see that the age of the place was an interesting question for her too.

"None work," replied Mikey. "Except for the ETs themselves, there's no natural carbon, for example, to establish a reference. That's the problem with all the techniques. No references."

***

They were soon at the inner chamber that had denied them entry for so long. Wong went right up to it, placing her hands on it.

"It strikes me as unusual that the rest of this artifact was so accessible and this is not. What do you make of that?"

"My guess," Lewis said, "is that it must be some protected area. But it's anyone's guess what it might be protecting."

"Maybe some special cargo. Or the ship's guidance, if it is a ship."

Mikey walked around it, touching the surface with Wong.

"Maybe the artifact is a ship and this is its computers, its ops center, if you will. We've found no signs of anything else that could play that role. And it lies at the approximate center of the E.T.O."

"Quiet!" Wong raised one hand and put her helmet against the smooth alloy. "It's making a very low frequency hum." She almost added that within the hum she could hear Henry Posada's voice.

*I don't want them to think I'm crazy. Henry, how can you be here?*

As if he were answering her thoughts, Posada responded. "Follow my voice."

.

***

Montero and Lewis also placed their helmets against the metallic wall and they both heard the hum. None of the reports had mentioned the hum at all. Perhaps it had only started recently. They also heard Posada's voice when he repeated his command.

Lewis' nerves started firing overtime. Beads of sweat were forming on his upper lip and his kidneys started to function in high gear. The hum picked up intensity.

"I suggest we leave fast," Mikey said. "This is something new!"

Before the other two could concur, that part of the surface that Jenny Wong was leaning against turned an intense bluish white. The light was so intense that the protective sun shields of Lewis' helmet came on, throwing everything else around him into darkness.

Mikey and he both reached instinctively for Wong, but the chamber swallowed her. It happened in the blink of an eye but it

194

took long enough that Lewis had the distinct impression that she was shrinking. Or fading into the distance. The inner chamber then disappeared, leaving a large empty space at the center of the artifact.

He would remember Mikey's scream for a long time.

# Chapter Thirty-Nine

Isha Bai studied her tablet but her mind was not on the figures. With Posada dead and Wong missing and presumed dead, she experienced a chill caused by her isolation.

In a world supersaturated with information, she was lacking what was necessary to make decisions about alternate courses of action. First, it would be nice to know details about what Martinez was plotting. She and Bridges knew more than they did some weeks ago. They also had Henry Posada's warning, as strange as it might seem.

*Is Clinton losing his mind?* That made her sad. The astrophysicist was brilliant but Alzheimer's was still a threat for some of the elderly, especially if there was a genetic predisposition to develop it at a young age.

*Second, why the firewall of secrecy in Project Saturn Watch, a firewall even I can't break through? If I believe Clayton, Moravcsik is up to no good and may be responsible for killing my best agent and for whatever Henry Posada has become.*

She began her re-examination of the personnel records of the Project Saturn Watch staff. They were complete up to the time most of the Spacers had pulled out of LEO or one of the U.N.S.A. posts in the outer solar system.

Michaela Montero had done one of her PhD theses with Clinton Bridges.

Bridges had been a close friend of Bai's when she was at Cornell. He often talked in glowing terms about his prize student, Michaela, who was going to throw her promising academic career away to become a Spacer. How sad it was, but if Isha ever needed someone she could trust to head up a project, keep her in mind; and no, she hadn't asked him for the recommendation since she was too proud, but he was still giving it.

In her mind's eye, she could see Bridges twirling that big handlebar mustache as he said it. That tickled a lot during those cold winter nights at Cornell.

*All right, Michaela. You are going to have your chance.*
It was two in the morning on the night of July 3, 2132.

***

Not far away from where Isha Bai pondered the future of U.N.S.A., George Blake and Amanda Chu led a handful of mercenaries towards the spaceport. They stopped their vehicles about two kilometers from the west gate, the smallest entrance to the spaceport and the least guarded.

They all removed their radiation suits, which they had needed to leave their base near Bogota. Underneath those suits, they were dressed as U.N.S.A. Security agents. Some didn't look or speak the part—mercenaries were scruffy and some didn't even speak good English or Spanish, the *lengua franca* around the Villa de Leyva spaceport.

The troops moved swiftly towards the gate on foot while Blake and Chu waited in the jeep they had come in. Twenty minutes later, the two started towards the gate again, having received the signal that the troops were in position.

"Evening," said the guard at the gate, shining his flashlight into the jeep. "You have the wrong entrance, I'm afraid." His was a Texas drawl, as out of place here as Japanese might be. His nametag said Sgt. Dwight O'Hanlon, U.N.S.A. Security.

"We're in a hurry," Amanda said with a sweet smile. She flashed her fake U.N.S.A. Security badge. "We need to talk to Director Bai."

"You guys must be from out of town. The main entrance is around on the other side. Let me have your badges and I'll give the main building a call. If they OK it, you can drive through here, but you'll have to follow the perimeter road around the base. Still, I guess you'd save about five kilometers. I'll call them up for you."

He trotted off to his kiosk with their badges.

"Nice guy," said Blake.

"Shut up, stupid! We're not here to socialize."

As Sgt. O'Hanlon bent over his com set, a stealthy figure streaked out of the shadows and smacked him on the head with a blackjack.

"Ouch!" said Blake.

"Let's go," said Amanda.

The plan was for their mercenaries to cut straight across the spaceport to the main building by foot while Blake and Chu circled around the perimeter road in the jeep.

\*\*\*

Inside the spaceport, another small contingent of U.N.S.A. Security waited.

"Here we are skulking around like some prehistoric band of hominids in search of their weekly meal of meat," said Bridges. "Doesn't it make you wonder what it all means?"

"This is not a good time to philosophize, Clinton," replied Bai. "Yes, mankind is condemned to wonder because we're sapient. That said, now be quiet. George thinks he hears a jeep."

"No fucking way they're all coming on a jeep. I still can't believe they'd try anything."

In case the July 4 in the Amanda Chu's intercepted message had any relation to them, Isha Bai had decided to put all the U.N.S.A. spaceports on maximum alert over the 48-hour period that overlapped July 4 in the Mid-Atlantic Union. Since Villa de Leyva possessed the same time zone as Philadelphia, their alert started at 12 noon on July 3 and ended at 12 noon on July 5.

"If I were them, I'd send the troops right across the launch areas, assuming they come in from the west gate. We don't launch at night yet."

"West gate doesn't respond," said Lt. Jorge Sanchez, the George of Bai's earlier reference and leader of the U.N.S.A. Security personnel at the spaceport. "They have Dwight. I hope he's all right."

"Looks like we're a go then," said Bridges. "Shit, this is almost as exciting as sex!"

Action occurred even before the jeep arrived. Mercenaries began a seize-and-control-with-prejudice mission that would have left the U.N.S.A. people hapless if they had not been prepared. Even at that, the firefight was furious for about ten minutes. Then silence.

The next time Lt. Sanchez appeared before them, he was worse for wear, but happy.

"It's all over except for attending the wounded," he pronounced. "I believe we have two of Martinez' biggies, Dr. Bai. Amanda Chu and George Blake, from his corporate security ranks.

No one dead, but some of ours and some of theirs are shot up a bit."

Isha Bai nodded.

"Call Ruffini," she told Bridges. "Hopefully it hasn't started there yet."

\*\*\*

On that same night of July 3, 2132, Otto Bonafacio met General Judith Marshall again at the state reception in Craig Ruffini's residence.

"What a pleasant surprise, General," the Man said, taking her hand and kissing it. "President Ruffini does throw a nice party, don't you think?"

The President of the Mid-Atlantic Union was halfway across the ballroom from them. From the way he cocked his head, both Bonafacio and Marshall knew that he was listening to his data link, not to the conversation of the various politicos around him.

"It's always a grand occasion," said Marshall. "I'm British, you know, and I don't think we ever were this excited about the independence movement in the colonies. Besides, it all seems ancient history. The yanks do put on a good show, though. How's your speech coming?"

"Not even started. I'll become inspired sometime early this morning. It has to flow from the heart, you see. I suppose I will work in something about how the old United States led the world towards democracy long ago and how Philadelphia was the center from where many of those noble thoughts sprang."

"Do you think the U.N. plays the same role now?" asked Marshall.

"I would like to think that but I believe we must expand our horizons. Our destiny lies in the planets and the stars. One day our solar system may be only a backwater and some other place, perhaps Tau Ceti and its planets, will be the center of enlightenment and economic power. All our petty squabbles here will be put into proper perspective then. However, in the interim, we must all try to work together in peace and harmony, don't you think?"

"The Chaos hasn't helped much there," said the General.

"No, it hasn't. People depend on mercenaries too much to solve their problems, when I think they should learn to solve them alone. It's part of becoming mature as a people, correct?"

"You're talking to an Englishwoman, Mr. Secretary General. We invented courtesy and correctness, remember?"

*And we've paid for it ever since,* she thought.

The Man laughed. "Yes, which is why it irked you so much when those colonists threw out all that lovely tea!"

# Chapter Forty

Moravcsik was a man of mixed emotions. He was unhappy that they had lost the yolk of the egg, that is, the impenetrable ellipsoid at the center of the S.E.T.O., which had disappeared.

*The scientist in me might really give a damn about what was in it, but not the bureaucrat. Too much on my plate.*

On the other hand, Jenny Wong, a thorn in his side for some time, was gone. This also had the positive effect of allowing him to clamp down even more on S.E.T.O. security so that Lewis' information about what was happening there became more and more sporadic.

Moravcsik had also commanded that Project Saturn Watch go into slow motion while he assessed their situation, or so he told his people. Those not involved with S.E.T.O. had more time on their hands. Lewis even had time to start some primitive observations of Saturn's turbulent atmosphere using some old probes that Cecilia Romero had brought out on the Valiant. Moreover, Mikey and Gus had time to help him.

Soon after Jenny Wong's disappearance, Mikey received a strange e-mail from Buenos Aires. She net-transferred Lewis a copy and they both studied it with eyes closed.

Lewis knew people who could 'see' copy even with their eyes open, others who needed to close them, and still others who couldn't do any of the visual tricks at all, only auditory. The data link technology was, in many ways, like trying to learn how to use one of the new prosthetic limbs—it took a lot of training and motivation. Mikey and Lewis were about average.

The message was from Mikey's aunt. Liliana Puentes talked about taking care of Mikey when she was young and wondered what she was doing now. So on and so forth. It was a very pleasant e-mail.

"The only problem is that I don't have a *Tia* Liliana."

Lewis thought Mikey was trying to pull his leg.

"You don't? She seems to know you very well."

"My family fled Argentina during the war to live in Asuncion. You know that."

"You didn't leave anyone behind?"

"Jon, none of these things she talks about in this message ever happened. I have no idea who this person is, but I know she's no relative."

"Maybe an old flame still in love with you, but he's in hot water with Calderon." Guillermo Calderon was the Democratic Socialist Republic of Argentina's dictator. While flamboyant and still popular among some of the Argentines, he was not a nice man. "Or maybe a bill collector from your graduate studies."

"I did all my graduate studies in North America, first at MIT, then Cornell." A smile crossed her face. "That's it! It's a coded message."

Lewis was confused.

"Why would someone send you a coded message from Argentina?"

"No, it's Clinton, Clinton Bridges, my ex-advisor. *Comprendes*? *Puentes*, Bridges—same word. In addition, she refers to how she's had facial hair problems in her old age. Clinton has an enormous handlebar mustache."

"What's he doing in Buenos Aires?"

"He's not in Buenos Aires, silly. He's made the message appear as if it came from Buenos Aires. That way it appears natural that it's in Spanish, but it allows him to hide tidbits from anyone who intercepts the message."

"How so? Many people know some Spanish. Ten percent of the world speaks some version of Spanish. I know a bit myself."

"Yes, but each region uses different words for things and has different meanings for the same words. I doubt that anyone here would catch that. It took me a while even, and I'm a native speaker. There are words here that are only used in certain regions of the Spanish-speaking world. It was done purposely and is probably a code. Maybe if I filter out the ordinary language and leave the regionalisms?"

"Does your former advisor know Spanish that well?" Lewis asked.

"No. He has some Latin blood, but he doesn't speak Spanish well. He had help. If it's from him. I think it is, from some of the bawdy humor. Be quiet and let me try to decode this."

Lewis stretched out on her bunk and tuned into a newscast. He was curious but he knew she didn't like to be hurried. After some ten minutes and many notes and calculations, she was ready.

"As near as I can make out, Director Bai wants us to spy on Moravcsik and company."

"Isha Bai? The Director of U.N.S.A.? Why wouldn't she know everything that's going on here?"

"Well, apparently they don't know much about S.E.T.O. They won't divulge their source but now they know Moravcsik has been hiding a lot."

Lewis was dumbfounded. "So who are they sending all that information to? And why?"

"That's what we're supposed to find out."

Lewis thought back to his conversation with Jenny Wong and answered his own question.

# Chapter Forty-One

"All right, everyone, any questions?"

One of Ruffini's security officers looked unhappy.

"How will we know if it's him? There are a lot of weirdos at these events."

Sylvia Hunter, U.N.S.A. Security agent in charge, fielded the question. She was a striking woman with a reputation for not tolerating failure, but she was harder on herself than she was with any of her troops.

"You have the profile. He will attempt to shoot Secretary General Bonafacio and possibly your President from far enough away that he can make an escape."

There were grumbles when the Mid-Atlantic Union's Secret Service agents realized that a battle might occur without any help from mercenaries. They weren't accustomed to sticking their necks out alone.

"Why aren't other U.N. Security personnel here?" asked another Ruffini agent.

"I have informed President Ruffini that we suspect that U.N.-hired mercenaries are probably involved, so we prefer to keep this to ourselves. Clinton, any comments?"

Clinton Bridges twirled his moustache nervously. They had already shut down the whole operation around the spaceport in Villa de Leyva. George Blake had died of wounds received in the action. Isha Bai had offered leniency to Amanda Chu if she cooperated, which she did. Bridges then had flown by scramjet to Philadelphia to meet Hunter, who had called Ruffini at the party on July 3. It had been a busy twenty-four hours.

"I don't have anything to add. Well, maybe one point: this jerk wants to kill a very good man. Don't let him do it."

\*\*\*

The old homeless hunchback pushed his rusty shopping cart through the streets, his off-key humming accompanied by the irritating squeak of the wheels. From time to time he would scavenge through a trashcan or a pile of refuse, emitting an "aha" or "Eureka" while putting what little of value he found in the cart.

Philadelphia was still part of a consumer economy where people threw away good items that they were tired of. It made life easier for those who couldn't afford the luxurious apartments in the downtown high-rises and eked out a living by sifting through the garbage piles.

Downtown sprawled across both sides of the river, far into both New Jersey and Pennsylvania. People from all over that area were streaming into the old downtown that morning, hoping to obtain a view of the grandstand and the dignitaries that would be there making speeches, or at least to find a comfortable place to watch the fireworks.

The maglevs were packed. Air taxis and street taxis moved thousands. Bicycles filled the bike paths. It was not sensible to bring your own vehicle, so people took advantage of public or simpler transportation.

Some even had camped out the night before in one of the pretty little parks around the central one in front of Independence Hall where the grandstand was. They would be stiff and sore by evening but they would also have the best seats.

The old man passed some of these groups. Some of the children called him names or sung deriding songs about him, bringing a smile to his parched lips. But mostly they ignored him.

*Better for me. He who stands out is remembered.*

There were thousands like him, victims to bad luck in a society where bad luck was common in spite of the number of people that could afford to come in and be part of the annual celebration. Even public transportation was not cheap.

He roamed the streets of the inner city all day. For lunch, he begged a handout at a pastry shop five blocks from the grandstand. He then curled up in an alley with his cart and took a long nap.

When he awoke, it was dinnertime. Many in the crowds around the grandstand had broken out wine, cheese, and other edibles. Two teenage girls offered him some bread, cheese and Polish sausage. He accepted it gratefully.

*Not all people are insensitive*, he thought.

Another nap in another alley. This time the sound of the band awoke him. It was eight o'clock in the City of Brotherly Love. He hoped the overcast sky did not portend a thunderstorm.

*Wouldn't want to put a damper on all the festivities, would we?*

He chuckled to himself and headed towards the tall, abandoned tower that already cast a long shadow on the buildings that surrounded it.

He was expecting to run into security and did.

"Can't go up there, old man," a brawny cop told him.

"I always sleep up there," he lied. "Why can't I sleep up there tonight?"

"You won't get much sleep. You know about the fireworks?" The cop backed away from the smell of urine and old beer.

"All the more reason to go up, young man. Plenty of time to sleep afterwards. And my eyes aren't as good as they used to be."

That brought a smile to the cop's leathery face. "All right, go on up. I didn't see you." He walked away to finish the rest of his patrol.

The assassin pulled an old rolled-up rug from out of the shopping cart. To a careful observer the rug would appear to be heavier and more bulky than it should be. However, there was no one to observe while he headed up the stairs.

Karpinsky knew the schedule by heart. First the mayor would speak, then Ruffini, then Bonafacio. How long he had to wait depended on the speech durations of the first two.

Inside the rug were the pieces of a light, new sniper's rifle. He had engineered and machined it to perfection. He put the other contents of the rug to one side and assembled the gun.

As was expected, the speakers followed the pecking order: the mayor's speech was only five minutes. Ruffini was much more eloquent and spent twenty-five minutes extolling the virtues of the city and his country.

*You would think that he was Thomas Jefferson*, thought Karpinsky. *But he looks like an annoying little ogre.*

Bonafacio rose to speak. He was a noble presence on the stage. When he shook President Ruffini's hand, it was like a kind and gentle father taking the small hand of his child.

"My friends of Philadelphia and the Mid-Atlantic Union, my friends all over the world, good evening. We come together here in this cradle of democracy...."

Eagle Talon supposed it was a good speech. Most of Bonafacio's speeches were good. Moreover, the old fool seemed to believe what he said. *Thanks to democracy, I can make a good living.* He was looking forward to retirement. *Maybe buy a little island in the Caribbean close enough to a big one where I can find some action when I need it.*

He sighted along the rifle. With his experience, it would not be a difficult shot. *If the senile idiot wouldn't wave his damn arms about so much—*

"Drop the gun!"

He turned and laid down the rifle. The man motioned to him to back away.

Karpinsky recognized one of President Ruffini's security agents, not the cop from below. He knew them all since he had researched this assignment. This was Secret Service Agent Antonio Jaramillo, forty-six, who had a wife and four children. *Too bad. I hope his life insurance is good.*

Jaramillo was out of breath and sweating in the heavy air that signaled the coming storm. *Still, he's in good enough condition that I didn't even hear him come up.* He bent over to pick up the gun.

It was what the assassin needed. One step, another longer step, and then a kick.

He tried to find a pulse, just in case, but he knew Jaramillo's neck was broken. He reached for the gun, thinking to make certain, but he was interrupted by pounding feet on the rickety stairs between the first and second landings of the tower.

*Shit,* he thought. *Someone's screwed me big time on this one.*

He'd be damned if he'd give Martinez his money back. Maybe he would kill him instead.

He left the rifle lie and reached for the other contents of the rug. He turned left and ran the length of the landing, jumping wide over the ledge into the twilight, as the first face peered over the top of the ladder.

A short pull on a cord was all that was needed to open the hang-glider. He landed and cut himself free before the agents on the tower could even locate him. He shed the disguise in seconds.

What looked like an old water storage tank broke apart to reveal a small aircar. The motor caught, he hopped in, and sped off into the darkening twilight. The tower and the frustrated agents dwindled behind and below him.

*** 

"There he is," said Sylvia Hunter. The blip showed clearly on her screen and the software announced that its origin was the tower where the agents had nearly caught Eagle Talon.

She and two others in one aircar stared at their radar screen. Another group was riding in a nearby car. She hit the button that would start the software calculating an intercept solution.

"Let's take him down!"

Two air-to-air missiles streaked through the night from different angles. They hit Karpinsky's aircar with a one-two punch. People assumed the light and sound of the explosion was only a precursor to the fireworks.

# Chapter Forty-Two

Moravcsik had to assume that Martinez' plan was proceeding on schedule. Otherwise, there was no way to synchronize. Soon a powerful oligarchy would completely control Earth and then turn its attention to bringing the independent-minded Spacers under its control. His next steps would be the first battle in that skirmish.

As Eagle Talon climbed the stairs of the abandoned tower in Philadelphia, the Dione chief made his way to the command and control center. Security checks complete, the door whooshed open to reveal a space that looked like an airport control tower.

Dan Coates turned to face Moravcsik when he entered the cramped space.

"What brings you here, Ted?" asked the puzzled man. "You're always chiding us for wasting time with personal chit-chat when we could do it over the intranet."

The smile on his face told Moravcsik that the man was only needling him in a collegial manner. At any other time, Moravcsik might have appreciated this attempt at camaraderie, but not today.

He pulled the small but lethal gun from his service coat.

"Hey, what's going on?"

The three others in C&C swung around, reacting to the fear content in Dan's voice. Facing them made shooting his colleagues more difficult. He shot Coates first, then the others.

In less than two seconds, he was standing alone. His thoughts didn't dwell on what he had done. Like that day long ago when he had defended his less than brilliant doctoral thesis, he was focused.

*A migraine from the stress, but focused. You have to be focused.*

He had reluctantly told Jenny Wong about the missiles. She was now dead and four others that knew about their existence were bleeding out on the floor. Only a few others outside the C&C, Coates' other shift, knew about them.

The guidance programs for the missiles had simple inputs. *Two steps. One, load the programs into the fire control app. Two, type in Helene.* The C&C computer did the rest.

"Testing for authenticity," said the computer in its metallic voice.

Moravcsik stared into the retinal scanner and applied his thumb to the appropriate pad at the same time. While it was possible that someone could cut off his thumb and hold it up against the pad, it would be hard to do it at the same time with the retinal scan. Since Project Saturn was a U.N.S.A. scientific program, people considered this fail-safe mechanism sufficient. No one had contemplated that the head of the program would be up to no good.

"System armed."

Moravcsik flipped the flyaway switch.

*Done. Fifteen men and women condemned to their deaths,* he thought. *Plus the ones here. You're doing well today, Dr. Moravcsik.*

***

Elsewhere in Dione, Mikey had received Clinton Bridges' report on the plot to kill the Security General and their moves to stop it. Amanda Chu had already implicated Rudolfo Martinez. Bridges recommended that they place Ted Moravcsik under arrest until they sorted things out.

"We have to find him," Mikey said.

"I'm buzzing him now," Lewis said. "He's not responding."

"Let's then go to his cubicle and wake him up. This is important."

Ted was not in his cubicle, though, so they were at a loss for a moment about what to do.

"Locater," said Lewis.

Many of the scientists had installed locater software in addition to the standard software used to run their wi-fi device. With the proper command, your device (actually the main computer) told you where the wearer of the other device was.

"Locate Ted Moravcsik," said Mikey.

"Dr. Moravcsik is in C&C," responded the computer.

They rushed off towards the command and control center.

As mere scientists, they were not cleared to enter the center. Mikey found a crowbar in a maintenance closet. Lewis set himself to the task of forcing the door.

"Unauthorized entry is being attempted," said the AI that controlled Dione and the center.

"Oh, shut up!" said Mikey.

Lewis opened the door as if it were a lid to a can of sardines. It would need repair.

He entered first and Mikey followed. She ran into Lewis when he stopped dead in his tracks.

The scene that greeted them would remain etched in their memories forever. There were five dead in C&C. Moravcsik's head rested in a pool of blood.

The scientist had shot himself. Lewis turned the body over and Mikey turned green. Half the face was blown away. The other half had an expression of sorrow frozen on it.

It was not a pretty sight. Four of their colleagues were also dead. There was only one monitor screen on. It showed a star field.

For a moment, Lewis thought there was something wrong with the station's computer and that it was a frozen frame, but then he noticed that points of light in the star field were moving. Better said, a wide-angle lens of something moving around Saturn was picking up rubble in the outermost ring. Moreover, a brighter speck of something right in the center of the field of view was growing in size.

Mikey pushed aside Dan Coates body and fiddled with the controls while Lewis looked over her shoulder.

"Whatever is carrying this camera is headed directly towards Helene," Lewis observed, reading the instruments.

"You don't think—?" She left the question hanging.

"Shit, there are two shifts out there at S.E.T.O.!" He reached for the switch that would connect him with Helene.

The missile was already near its target. The warhead detached and fired on its own, speeding out in front of the main rocket that had been carrying it and now only carried the camera. It passed right through most of the S.E.T.O. with tremendous speed and came to stop under it before the detonation occurred.

The little moon imploded for a few seconds. Helene then expanded and shattered, all in slow motion, as the various delta V's associated with its debris combined with the orbital velocity of

Helene to spread the debris along the old orbit, forming a new ring around the planet.

Mikey wept. S.E.T.O. was no more. Fifteen of her colleagues were dead.

It was not one of humanity's prouder moments.

# Chapter Forty-Three

It didn't take the Man long to take charge of events.

They rounded up the leaders of corporate mercenaries involved in the plot, at least the ones they knew about from the confessions of Amanda Chu. General Judith Marshall committed suicide before they could capture her.

They caught Martinez on the Philadelphia-to-Toronto mag-lev on his way to the Great Lakes Confederation. It was a natural escape route; the Confederation had no extradition treaty with the U.N., so he would have been safe if he had made it.

The CEOs of the world's largest multinational corporations, whether they had participated in Martinez' plan or not, were rounded up by U.N.S.A. Security and put into "temporary quarantine," like the press release said. They then forced them to attend a meeting in Bonafacio's conference room—in person, no avatars. Armed security agents stood guard both inside and outside the doors. Bonafacio presided.

"This is a terrible setback for the U.N.," he began. "We have seen again how greed and lust for power can bring men and women to perform hideous acts against humanity. We have had political setbacks before, though not of this magnitude, but these tests can only make our very imperfect union that much stronger as the U.N. tries to create some semblance of order during the Chaos."

He looked at the magnates assembled before him. They were a captive audience but their stake in every word was apparent.

"We all know this is mostly the work of one man but many of you have been willing if not active accomplices. However, in some sense, we all are. Although this will never be reported on in the press for security reasons, to those participants among you, your punishments will be handed out here today."

\*\*\*

"What, no judge, no jury?" asked Denise Andersen. She sat at the other end of the large conference table, a position recognizing both her importance and her innocence compared to some of the others present.

His first answer to a question was a scowl. It was not pleasant on a face that was usually gentle and kind.

"You, above all, the person that has taken justice into her own hands all too often, are lucky that I consider you only a minor player in Mr. Martinez' scheme."

Ruffini, who was also present and sitting in a corner, squirmed. It was like a tongue-lashing from a benevolent father. Not part of the plot, they had nevertheless invited him to participate since he was instrumental in thwarting it. *Sometimes you need to better plan your success in order to not become a victim of it.*

"I can provide a public trial to those responsible, but then this all goes to press. You and your corporations will be severely affected or even ruined. I guarantee it. Your lives may not be worth much either. In fact, I would be surprised if your own Boards of Directors or security organizations didn't put out a contract on you. Do you want that?"

"Maybe we should take our chances," said Denise, who found herself in the uncomfortable position of speaking for her colleagues, many of whom she disliked. "Depends on your alternative."

"That it does. You all know Isha Bai. She and Clinton Bridges have worked out a plan that involves many of you. Originally, she was worried about how she was going to convince you to accept it. Now, that's no worry, not for me. If anyone doesn't accept it, you will be carted off to jail to await your trial for crimes against humanity."

"So how are you going to keep the story from the press if Martinez goes to trial?" asked a third member of the group.

"The press has been informed that Martinez regrettably died in an airtaxi crash on his way to the Great Lakes Confederation. In fact, he sits in the same Turkish cell that I believe the Alternate Pope once occupied. At any rate, for all intents and purposes, he is dead."

"So let's hear your offer," said Andersen, piqued by curiosity. She was safe since she had known nothing about Martinez' plan. Nevertheless, she was a businesswoman. What Bonafacio offered might have attributes she could use.

"Isha? Please explain your plan to these people." Otto Bonafacio sat down. He looked tired.

\*\*\*

Isha Bai's avatar appeared. To Ruffini, in spite of her size, it was like Moses coming down from the mountain. He nearly laughed. *This is worth the entrance admission price.*

"It's called Eureka L.T.D.," she began. "The idea is to make R&D related to space exploration and exploitation independent of you people while at the same time make you foot the bill. Let me go into details."

At the end of the presentation, the Director of U.N.S.A. asked if there were questions. There were none. She had trumped them.

"I consider then that this plan is ratified. Your legal departments will be receiving copies to sign very soon, but that is a formality. Any wavering and there'll be hell to pay by the guilty. You're all free to go now. Good day to you."

Most in the room cleared out fast, glad to be free from the stern looks of the U.N.S.A. Security agents. They rushed Otto Bonafacio away to an appointment in another part of the building. Denise Andersen and Craig Ruffini lingered on along with Bai's avatar.

"My ancestors believed in hell," Ruffini said. "We are working with the devil here."

"I agree," said Isha. "Make no mistake, this is a devil pact we are making, but it's the only possible solution, given the circumstances. If good comes from it, we will be lucky. Good day. Never fear. I will keep in touch."

\*\*\*

They watched the avatar fade away. They both recognized that Isha Bai was one very small woman carrying some very large problems on her shoulders.

Ruffini cleared his throat. "Well, I for one, could use a drink. Denise?"

The CEO of WorldNet nodded. The disaster with Project Saturn and S.E.T.O. was not common knowledge but she and Isha Bai were tight—the U.N.S.A. Director had informed her that Moravcsik had managed to destroy all S.E.T.O. remains with Helene. There was no physical evidence left of the greatest archaeological find in human history.

With respect to the exploitation of space, Denise Andersen realized that her business model was about to change. She looked forward to it with only a wee bit of apprehension. *If I can do my small part to make it better, as I've been doing, I will be satisfied.*

She followed Ruffini out of the conference room.

# Chapter Forty-Four

In the half-light of her bedroom, Clinton Bridges snuggled up to Isha Bai. With one hand, she twirled his great handlebar mustache and with the other, she played with his limp member.

"Isha, I have to go back to Ithaca, you know. I'm stressed out with this political crap."

"I know. Nonetheless, you did a good job for me. On many fronts." He smiled when she smothered a chuckle.

"Come back with me."

"Someday. However, I have to make sure this Eureka L.T.D. takes off. You helped a lot there too."

"It was your idea."

"But it was your brilliant tweak that made it independent of everything. Yet it could still die."

"Not with you nursing it along."

"Eureka L.T.D. Doesn't that sound good?"

"Names are unimportant." He stroked her hair. "I'll be waiting for you in Ithaca."

"I'll be there before you know it."

***

"She's a nice lady," observed Juanito.

Clinton Bridges released his hand to grab his suitcase when it came by on the carousel. He knew the kid was referring to Isha Bai, who had given him a big hug and kiss when they were leaving Colombia.

"You'd better believe it. Say, before we try to catch a local to Ithaca, how about you and I finding some ice cream?"

Juanito nodded and followed Bridges to the escalator that led to the level where the fast food places went about their business selling unhealthy food to an unsuspecting public. Naturally, the kid wanted sprinkles on his cone.

They found a table away from the commotion of the busy terminal and sat down, both tired and happy.

"Say, about those voices. Did I tell you I saw Posada? He came to me in a video game. Very clever of him."

. "I rarely hear the voices now," said Juanito looking out the huge windows over the tarmac where the scramjets lined up to take off. "But Sr. Posada spoke to me just before we left Colombia."

"He did?" *Both Posada and Wong are among the missing since Wong disappeared into that egg at the center of the artifact. So did this little guy receive a message from Posada after that?*

"*Si, Sr.* Bridges, he said not to worry. He and *Srta.* Wong will be fine. And he thanks you for adopting me."

Bridges choked on his ice cream that didn't even have sprinkles. *Now, how the hell did he know I was going to do that?*

"*Si, si senor,* tomorrow we will visit the immigration office in Ithaca and start the paperwork. With me as your new guardian and Isha Bai as a reference, I don't think we'll have any problems."

"I thank you too, by the way," said the boy, his wide smile smeared with ice cream and sprinkles.

. **\*\*\***

Henry Posada had never experienced a computer like the one that now contained the many terabytes of his essence. It seemed more like a living being but was also a vast labyrinth that he was afraid to start exploring.

He was aware of the "others." The computer itself seemed to be sentient, a protective presence surrounding him like a womb. Yet there were other strange minds too, alien minds, weaving in and out of the computer's memory. And a more familiar Human, a female, somehow with them, but outside the computer too. They all seemed to be outside space and time.

Subjective time also seemed immaterial while he laid out two tasks. The first priority was to explore the labyrinth and try to understand where he was. It seemed like an almost insurmountable task compared to the one he had undertaken when he died. The second was to return the Human female to her lover. Physically.

*A resurrection. A rebirth. Call it what you will, it might take some doing.*

But he was patient.

***

The scientific colony known as Project Saturn recovered from the shock of what Moravcsik had done. The healing process was catalyzed by Gus Hanson's election as new project director. Lewis was surprised that Hanson even wanted the job.

He smiled across at his new bride. Mikey smiled back while she torqued a recalcitrant bolt into place.

They were on Calypso putting the finishing touches to a new research station. With Helene gone, the Trojan trio of Tethys, Telesto, and Calypso had become a substitute for the original design. Hanson had proposed the change to Denise Andersen and she had accepted.

*It's nice to be back on that hedonistic stool that Tanglevsky pulled out from under me. Maybe good things do come to those who wait.*

# Part III

## Billy

*Never let your sense of morals get in the way of doing what's right.*

– Isaac Asimov

# Chapter Forty-Five

"Nice job."

Chang watched the scruffy man drop a fifty note into the upturned hat on his piano. The musician couldn't see how much money was in the hat due to the low light of the lounge, but every bit helped the cause.

The stranger offered a hand. "Billy Clarke. How do you keep all those songs in your head? I heard some that go a long way back."

Peter Chang studied the man. *Not your usual single fellow in a piano bar,* he observed. *This guy's old, not looking to score. Unless he thinks it's a gay bar?*

Chang had mostly Russian and Chinese blood. The former had more influence on a genetic makeup that gave him big feet and large hands. The hands were not as big as Rachmaninoff's but the long fingers stretched over the keys with ease. The Chinese blood from his mother had given him a talent for music and perfect pitch. At least, that was his theory.

He didn't trust this man, although he had no reason for the distrust. It was only a premonition.

"It's an old trick," he said, showing the stranger his music books. "These are called 'fake books.' I don't know why. But, you see here, there's only a melody line. Above that are the chord progressions."

The stranger seemed interested. "So, what about rhythm and all that? You're doing an awful lot with your hands, friend."

Chang wasn't sure he liked the assumption of friendship, but the stranger was the only one in the bar that didn't seem drunk. Moreover, he had thrown in a nice tip. The pianist took a sip of his whiskey, now too watery with the melting of the ice.

"It's hard to explain to someone who doesn't play. For someone who does, no explanation is needed. However, here's an attempt. Take the song I just played. It's a slow waltz. So, there's a basic rhythm. One-two-three, one-two-three, or three quarters time. I mess with that using some standard embellishments. Or my own. I can change the chords too, if I want." He played the song several ways. "It's like anything else—it takes practice. I'm a pro. It's what I do."

"Fascinating. Have you been doing this forever?"

"Long enough. What do you do for a living?"

"Security. Insurance. Nothing as creative as music. Thanks for talking to me."

Chang watched the man walk back to his table and then put him out of his mind.

He looked at his watch. He had a few minutes more to go before his break, although he figured the owner of the bar wouldn't care enough to time him.

He headed for the men's room.

*** 

After Clarke sat down, he took a sip from his own drink, but he didn't focus on its quality. He surveyed the bar, noting the newcomers. He had already sized up the other clientele. The owner had stepped out and there was no bouncer. The bartender was a woman who was less animated than her robot helper.

When Chang took his break, Clarke followed him to the men's room and listened from outside. When he heard the urinal flush, he stepped inside and locked the door.

"Funny thing about insurance," he said, "is that you can buy it for most anything."

Clarke saw that Chang was surprised to see him. In the harsh light of the bathroom, Clarke knew that his scruffiness clashed even more with the appearance of the bar's usual patrons.

"What do you mean?" Chang asked.

Clarke put leather gloves on. They had enough padding that his knuckles would not suffer from the thrashing he planned for the pianist.

"My organization insures all sorts of stuff. In your case, a drug debt. Our clients get their money up front and we do the collection."

Chang turned a pasty white and backed away. "I told your other people that I would come up with the money. I get a lot of action from lonely women here. Some of them are rich and pay me well for my services."

"As I understand it, you made that promise last month. What about now?"

"I'm working on it. I'm using my free nights but the women on top of my list are traveling. You have to give me more time."

"Oh, you'll have time," said Clarke, approaching Chang.

The pianist whipped out a vibrablade. It looked puny in his big hands.

*This dickhead's very foolish,* thought Clarke. *And he's going to make my job difficult.*

He feinted once and decked Chang with a left hook. He then reached down and pulled the man up by the collar, deciding that the pianist deserved a facelift for pulling a knife on him.

Too late, he saw the vibrablade arcing toward him. He deflected it with his left hand, but Chang was strong enough to continue the thrust. The blade went into Clarke's arm just below the left shoulder.

He let the collar go and grabbed the wrist of the arm holding the knife. Pushing it to the floor, he stomped on the hand until Chang let go of the blade. Clarke kicked it and saw that it slid under the door of a toilet stall.

"You got some nerve, I'll say. You're a pro at your music. I'm a pro at what I do. I've been doing it longer than you've been tickling the keys, Mr. Schumann." He stomped the man in the face for good measure. "You're pathetic."

Chang writhed in pain, clutching at his hand. The blood from the broken nose didn't seem to bother him.

"You could have gotten away with just the face job, pretty boy, but no, you had to be a macho and pull a knife." He knelt down and whispered in his victim's ear. "Be forewarned: I'm just second tier, friend. The next time you might become a quadriplegic. The third tier guys even scare me."

He kicked the pianist in the ribs for good measure. He left Chang moaning on the floor and walked to the nearest washbasin to see what he could do about his arm wound.

\*\*\*

*Making an honest living is becoming harder and harder.* Clarke stumbled out of the maglev station over to the tracks and vomited yet again. *Life sucks. Chang sucks. I should have killed the bastard.*

The sensual graphics and sound of the portable zookie were not enough to sweep the memory away. From the socket behind his ear, Clarke unplugged the wi-fi device of the VR set. Memories clamped down on his mind like a vise.

*Trapped.*

Lately he often experienced that feeling. The night before he had felt it. The painful memory was as pungent as the new, sour taste of the vomit, the former overriding the pain from the cut in his arm.

*Would Chang ever play again?*

He had gone to Lawrence to seek comfort in drink and the arms of Rosita, but she had mistakenly smashed a bottle over his head while she put an end to a brawl in her bar.

*And I wasn't even in the fight.*

He wasn't sure whether he had even spent the night with her—rather morning—she wasn't with him when the dawn streamed through her dirty bedroom windows.

*Rosita always looks good sleeping like a bronzed angel in the early morning light. Where the hell did she go?*

He couldn't even enjoy a warm shower (was it Rosita's water ration day?). His shoulder throbbed. He headed for his apartment.

*Not a moment's rest.*

\*\*\*

The dragon lady's avatar was waiting for him at his apartment. She was a great believer in multitasking. Like some modern Medusa, from her HQ she would send out avatars to her various enforcers. The vast bank of the syndicate's servers managed all of this with ease, making electronic clones out of each avatar. The vast computer power also made her enforcers miserable. It was hard to negotiate with an abstraction.

"Good job with Chang," said the avatar.

Clarke studied the avatar. The holographic projection beamed down from a ceiling projector and appeared to languish on his bed. He wondered if the boss-lady looked that good. He was sure the computer edited out the drug-red eyes and limp hair of the original. He had seen too much of the real thing on the streets. Yet her avatar still had an aura of sensuality.

*A cheap Cleopatra to my Anthony?*

It was an impersonal sexuality, soft porn for the internet crowd of pimpled boys hoping to get laid. She could have been a robot for all he cared. Rosita was more human. Yet the new boss could also be the Sphinx—she was just as mysterious.

"Chang did a good job on me," Clarke said, pointing to his shoulder. "I should receive a bonus for hazard pay."

"You know the risks. And why would you think I give a fuck? I only expect you to do your job. Either get my money or soften up the asshole for the third tier."

Clarke went to the washbasin. His studio apartment consisted of a galley kitchen, toilet, and washbasin, plus enough room for a single bed. It was all he needed.

He stripped off his shirt and bathed the wound. It hurt like hell.

"You'll need some stitches for that," observed the avatar.

"Your concern is touching."

"My concern is that you are in good enough shape to perform your next task. A few stitches and antibiotics will keep you from having an infection. I wouldn't much care, but I've already tasked you for your next job. To reassign personnel is inefficient. I like efficiency."

"I think you only like money. You're one greedy bitch."

The avatar laughed. The projection shimmered a bit when she did so. *Damn juice*, thought Clarke. *They're always screwing around with the electricity.* The projection stabilized and the avatar turned on its side towards Clarke, left leg on top of right. It began to repeatedly raise and lower the left leg. Clarke watched the hairy triangle between her legs shrink and expand, shrink and expand. On the expansion more was visible than he cared to see.

*Maybe not soft porn. This is hard-core. Is she taunting me?*

As if she was reading his mind, she laughed again. "Don't get your hopes up, little man. The only thing I would ever do with your dick is eat it on a bun if you ever cross me. Don't ever forget it." She stopped with the leg raises. "Go to Heinrich in Alston and he'll sew you up. Then contact HQ for the assignment."

"If Heinrich says I'm not able to work?"

"That is up to him. He has to make that decision. I can get some good money for your body parts, so you'd better hope that he gives you the OK."

\*\*\*

227

Heinrich gave Clarke the OK.

*I don't know whether I'm disappointed or not. Sometimes dying seems the right way to go.*

The computer voice sent him downtown, so he returned to the maglev station. Trapped yet again into going after someone he didn't know or care about.

*Until after the violence. And so much for the psychological benefits of a well programmed zookie. The U.N. Medical Association hasn't catalogued the mental health hazards of my profession yet.*

He switched from the maglev express to the local at Porter Square and disembarked at the Charles Street station.

*Trapped.*

The word had taken on new meaning in recent months while the new boss moved in to consolidate her territory. It ate at his brain like one of those monsters in a zookie game. It was like a bad hangover.

Clarke found the centuries-old brownstone. The door sagged as if to mimic the sagging of his tired body. He entered, wondering how to better his life.

*Trapped in my job. Trapped by my boss. Trapped in my love life.*

Boston's Back Bay was no longer a rich man's neighborhood. Flooded by the rising waters produced by global warming, it was dry now and protected by dikes. The Chaos had made it into a war zone. That also meant that rent was cheap. It was a slum with cache.

*What a hangover!* A hinge whined an accompaniment to the percussive pain in his arm muscle. *There was a time when I thought I had a future,* he mused, while he counted the steps he had to climb. The ele no longer worked. *As a kid, I dreamed I was going to be a rig pilot. I identified with them. I still do.*

He even had adopted their religion, the Church of the Universal Way, and meditated for a time, usually with old Buchman, the neighborhood Guide. *Cantankerous old SOB.* Although meditating didn't help him much, it seemed to keep the Spacers sane.

*'Course I don't know any Spacers,* he thought with a smile. *The rig pilots are Spacers and the Spacers are all misfits, just like me, generally running from something or someone on Earth, or fed up with Downy society in general.*

How he had liked to watch the launches of the big rigs on the newsnet. Sometimes his old man was sober enough to go outside with him and look at the stars. They'd pretend that they could see the big rigs leave orbit and head for Mars, the asteroids, whatever. The old man then bought him a telescope and they could really watch them.

Somehow, the pretending was better.

*Then came the Chaos. The old man left Mom and me to go off and die in some dusty mine in the Northwest Republic.*

# Chapter Forty-Six

With its impersonal electronic voice, the wi-fi device whispered to his inner ear, "John Wade, Apartment 327." Somewhere one of the boss-lady's computers was directing events, electronically feeding off the chip in his shoulder.

Such surveillance and pursuit were legal, but he was on an illegal mission. On the local crime scene, Clarke was a savvy jack-of-all-trades but master of none. There were thousands like him, feeding off the decay of the cities.

Nevertheless, he figured he was special. For one, he was older than most of them, a survivor. He had grown into manhood during the turmoil of the Chaos, those years of near anarchy in the big cities, by working for a number of warlords, as the news media liked to call them.

*Warlords in Boston!* He chuckled at the name, since it seemed to be too dignified a term to apply to people who had so scrambled their brains by drugs, booze and lust for power that they considered themselves not only above the law but the creators of the law as well. *They once owned Boston. But no more.*

An unstable status quo now existed between the local U.N. mercenaries and the new bosses, who passed themselves off as upstanding bizpers. "You get some, I get some" had become the day-by-day mantra of existence. *Better than the Chaos, at least.*

He used to love his city. It was still important to him in some ways. But he was trapped in it. He had lived most of his life here and knew that it held no future for him.

\*\*\*

Wade's girl friend opened the door. Her eyes were dull with lack of sleep and blackened by smeared mascara. She was dressed in a bathrobe that had once been stylish but now was in poor taste.

In a drab hall made gloomier by the rachitic sunlight of a Boston winter, the woman could barely make out Clarke—and didn't like what she saw.

She knew that through the partially opened door he was able to see most of the apartment. While the hologram ID plate on the door had the words "John Wade - Communications Hardware Specialist" swimming in 3D, he could see that she was alone.

She had kept the chain on the door, yet knew it would be only a minor nuisance if the unkempt stranger decided to enter by force. Wade, like the other tenants in these buildings, could not afford the peace of mind that a modern security installation offered.

"Lookin' for John Wade," Clarke announced. She decided that his smile was not genuine.

"He's not here," she answered. "He left early this morning and hasn't come back. I don't know where he's off to." She hesitated a moment, sizing him up to see if he merited more confidential information. She had her doubts but couldn't resist justifying her presence. "We're going to be married, you know."

"Yeah, sure," said Clarke, matching her certainty about that. "Give me your com code and I'll let you know if I find him." She fell for that. "Could he be at the Toot?"

She decided then that Clarke was an enforcer. Only the mercenaries or the gangs would know Wade worked for MIT. As an assistant professor, her man made only a little more than a research assistant and would never make tenure and associate professor. The prestigious MIT would squeeze him dry and move on to hire another dupe.

She told Wade this all the time. She was the pessimist; he was the optimist. He believed that it was a privilege to work for a world-class institution. They both knew that he wouldn't make much more money at another college or university.

His answer was to go and try to make money gambling. Like many addicts, he believed he had a system. It didn't work very well, but he had met her at the tables, so she tolerated his self-indulgence.

She sometimes even went with him to the backrooms of bars in Chelsea where some of the big games took place, hanging on to him as if he were a trophy to her womanhood. He was, after all, smart and elegant.

*The cards are his addiction and he's my addiction,* she thought.

"He's on a two week vacation," she lied. "To Chicago. You'll have to come back then."

*Let him think that Wade skipped out on his gambling debt and left me behind.* It didn't register that she was contradicting her statement about marriage.

Clarke looked over the chain around the apartment again. She watched the bloodshot eyes search and then come to focus on her breasts.

"He doesn't deserve you," he said.

She watched him walk back down the corridor to the creaky stairs and shivered.

*Perverted asshole,* she thought.

***

However, Billy Clarke was more a professional than an asshole or pervert. He was thorough. He also was greedy enough to want his commission, so he went to MIT and broke into Wade's office.

*Although this is a high-tech place,* thought Clarke, *the security is laughable. They probably want to make it easy for the homeless to find a place to sleep in these hallowed corridors.* He smiled. *Maybe a Nobel Prize-winning homeless person?*

He had read a study some time ago that said that major colleges and universities all over the world were hit hard by the Chaos. He didn't find this surprising. The People's Republic of Cambridge, home to MIT, had become a war zone.

At night the drunks, thieves, and homeless warmed themselves via bonfires set on Mass Ave. Police presence was non-existent and only a few U.N. mercenaries spilled over from downtown Boston. It was safer to sail through the city on the maglev.

The Toot most likely figured that a common thief wouldn't find much of interest here. To support that idea, the only item he found that was interesting was a well-thumbed and coffee-stained newsnet printout, a two-month-old bulletin about another crazy starship project that Eureka L.T.D. was sponsoring. It was entitled "Last Chance for Scientists and Technicians to Sign On to Eureka's Magellan."

Magellan was both the ship's name and the project's name, Clarke recalled. He read the bulletin in its entirety, put it into his pocket, and left.

His puzzled expression became a smile as he read. The girl friend was lying about Chicago. His opinion of her improved because he realized that she had put Wade's interests above her own. *Love makes the world go 'round. For some, at least.*

Clarke knew how to fool network security on most of the computer networks in the greater Boston area. It was part of his job. He had help from some excellent software the syndicate had pirated, but he was no novice all the same.

After three hours of work in his apartment, he had a good guess about John Wade's next move. The man had bought a ticket to Villa de Leyva on the New China shuttle. It left at 3 p.m.

He frowned. He knew the boss would consider the money used for that ticket to be her own money.

He looked at the clock on the wall above his computer terminal. He could make it out to Daniel Shay Airport with time to spare.

Being a man of caution, he informed HQ of his plan, subvocalizing on his way downstairs and to the street to find a taxi. Lil' Sam, one of the boss' lieutenants, OK'd the plan.

*Good,* thought Clarke, *that way the boss also pays for the taxi.*

Greed is such a powerful emotion. The boss would pay little expenses like a taxi or maglev in order to either collect or have the satisfaction of hurting the person who was in her debt.

She was no different from any of the others who had employed him.

***

They used the new airport exclusively for international exoatmospheric flights, in contrast to the old Logan airport, used only for local commuter flights, and Devens, used for both. Shay was also the farthest from his apartment in Dorchester.

It was not a busy time of day, however, so it was not difficult to find an airtaxi. He was soon winging his way into western Massachusetts, the many dingy areas of uncontrolled development, the factories and slums of the latest New England economic boom, speeding by below.

The traffic was heavier the closer he was to the airport. Daniel Shay was nearly as busy as the Henry Hudson in the New York City metropolitan area since it served the urban sprawl that started south of old Hartford and reached all the way beyond Portsmouth.

It took Clarke over an hour to arrive at the busy airtaxi complex off to one side of the huge airport. He had been there many times, so he knew where the New China terminal was located. The computer's voice behind his ear told him the number of the departure gate for Villa de Leyva.

Wade was not in the waiting area.

*** 

Clarke waited around for a bit. He then went to eat a late lunch. When he came back, Wade still wasn't there.

They started loading passengers at 2:30, but Wade still hadn't made an appearance.

Clarke then saw Wade's girl friend. She was much more presentable than when he last saw her.

*Not bad looking at all. What's she doing here?* She approached him with a peculiar smile that was both attractive and rang alarm bells. *What's going on?*

She didn't leave him much time to come up with answers. She reached into her purse and took out a bottle of perfume. Only it wasn't perfume, he discovered, when the pepper spray hit his face.

Coughing and gasping, he fell to his knees, cursing his stupidity. Even with the stinging tears in his eyes, he managed to catch a glimpse of Wade running to board the shuttle. The woman waved to him while she gave Clarke a kick in the solar plexus.

Airport security, sweaty mercenaries dressed in ragged U.N. blue uniforms, were moving in on the two of them. Embarrassed and still sucking air, Clarke was limp as they straightened him up.

"This man was stalking me, officers," said the woman.

Clarke could only glare at her. Words required oxygen he didn't have.

# Chapter Forty-Seven

*The South American sun feels good*, thought Clarke, *even though it is setting.* Although he didn't have too much time to soak it in, it warmed him in comparison to Boston sunshine. *One of the perks of my job,* he told himself. *Or, a temptation to tell the boss-lady to shove it.*

After the debacle at Shay and in spite of the woman's protests, some well-placed bribes from the syndicate earned him a quick release. Wade's girl friend had disappeared. After checking it with the boss, Clarke caught the Nueva Granada shuttle, which left an hour after the New China one.

Villa de Leyva was not that familiar to him, but, at the busy Simon Bolivar airport, Clarke followed the whispered directions of his wi-fi device to meet his contact, a spry, short woman, maybe in her thirties.

Mercedes Prato worked for an old friend of the new boss. Clarke had a gig with her before and was fond of her. She went out of her way to be helpful and even showed him how to penetrate the Magellan complex.

"*Gracias, Mechitas,*" he said.

He was indeed thankful. The years had treated her better than him. She could have been resentful. Instead, she was amused that he needed her aid.

He gave her a good thank-you-you-saved-my-ass squeeze on her butt. She gave him a kiss full on the lips.

"*Cuidete, mi'jo,*" she said.

*Take care of yourself. Don't worry, kiddo. I'm a survivor too.*

He swung himself in behind the wheel of the laundry van that was to be his transportation to the spaceport. Her smile was warmer than the low Andean sun as he waved goodbye.

\*\*\*

The drive to the Magellan complex took over an hour. The squalor of urban development run wild around the airport area was even more recent than New England's, but just as bad, in spite of recent attempts to clean it up.

His mind wandered while he drove, back to his first meeting with Mercedes.

"Ever killed anyone?" she had asked, as they cowered behind some cement statues at a park in the Bronx, fat people sculpted by some old Colombian named Botero. The man, woman, and kid were recent relocations from some more dangerous part of Manhattan.

*Is any place safe in this city any longer?*

Clarke wondered if the sculptor would mind a few bullet holes in his works of art. Or, that they were taking refuge behind their grossness.

A street gang thought the two were horning in on their drug territory. They had pinned down the youth and the woman who was five years older.

"Not that I know of," answered Clarke, "but I've shot a few and taken some shots. You?"

Prato laughed. "I'm Latina. The low-lifes assume that I'm working the streets, especially the gangs. I've had to defend myself. With prejudice, as some old spies used to say."

"I don't know any old spies." He peered around the huge waist of the gentleman-statue. "Think we're going to get out of this?"

"See that alley?" Clarke nodded. "Halfway in there's a fire escape on an abandoned building. You're tall enough to reach it and pull the ladder down."

"What good will that do?"

She pointed to his automatics, then hers, and a third, once belonging to a gang member, which was stuck in the belt behind her pants.

"We have some fire power. If we can get above them, we'll have a chance."

The plan was good, up to a point. She covered him while he dashed for the alley. She fired some more rounds and ran after him.

Clarke jumped and brought the fire escape ladder down even as the bullets zinged around him. He fired a salvo and then gave her a hand. He struggled to keep up with her while they climbed.

*Wings on our heels,* Clarke told himself. *We're climbing for our lives.* She was the one in better shape. *Billy boy, too many hot dogs and donuts under your belt.*

They went up two stories and then turned to watch the alley.

At the same time, they saw some movement below, the window behind them opened. A long-barreled Glock covered them.

"Not too smart," the man said.

Clarke pointed his guns down at his sides. Prato did the same.

"You don't look like one of them," said Prato.

"I'm not. My name is Zeb Lane and I run the Angels of Justice."

"I'll be damned," said Clarke.

Prato dropped to a crouch, aimed, and fired rounds at a nearby window while Lane spun to his right to follow her aim. One gang member toppled to the alley below while another hung lifeless over the windowsill.

"Pasqual, take the rest of them!"

On the roof three stories above, separated from them by the remnants of the rest of the fire escape, Lane's Angels appeared. Machine guns and shotguns made short work of the gang members that didn't flee.

"Hey, thanks," said Clarke to Lane as the latter took the ladder down to alley level to check on the gang casualties. His stomach churned a bit when the mercenary put two gang members out of their misery.

"And I thank your girl friend," Lane called, waving at them from below. "Take care of her. I have to go. The cops will be here soon."

It was then that Clarke realized that Prato had taken a bullet.

Her recuperation made them close for a while because the patient developed feelings for the nurse. Like all his affairs, this one had ended.

*Not badly. And it was my fault, not hers.*

\*\*\*

Besides traveling as a crewmember on a big rig, Billy Clarke had always wanted to be like Zeb Lane. The man had become a vigilante legend, a force for law and order, while Clarke spiraled down into the world of crime, becoming an enforcer for a syndicate whose only redeeming quality was allowing him to scratch out a living as long as he had enough muscle and guts to do it.

*Trapped. The story of my life. Trapped by my own choices.*

The urban squalor saddened him.

*And, to make things worse*, thought Clarke, *the day's hot equatorial sun leaves it a stinking mess. We can't keep up with our waste products anymore, even with all the research and technology that we throw at the problem.*

The thought startled Clarke, who was surprised that at least some small part of him cared.

*Shit, maybe I only need some down time to think and I'll become an urban philosopher.*

The Magellan complex sat in another valley some kilometers down the eastern highway and about 10 klicks off it. While he drove along, he thought more about his past.

It haunted him, causing a major confusion with the memories that bubbled up above the threshold determined by his pain.

*If I had just made the right decision then, or if I had another chance to change things there....*

The ennui made him dizzy. He was not at peace with himself. Far from it. He was trapped by the choices he had made. There was no way to go back in time.

*Time machines only exist in zookies. No one can change the past.*

He had lost control of his life early. It was like losing your queen and knights at the start of a chess match. You could struggle, but you knew the inevitable outcome would be checkmate.

*Unless you were very good.* And he knew he was not very good. He was only an average shit muddling along through life. In disgust, he turned on the van's music system so loud that it seemed to drive the black thoughts from his head.

Only at the end of his journey, before the turnoff, did he leave the city.

*Too many people*, he thought. *We're going to ruin the planet. Then what?*

He didn't think the Magellan and similar programs would work. *Too little too late.* Surprised again at the thoughts, he decided that it was peculiar that he had become so concerned.

*That's it,* he mused. *Now I know I'm crazy if I have nothing better to do but think of the world's problems.*

He spit out the window into the eerie twilight.

# Chapter Forty-Eight

The long shadows of the Andes were teasing with the dusk when he pulled up to the main entrance of Eureka L.T.D. The main building was a modern one, a tower of concrete, metal, tempered glass, and plastic, all askew and looking like it could fall in any direction. It was a uniform dark blue, every window a one-way indigo mirror that hid inside activities from prying eyes.

He could see several shuttles in the distance, their rounded prows pointed to the heavens. He guessed that one of these was destined to ferry the last of the starship's crew to LEO.

At the gate, the guard passed Clarke's fake ID disk through the scanner. Mercedes' hackers had done their job. The guard motioned Clarke through.

As he drove along, he enjoyed looking at all the other shiny, new buildings and watching the people.

*Here I am*, he told himself, *the kid who once dreamed of being a rig pilot, now inside the Magellan complex.* He smiled. *Like being in a candy store.*

He knew the starship was nothing more than a refurbished big rig. He'd read that somewhere. Instead of the outer planets, its destination was a star too far away for Clarke to comprehend.

*Think of all the money spent on this*, he observed to no one in particular. It was one of the oddities of recent years that Eureka L.T.D. had money to burn.

For more ambitious projects like Magellan, U.N.S.A. had launched Eureka L.T.D. It was a non-profit organization designed to finance long-range programs associated with space exploration. Funding still came from the huge corporations. However, part of it was dedicated to pure science—far-out research that left Clarke's head spinning.

The creation of Eureka L.T.D. had occurred five years after the Chaos ended. He had watched it happen and thought U.N.S.A.'s Director Isha Bai was crazy. *Crazy like a fox.* In spite of disbelievers like himself, the venture paid off, as more companies contributed. Projects considered risky turned out to be profitable when turned over to the member companies after the initial R&D. Eureka L.T.D. grew.

As far as Clarke was concerned, U.N.S.A. and Eureka L.T.D. were now the only organizations in the labyrinth of his bureaucratic world that halfway functioned. That wasn't counting the corporations, of course. Their tentacles held a rotting world together in a tight embrace.

*Is there a better way?* Billy Clarke asked himself.

\*\*\*

Since the Magellan project was not military, security was just enough to be a nuisance. However, the laundry deliverer's uniform was the same color as everyone else's, so not many people even gave him a sideways glance.

The same lack of security meant that he had a complete diagram of the whole complex available to him from his wi-fi device. In this case, the device fed the graphics signals into his optical nerve, so that he "saw" the information instead of hearing it. The same technology that made the zookies so popular provided the 3D map that floated in front of his eyes. Subvocalized commands allowed him to magnify or shrink portions of the map.

Even with that aid, it took him a little more than two hours of walking through several buildings and a labyrinth of mostly empty corridors before he located John Wade. He had to break into a Eureka database to do it, something the wi-fi device couldn't do for him.

He found an electronic file on Wade with a last entry that said 'MedicalStation2/CryoSleepPrep/20:30/w/JOrtega.' From the map, he knew where Medical Station 2 was located. He cursed. *In this complex, nothing is close.* He wondered if everyone used avatars for meetings like the boss.

Clarke also knew from the original newsnet info stolen from Wade's MIT office that most of the crew of the Magellan would sleep through the journey in a drug and cold-induced hibernation perfected some fifteen years earlier. That technology made Eureka's exploration of the extreme reaches of the solar system possible. It was also used in two other colony ships that were already outside the solar system. Magellan was to be the third.

They were all heading for planets already determined by the Terrestrial Planet Imager Project to be Earth-like with landmasses, oceans, and atmospheres similar to the home planet.

*The greatest adventure of humankind: Three steps into the night.* He smiled when he recalled the advertising slogan. *Give the spin-doctors credit. They can even sell a death sentence.*

Cryosleep technology had also made the whole colonization program a volunteer one. Some people would not wake up. It was simple statistics. Clarke wondered what kind of person would be willing to gamble with the nine to one odds. *But then, Wade is a gambler!*

As for Ortega, Clarke figured he was another sleeper that would undergo treatment with Wade.

It was close to 8:30. Nearing Medical Station 2, he came upon a changing room. He heard noises inside and decided it was either Wade or Ortega.

If Wade, he would nail him right then and somehow haul his ass out of the Magellan complex. If Ortega, he would take the man's place and then proceed with his plan for Wade, once he found him.

***

Dr. Juanita Ortega was changing into a smock when Clarke burst through the door. He put his hand over her mouth to cut short her scream, but she bit the hand.

"Do that again, Senorita Ortega, and I'll stuff you into that locker. I'm not going to hurt you!"

She relaxed a little.

"OK, here's the story. I'm going to have to become you for a bit. If you promise not to scream, I won't gag you."

She nodded, so he released her. "Who are you? What are you doing here? And it's Dr. Ortega."

"I'm with U.N.S.A. Security," he lied. "I'm after John Wade, the man that's receiving the sleep treatment the same time as you. I need your help."

"Let me see your ID disk."

He knew she didn't trust him. He had a two-day-old beard and probably the eyes of a wild man on crystal meth. He didn't look like security.

"OK, Doc, you're a cute little number but a little slow on the uptake. I'm disguised as a laundry deliverer, so I'm carrying a fake ID. You'll just have to believe me."

She looked doubtful. Nonetheless, she handed her own ID disk over to him.

"When you capture him, I'll accompany both of you to our internal security office, and you will confirm to me that you are who you say you are. *Comprendez?*"

He nodded. "Look the other way." He stripped down to his underwear and put on one of the hospital smocks. "Wait here."

He exited the room and pulled the door shut. He heard her try to open it and then realize he had jammed it. He received a brief lesson in both English and Spanish curses.

*You're one hot number*, he thought, admiring her energy. *Sorry, Juanita.*

***

As Clarke trotted off down the sterile corridor, he was hoping that his scheme of assuming the doctor's ID would hold up, at least for a time.

By international law, there could be no record of the sex of J Ortega on the disk. Long ago ID disks had become unisex to prevent sexual discrimination in the workplace or by authorities. And the U.N. would follow international law—they made it. If he was lucky, the good doctor also chose the option of not having her holoimage recorded there either, a choice recommended in the same spirit, although current hairstyles made it difficult to separate men and women via head shot alone.

If all that was true, he figured he had a chance. The sleep doctor that was putting Wade and Ortega into deep cryo wouldn't know Ortega personally. He also wouldn't check the other ID info like retinal scan, DNA, dental records, and fingerprints, which was required to be on the disk.

Medical Station 2 was only four doors down. The sleep doctor wasn't there yet, but Wade was.

"Come on in. One more zombie to put to bed." Wade's voice contained some signs of hostility as well as boredom. He was lying on a gurney, facing away from the door, so Clarke came around so Wade could see him. "Hey, you're not Juanita Ortega!"

"No, I'm Billy Clarke, here to remind you of your gambling debt. If you come along quietly, I won't hurt you too much, and I'll dump you then in some tourist spot near the local bullring. If you're nice, I'll even call your girl friend and tell her where to find you. For some reason, she thinks you're hot shit."

Wade did not intend to come along quietly. His response was to jump Clarke. The larger man would have overpowered him if Clarke hadn't known some dirty tricks picked up in his turbulent young life during the Chaos.

Even with those, he only managed to achieve a face-to-face standoff with Wade—he was that good. *First Chang, now Wade. I'm too old for this shit.* They circled each other like boys in a schoolyard, looking for the next opening.

Clarke gasped for breath, blood dripping into his right eye from a gash above the eyebrow. The stitches in his left arm were also throbbing.

Wade, bleeding from the nose onto his white smock, was clutching at his crotch.

*This fellow is a fighter. And desperate. Who is more desperate?* Clarke was not in a panic, though. Wade was not a pro. He would make a mistake. *It's only a matter of time.*

***

"What's the sense of this?" asked Wade. "What have I done to you?"

"You don't know how many times I've heard that. I'm only a bill collector. If you'd paid on time, I'd never have come after you."

"What a life! Beating the shit out of people!" Wade dabbed at his nose with his hand and then wiped the blood off on the smock. He was wild-eyed but coherent. "I'm not impressed. You must have some intelligence if you could avoid security and find me so fast. I thought I had lost you in Daniel Shay. Why not do something better with your life, man?"

"My life's not your concern. And, talking about intelligence, why did you run up a gambling debt?"

"It's a bad habit, I know. I have an addiction, all right? But there are no casinos where I'm going. And your stupid syndicate won't be there either."

"What about your girl? She seems to be a doing a lot for you. Is she catching a later bus?"

"We both agreed this was the best way. She knew your syndicate would find me and kill me. I don't have any money and she doesn't either. She prefers to have me alive on Magellan than dead in Boston."

"Why not both of you?"

"She's an artist who wants to make it big time. I honestly think her work is crap, but she's a good person. However, Eureka L.T.D. only accepts certain skills. Painting in acrylics is not one of them." Wade dabbed again at his nose and laughed. "Let's make a deal. You let me start a new life, and I'll sign over my entire signing bonus to your syndicate."

"What signing bonus?"

"The Magellan colonists won't be paid, but their immediate family receives a one-time lump sum payment. Eureka L.T.D. offers an advance life insurance policy due to the cryosleep risk. Just another enticement to generate volunteers." His speech was slurring with the swelling of his lips.

"Not interested. Your body's enough guarantee. You're young and healthy. The syndicate could generate enough from selling your body parts on the black market to more than cover your debt."

Wade's mouth twisted into a distorted grin. "I bet you would be there cheering them on." He jumped over one of the gurneys, keeping it between them. Clarke was glad to have it to lean on. "There's another alternative," Wade said. "You can go with me, you know."

***

Wade had taken Clarke by surprise. It was hard to collect his thoughts through the pain.

Some of the collectors enjoyed the violence, he knew. He hated it. He still remembered how sick he had become on the maglev platform, remembering the dry crunch of Chang's fingers and the blade sawing through his shoulder flesh.

He shook his head to clear away some of the fatigue. *Is Wade crazy enough to make that kind of bargain with me?*

He answered his own question by realizing that the engineer had nothing to lose. He had already given up his girl and a job at a prestigious university. Although he had family, he was willing to give up his signing bonus to the syndicate.

*It's a pact with the devil, but why not? I have nothing to lose either. Not really.*

He raised his hands to shoulder level, palms outward—the universal sign the kid from the street gang used to indicate that he wasn't a threat.

"Let's talk about it."

It didn't take them long to come to an agreement. After some frantic minutes of cleanup, they were ready for the sleep doctor.

When he appeared, there was no sign of a struggle. He saw two men, lying on gurneys, chatting as if they were old friends, so he began the procedure, unaware that anything was amiss.

*Maybe not so trapped*, Clarke thought, as he faded off into dreamland.

*** 

"Are these the last of them?" the space station dockworker asked.

"You got it, man. All freeze-dried and ready for the long haul." He chuckled at his own joke.

"Ever wish you were going?"

"Sometimes. But the 10% mortality! That's not good odds when it's my life."

"They all know that," said his friend, "but they still volunteered. I kind of admire that."

"I guess so."

He helped his comrade stow away the two new colonists into their cryosleep slots on the starship Magellan, joining over five hundred others already aboard in their temporary coffins that would hopefully keep most of them alive during the long trip to 82 Eridani.

"Bon voyage."

# Chapter Forty-Nine

Clarke dreamed. The dreams came fast, moving through his troubled childhood, to Mechitas and Zeb Lane, to Chang and Wade, and to his boss, then round again—different scenes, some pleasant, some dull, some horrible, and some uplifting.

Far-off voices disturbed his reverie. He tried to clear the wispy tendrils of the dreams from his mind. The tendrils wouldn't cooperate.

"There's been a mistake."

A woman's soft, soothing voice. It had an Asiatic lilt to it, although she spoke Standard English. *I'm certainly not in hell,* he concluded. He then remembered the cold pinch of the doctor's needle and groaned. *Not hell—only a long sleep.*

He supposed death was like that sleep. Only death lasted for an eternity. He was not religious. When his time came, he would fade into that same void, losing himself in it, finally at peace.

*Well, maybe I am religious, but as a follower of the Way. No Christian salvation for me. I can't believe in symbolic cannibalism. Too much Zen in me for that. I wish Buchman were here.*

\*\*\*

"He's coming out of it." A man's voice, more gruff and filled with impatience. No lilt, this fellow's voice had drill sergeant potential.

"This is not who the computer says he is," said the woman's voice.

Clarke wished both of them would shut up. His head still throbbed. His nostrils filled with the nauseous odor of hospital fluids mixed with the smell of unclean bodies. Since he couldn't imagine the odor coming from the woman with the sweet voice he had just heard, he tried to look at himself. He realized then that he couldn't see.

"I'm blind," he rasped. His voice sounded like that of a man dying from thirst. *Or, one back from the grave. In fact, I am dying of thirst. I need a well.*

"You'll be fine," the woman told him. "This is normal post-cryo. Now, we know you're not Juanita Ortega, although you were frozen as J Ortega and have her ID badge. Who the hell are you?"

He didn't answer. He wasn't physically capable of doing so. Moreover, Wade and he had made a pact and he would stick by his word. He tried to access his data link device. Neither words nor images. He felt very much alone.

He wondered if they had any good zookies on the Magellan. Or, maybe a meditation room where he could say some mantras to the Way and end his case of nerves.

*I feel like shit. I smell like it too.*

"Well, don't try to answer now," said the man. "We'll get you through the initial steps first."

During the following hours, the people belonging to the two voices and others did uncomfortable things to his body. They removed tubes from various orifices, cut body hair and nails, and pumped liquids into him and out of him.

***

Clarke began to feel better, especially when his eyesight started to return. He feigned sleep to buy some time to get his bearings.

When it had been quiet for some time, he ventured a peep. When the room stopped spinning, he decided that it didn't look much different from Medical Station 2, but there were enough differences to know that so far the scheme was working.

If he had been at all religious, he would have counted his blessings. A traveler of the Way didn't believe in blessings, so he could only consider himself very lucky. He wasn't sure if Guide Buchman would approve of what he had done, but at least Clarke thought he had taken steps to improve his life.

With the exception of the terrible headache, he decided he was all right. The bruises from his battle with Wade were gone. He tried to stand to look at himself in the mirror and nearly fell flat on his face. He was able to see that he had lost some excess kilos, maybe five or so. At least the cryosleep had something positive about it.

The door swung open and a woman in a lab smock walked in. "Well, Mr. X, you seem to be better." She squeezed his biceps. "We'd better find you some clothes. How do you feel?"

"Like hell. What hospital am I in?" Since he already knew that she knew he wasn't Juanita Ortega, he decided that he would feign amnesia. Many people had amnesia coming out of cryosleep, or so he had heard.

"First things first. Do you remember your name?"

"Billy Clarke. What's yours?"

"Fair enough. I'm Linda Ting. I'm a microbiologist helping with the awakenings. Dr. Takahashi was the other doctor you might remember from your awakening. He'll see you later." She paged through some screens on her portable data readout and shook her head. "Not even close to Juanita Ortega. So now, it's your turn." She walked around him in her inspection mode. "Can you remember anything? What do you do?"

He decided he liked this woman and didn't want to deceive her. Nevertheless, he stuck to his story. "Get me some clothes and I'll be out of here. I think I work in Boston somewhere. Yes, I'm sure I work in Boston, but I don't know who I work for."

She laughed. "I think you're still on some of the gas. Boston's a long way from here."

"I know that. How long have I been in a coma?"

"You weren't in a coma, Billy. You were in deep sleep like the rest of us. We're well into the 82 Eridani system and we'll soon need everyone's skills. Now, since you have cryo-induced amnesia, I'd better see if the computer can do a better job of finding out who you are."

She didn't have much luck at that, which was not surprising. Without offering any personal info, he was able to learn that he was one of the lucky ones. The cryogenic failure rate had been somewhat higher for this colony ship compared to the two others. Seventeen percent of the sleepers had died during the 115-year journey to 82 Eridani. Redundancy in personnel meant that this was not critical to the success of the Eureka colony, but it did mean that they would be shorthanded in some areas.

The process of waking up the deep sleepers continued. As they were aroused, their storage areas changed into living quarters. Stacked bodies, however, even in the large cryogenic coffins, still took less space than living, breathing, and moving people. Extra space on the Magellan was available due to the number of sleepers who hadn't made it, but it was becoming scarcer.

Yet most everyone seemed to be in a good mood, since the ship was nearing the end of its journey. Everyone that awoke tried to remember if he had met Clarke or knew his occupation.

*** 

Clarke didn't waste any time obtaining a new wi-fi device. His implant was now Eureka L.T.D. state-of-the-art technology. State-of-the-art meant one-hundred-fifteen-year-old, of course, measured from the time they left Earth. With this wizardry, he learned about the Magellan and her crew.

Like the two other ships before her, the Magellan was supposed to contain all the personnel, equipment, and provisions necessary to establish a new home for its crew. Although they needed a planet comparable to Earth in most respects, the possibility of living in pressurized habitats until they terraformed the planet had been considered and all the necessary supplies and equipment were available. They were on their own, yet they had everything they needed.

The Magellan, like her sister ships, was a converted big rig, an ore ship that Eureka L.T.D. had expanded and refurbished. It was a behemoth, so it had limited maneuvering and acceleration capabilities. Nevertheless, it had staying power. After its initial burn out of the solar system, which took nearly a year, the colony ship passed through the Kuiper comet belt at twenty per cent the speed of light and coasted the rest of the way to 82 Eridani, where now it was in its deceleration phase.

The ship itself was modular and could provide building materials on the planet if local materials were hard to come by. It looked like the end of a wire-mesh bugle, a huge, hollow oil drum, and three cubical blocks stuck together. The three end blocks formed the vertices of an equilateral triangle. Each contained a torch drive. This end of the ship did not rotate.

A seven-square-kilometer radiation shield with a high magnetic field was at the other end, used to protect the living quarters and to replenish some of the hydrogen, which it scooped up along the way. The shield did not rotate either.

The crew worked and slept in the oil drum, its axis forming a perpendicular to the plane formed by the three end blocks. This part of the ship rotated about the cylindrical axis. Since the outer radius of the cylinder was one and a half kilometers, a turning rate of somewhat less than five revolutions per minute gave a comfortable sensation of gravity throughout the living quarters.

The designers had mounted various communications and radar antennas of assorted sizes and shapes, as well as various kinds of telescopes and navigational aids, on the principal axis between the living quarters and the engines. The skin of the cylinder, as well as its axis, contained extra reactive mass for the engines, complementing that carried in the huge blocks at the end. That extra mass also provided additional protection from harmful radiation.

A member of the Earth media had described the starship as a flying junkyard. It was not pretty, but it had taken them to 82 Eridani. It had been their home for over a century.

The computer installation was located on the inside edge of the cylinder that formed the living quarters, midway between the ends. Like everyone else, Clarke could use his new data link device to access the main computer, an AI called Hercules, which handled the principal computer-human interfaces and avatars as well as many of the apps associated with their connection to the digital world.

For example, Hercules could tie you into the huge databases that contained most of the cultural and scientific legacy of Earth, which had grown in 115 years. Hercules also had at his command many other computers where he could delegate tasks like controlling communications, radars, life support systems, and navigation.

Clarke killed a lot of time at first by exploring more within the databases, catching up on what had happened on Earth. Many crewmembers did the same, especially those who just awoke from cryosleep.

At first Earth history seemed to be without any logic or order, but he soon made sense of it. North America was one political unit again, for example, but he wasn't sure it could be called a country. The major economic power was now in South Africa, and that wasn't a country.

All these changes were at least twenty-one years old, the time it now took for a radio signal to arrive from Earth.

\*\*\*

"Mr. Clarke, you are doing well."

He rubbed his butt where Linda Ting had applied the shot.

"Working out," he grumbled. He pulled up his gym shorts, the standard uniform on board the Magellan. "It's boring, but I feel better."

"Healthy food and exercise are as necessary here as on Earth. Even more so." She squeezed his right bicep. "Don't overdo it. Mental acuity is also desirable."

He winked at her. "I'm not sure what that means, but I like the way you say it."

*The exercise and the healthy if unappetizing food are making me a new man,* he decided. He experienced a new vitality that he hadn't felt in years.

"If you meet me for coffee—" She looked at her watch. "—in forty minutes, I'll explain what it means."

Thus began a new relationship for Clarke, the best of his life. Ting seemed to be a soul mate. They grew close. Ship gossips had a field day.

Ting's mental acuity sermon had degenerated into recommending that he become more familiar with the shipboard computers. He was soon helping process the awakening crewmembers.

One night after a recreational romp in the privacy of his quarters, she suggested that he start redefining his career.

"You know, Billy, since the computer doesn't know who you are and you can't remember, you can be anything you want to be. You seem to be interested in computers. Maybe you should take more of the computer courses we brought along and find yourself a new career." She combed his hair with her hand. "When we make planet fall, you'll be expected to help out. I'm sure you'd be happier doing something with the colony's computers, for example, instead of helping the robots in manual labor. Even overseeing the robots would be more fun, I'd think."

Clarke took her advice to heart. He began some more formal courses in computer science. After another two weeks, he was discussing some of the more elementary issues related to AI, databases, and fuzzy logic with some of the other computer staff. Raul Gomes, the computer section chief, seemed to like him and offered to give him work.

He also developed an interest in the art of navigation. Harold Nie, the Chief Navigation Officer, took him on as a pupil and seemed to be always ready to listen to any of the questions Clarke had.

Harry, as he was called, was the closest person they had to a ship's captain. He was also a microbiologist and would be working for Linda Ting when they made planet fall. Harry's days as a navigation officer were therefore numbered.

*** 

Clarke was even better at helping people iron out their problems, though, than he was dabbling into computers and navigation. And they had problems. Most of the 500 plus people on board were misfits in some way. They either had rejected normal society or been rejected by it, or both. Many had large egos, strong opinions, and quick tempers.

He managed to know most of them. Ting considered the ship a small city.

"You have all kinds here, lots of diversity and a full spectrum of personalities. I'm sure we even have some sociopaths and psychopaths, although Eureka did an exemplary job screening them out." She poked him in the belly and then slid on top of him. "Probably all kinds of sexual appetites too. Watch out for the women."

"I think I can help them too," he objected.

"And I'm sure you'll find that what they mean by help is flattering to your ego," she said, "but for now, I want sole possession."

"Works for me," he said.

He was a good listener and enjoyed hearing all their stories, although Ting was right about some of the women. *Some women are downright aggressive.* He knew just about everything one could imagine was going on. *Strange stories about strange relationships, but I don't care. People can be what they want to be—up to a certain point.* No story was as strange as his own, but there were some good ones.

He was wandering down one of Magellan's corridors when the most serious incident took place. The lights moved with him while the rest of the corridor was in darkness. He could imagine it lined with the cryosleep units that contained centenarian sleepers.

*A mausoleum for people buried alive.* He shuddered. *I was one of those. Weird. Nevertheless, here there is no Syndicate, no dragon-lady ready to cut off my balls.*

Two fighting colonists interrupted his thoughts. Dressed in their underwear and locked in combat, they fell into the corridor from one of the singles' quarters the crew had carved out of the cryosleep areas.

"Piece of garbage!" one said, trying to sneak in a punch to his opponent's bare midriff. The other said something in Japanese and landed a good blow flush on the nose. Both were wounded. Their blood spatters and perspiration managed to land on walls, floor, and ceiling.

Clarke, who was bigger than either man, stepped in and pulled them apart. The first man that had spoken swung at Clarke, who floored him with a blow to the solar plexus. He placed a foot on the man's back, grinding his nose into the floor, and faced the Japanese speaker. "Want to try me?"

The man dropped his arms and shrugged. "Fight's not with you, Clarke."

"You're Dr. Takahashi, aren't you?"

"The biggest asshole on Magellan," said the other man, wriggling free from under Clarke's shoe and standing, his face still red from the exertion, though his nose was turning a deep shade of purple.

"And Dr. Schwartz. You're both assholes." He counted a few beats and then gave his verdict. "You're tired from overwork, but you should know better. Before I knock your dumb heads together, return to your cubicle, find some clean clothes, and go play some chess or something less violent than beating each other senseless."

The two medics looked at each other, shrugged, and went back into their cubicle. Clarke continued down the corridor, whistling a popular tune from the Chaos years.

He was certain old Buchman would be proud.

*Maybe Ting too.*

# Chapter Fifty

The ship was now far into the 82 Eridani system. Their speed was that of a typical big rig in the Sol system.

The 82 Eridani system possessed twelve major planets. Three Earth-sized outer planets could be escaped satellites from the gas-giant. This large planet was larger than Jupiter. It still had three large moons, one the size of Earth, and two the size of Mars, along with several minor moons. Inside the gas giant's orbit were eight more planets, all slightly larger than Earth. The fourth planet gave every indication of being terraformable, if not immediately habitable; that much had been determined years ago by the TPI Project and by robot probes Eureka L.T.D. had sent to 82 Eridani.

They called their destination New Haven. They made corrections in the ship's trajectory to bring it into orbit around the planet. Clarke was proud that he had a small part in the calculation of some of those corrections, under Nie's tutelage, of course.

They had entered low orbit around New Haven when Nie called Clarke to his cubicle, which also served as a makeshift office. Nie didn't look happy.

"Something wrong?" asked Clarke.

"You know, Billy, you have some natural abilities that could make you a valuable member of this expedition. You also have a great talent for moving people past their differences so they can work together. I don't mix well with people, so I was happy for you to step in and help out there, talking to people, solving their problems. That's why I feel so betrayed, I guess."

He handed Clarke a computer printout. It was a rarity and made from a special recyclable synthetic paper. There would be no paper mills on New Haven for a while.

"This is a hardcopy of the message Magellan received 114 Earth years ago while it headed out of the solar system. Linda Ting, being the sensitive and helpful person that she is, long ago set up a background search program to find references to Juanita Ortega and/or Billy Clarke."

Nie paused and studied Clarke.

*I'm not offering anything. Not even a change of expression. This is like handling cops in an interrogation. Let him put his cards on the table.*

"The AI finally came up with this complaint," continued Nie, "signed by Juanita Ortega against an unknown assailant that prevented her from coming on Magellan. Juanita used a computerized drawing program to produce a sketch of her assailant."

Nie handed the sketch to Clarke.

"Talented woman," he observed. "A real Rembrandt."

"As you see, it cross-correlates well with the passport ID picture of William H. Clarke, from Boston, New England Confederation."

Clarke could only look down at his toes. *The truth has come home to roost.*

***

"Does the defendant have anything to say to the jury before they recess to consider your sentence?" Harry Nie's voice sounded strained.

Clarke looked at the seven jurors, then at the rest of the people crowded into the largest rec hall on the Magellan.

*These are good people*, he thought. *I've let them down.*

He had come to know most of them in the time since his awakening. Crewmembers that were on essential duty or just didn't fit into the room had tuned in via their wi-fi devices or sent avatars as they dreamed the dreams of REM sleep.

Hercules was also carrying both video and audio of the whole proceedings. He was also recording them for the ship's electronic archives and beaming them back to Earth where they would arrive in twenty-one years.

*At least, I'll be famous then. I'm the first stowaway in the history of star travel.*

Clarke liked most of the people on Magellan. They were all good people. Highly educated most of them, some with egos to match that education, they formed a special group of misfits, every one of them out either for adventure or escaping from something or someone. He also thought most of them were fair-minded.

*Will they understand my motives?*

Clarke knew he had taken the easy way out. It had been easier to become one of the many thugs out on the streets who apprenticed in the gangs on their way up to major crime, exploiting the hard-working people.

As a kid, he would have found it difficult to tell the gang leaders to go to hell and stick with his schoolwork. *I would have been ostracized. Or dead.* As an adult with little formal schooling, he would have found it hard to struggle to find and maintain a decent job in a world that wanted to keep you down and rub your nose in the dirt.

Many others in his circumstances might have made the same choices. However, he now regretted those choices. It would have been hard to make others, but the last weeks had shown him that he could have done better. Much better.

He looked at Linda Ting. She studied her lap, obviously uncomfortable and saddened by the whole proceedings. He regretted failing her too. She was the only woman in his life that he had connected with.

*Linda, please forgive me. I don't care what happens if you'll just forgive me.*

He thought of all the events leading up to his stowaway on Magellan—Chang's vibrablade, Wade's girl friend's kick in the crotch, the feisty Juanita Ortega, and the brutal confrontation with Wade.

*I'd have done it even more willingly if I had known I would meet Linda.*

John Wade, sitting beside Ting, winked at Clarke. He had already been on trial for his part in the scheme, his sentence being two months of community service.

*That's a good omen. However, Wade has skills I don't have.*

Moreover, he knew they considered his offense more serious: he had prevented a valuable colonist from coming with Magellan. Juanita Ortega was to have been one of the five pediatricians that would be busy when the first of the 10000 fertilized eggs stored in another part of the Magellan became babies. Eureka L.T.D. had taken very seriously the need for genetic diversity among the members of its colony.

"I've betrayed the trust of some people that I like a lot," Clarke began. "I'm sorry about that. You now know my reasons, after John's testimony. I haven't had much luck in life, but I didn't try to make the right choices and improve things, either. I've been mean and nasty to many people, but I haven't killed anyone. Hell, John and his girl friend kicked my ass more than I kicked theirs."

Some of the jury laughed. That part of the story had caused some amusement throughout the ship's crew. Many considered Clarke to be a cross between a bouncer and a shrink.

"I felt trapped in what I was doing, you know. Sometimes you just need to break out. Coming on the Magellan has given me a second chance. Dipping into this computer stuff, working with Harry, being with all of you, helping you solve some of your problems—that's something new for me. It wasn't boring either. I felt good about it. And I was doing something positive with my life."

He studied the expressions on their faces and decided that there was a general hostility. He shrugged. *Go for broke. I don't have anything to lose.*

"I think I can continue to turn my life around and still make something of myself if you let me. Besides, you're going to need all the help you can get. What are you going to do, build a jail for me and lose two or three valuable people to the job of guarding me? That isn't practical."

At that, Linda Ting looked up and smiled at him.

"Well, at any rate, do what you have to do. I'm ready to take my medicine."

***

They took Clarke to a small side room to wait on the jury's deliberations. The next moments were the worst in his life.

Sometime after the firefight when Mercedes Prato and he had met Zeb Lane and his mercenaries, he happened upon the infamous vigilante in a bar in the Village.

"Mr. Clarke, how's it going?" said Lane, taking a stool next to Clarke.

"SOS," said Clarke. "I see that you're making a name for yourself."

"I'm keeping busy, but Maria Helena's pregnant. I want to go back to my ranch and live a quiet life with my new family. New York City's not a great place to raise kids."

"Neither is Boston," said Clarke. "I can understand your yearnings. I was trapped into what I'm doing too."

Lane took a sip of the heavy Irish brew he had ordered. "I pray for the strength to leave this life behind. But there is so much need, so many people suffering. What's the solution, Clarke?"

Clarke laughed. "You're asking me? I don't have anything holding me back, but I don't have anywhere to go either. You're lucky in that sense."

"I don't even know if I'm still recognized as the owner of our ranch," complained Lane. "The Chaos has made a mess of everything."

"I'll agree to that. It'd be nice to think at least that I have somewhere to go, though. And a good woman to accompany me."

"Don't be so pessimistic, man." Lane threw a bill on the counter. "That should cover both our beers. Good luck, Mr. Clarke."

"The same to you, Mr. Lane."

Back in the little room, Clarke wondered if Lane had ever made it back to his family's ranch.

***

Linda Ting listened to the debate after Clarke made his defense speech and they took him away. The suggested punishments for him were various. Since there were no precedents, some people were creative in proposing unusual punishments.

Harry Nie, who apparently had it in for him, proposed one of the worst. Clarke had betrayed him. He proposed that they put Clarke back into cold sleep until they could send him back to Earth. Ting didn't like the thought of that—in fact, she told him that it was absurd.

The jury then recessed to deliberate. They only took a half hour.

Ting also felt betrayed by Clarke. It hurt because she had fallen in love with the scruffy stowaway. She knew that deep down inside that rough exterior there was a good man.

She knew that her future on New Haven was as much in the hands of the jury as Clarke's. It was not a pleasant thought.

She wrung her hands and waited for the verdict.

***

They waited while Clarke returned and took a seat. The foreman, the medic Dr. Takahashi, one of the physicians who had been in the fight Clarke had broken up, faced Harry Nie, who was acting as judge. Harry had a pained expression on his face.

*Here it comes, Billy boy. Expect the worst.*

"Harry, we have a problem here," Takahashi began.

"Let's just have the verdict, Gordon. We all need to return to work. This is becoming a circus."

"Agreed, but let me explain the problem. You see, Billy Clarke has changed all of us. Most of us like him, even respect him." Takahashi smiled at Clarke. "Yet he obviously did something wrong. Now, admittedly Wade should never have had the gambling problem that put him at the mercy of Clarke's employer, but Clarke has admitted that his job as a second tier collector was to 'put the muscle on him,' as they used to say in the old movies."

Takahashi turned away from Nie to address the assembly. "That was not only wrong, but illegal under the General Criminal Code of 2217, our present governing code, according to Hercules. Moreover, we have the complaint that Juanita Ortega filed. Hercules is not sure about the civil rights ramifications of that since both Juanita and Billy were citizens of countries that no longer exist, but it has most serious consequences for our future colony."

That started everybody talking. Most people had strong opinions about Clarke's taking the pediatrician's place on Magellan. Many had known Juanita Ortega. They had assumed she died in cryosleep.

All were voicing those opinions now, as well as debating again what to do with Clarke.

Nie pounded on the table in front of him with a heavy plastic coffee mug he was using as a gavel. People quieted down.

"Let Takahashi finish," said Nie. "This is taking far too long. Has the jury accepted my proposal for Clarke's punishment?"

Takahashi directed a frown at Harry Nie. "As I was saying before I was so rudely interrupted, what Clarke did was wrong. But, considering his exemplary behavior since his awakening, and the fact that our numbers have been considerably reduced by our cryosleep losses, the jury has come to the following decision: Clarke must provide three years of community service to our new colony, doing work the majority determines fitting for him. This jury hopes that he keeps on doing what he has been doing: solving problems and getting us to work together. Let's face it, Harry. You're completely incompetent at that job."

There was snickering from the audience. Harry Nie looked like he had indigestion.

"To set this up initially, until we can all vote on it, and to take the unwanted load off you, Harry, this jury proposes that Billy's community work be that of temporary mayor of our new colony." Takahashi smiled at Clarke. "You will have no choice in this matter, you realize."

Some were as surprised as Clarke. Others nodded, considering the verdict wise and just. Still others were aghast.

However, Clarke focused on two special people. First, Harry Nie had an expression of surprise and relief, like a tremendous burden was lifted from his shoulders. Second, and more importantly, Linda Ting was approaching him with a big smile on her face. She hugged Clarke.

"I may never forgive you for not confiding in me," she said, "but I love you all the same, Mayor Clarke."

He put his arm around her and kissed her. It seemed like the appropriate thing to do.

# Sing a Samba Galactica

Read the first two chapters of Steven M. Moore's new sci-fi thriller, *Sing a Samba Galactica*...

## Chapter One

The colonists first knew something strange was beginning to touch their lives when little Annie Li slipped and fell off North Bridge. The two visible moons of New Haven were low on the evening horizon as the picnickers returned to First Landing. They watched in stunned helplessness as the toddler fell the three meters into the swift waters.

Mayor Clarke, constantly in contact with the com hut through the data link buried behind his ear, immediately called for help. Two search parties in helicopters headed out from town, one on each side of the river, while the picnickers, silenced by their expectations for the worst, continued the walk home.

The wait was not long. Everyone in the colony was amazed when they found the girl four kilometers downstream, sitting on the bank, wet, coughing and cold, yet alive. There were strange marks on her body. Like rope burns, her mother said.

Gordon Takahashi had flown in one of the helicopters with Janet Li, Annie's surrogate mother, and the pilot, Ines Garcia, one of the civil engineers. Li and Garcia ran from the cafeteria where the latter had been complaining about the syntho coffee. They met Takahashi at the chopper. The physician was somewhat winded from his run from the clinic and embarrassed that the women were not. But theirs was the first chopper out.

"Garcia," said Clarke, "I have an estimate of the river's current."

Garcia was able to calculate where the current would carry the toddler and headed to intercept.

"There she is!" said Takahashi.

They passed over Annie, who was already sitting on the bank, and had to double back.

Upon landing, Takahashi examined her and found her healthy. Her survival astonished him. The child had just learned to walk. There was no way she could have swum to shore. Yet the child was unharmed and seemed amused by the incident.

Garcia and Takahashi had to comfort the mother, more than the daughter. Li was hysterical. She had been one of the first volunteers to implant one of the 10,000 fertilized eggs the colonists had brought with them. She loved little Annie as if she were her own.

Over the next ten weeks that followed everyone in the colony was as busy as usual, so no one would have given the mystery more thought if there had not occurred other incidents that were equally strange  Takahashi expressed this concern to the mayor.

"So, who am I, Sherlock Holmes? If you're interested in mysteries, solve them yourself."

Clarke had so far performed well as mayor of the new colony, so well that he had won easily in the first real election. The doctor and the mayor became friends even before the trial aboard ship to determine Clarke's unusual punishment, so it wasn't surprising that Clarke and Linda Ting, Clarke's new wife, often invited Takahashi over for dinner.

Such gatherings were informal, considering their simple diets, but that only meant that people and conversation took precedence over food. All three were travelers of the Way and often meditated a little before food and conversation, but often would forget about ceremony in their hurry to proceed onto the business of the colony. This time it concerned the strange happenings.

"People are so caught up in their work that they're getting stressed out, imagining things, you know," said Ting. "We're too shorthanded. People are making up things to have a distraction."

Takahashi was not about to leave it at Clarke's good-natured insults or Ting's more sanguine reasons. "But the incidents are real, Linda. There's the case of Annie Li. We also have several instances of lost equipment appearing. Then there's the case of Raul Gomes waking up in his own bed after passing out in a drunken stupor in South Common. And so on. And finally, there's your mystery creature, Linda. Why don't we see more of him?"

New Haven, the fourth planet in the 82 Eridani system, was the statistical anomaly in the short history of Earth's colonization of nearby stellar systems. Unlike the previous planets colonized in the Tau Ceti and Delta Pavonis systems, New Haven had an already established ecosystem. The other two colonized planets, while orbiting stars that were more similar to Sol, were in what might be called their Precambrian periods where prokaryotes of various forms—bacteria, algae, and so forth—floated in their oceans and on the oceans' floors.

The more complex ecosystem on New Haven was both a blessing and a hindrance to the colonists' work. They didn't need breathing masks since the atmospheric mix contained 20% oxygen, close to the same percentage as Earth's, unlike the two other colonies. On the other hand, the other colonies easily introduced Earth flora and fauna, whereas the New Haven colonists found the local flora and fauna very competitive with Earth's.

New Haven possessed abundant plant life, not unlike Earth's in its use of photosynthesis. It was also home to a not so abundant animal life that filled many of the same ecological niches as Earth's insects and smaller animals. However, local life was more limited in the sense that overall there did not exist the multitude of species that Earth had now or in its past since the Cambrian.

All of the local life forms had a DNA code based on the same four amino acids as Earth's code, but evolution had taken very different turns in its choice of stereo isomers. Consequently, Humans found the local flora and fauna mostly inedible.

One of the curiosities of the local ecosphere was that they had found no large animals. The largest discovered so far and the most numerous was a furry rodent-like creature about the size of a rabbit with six legs and two eyes sitting on short antenna stalks. They thrived on many of the plants and were everywhere. They filled the evenings with their calls, which resembled a turtle-dove's. They didn't have any predators, though, so it was interesting to conjecture what kept their numbers in check. Most thought there must be a large predator not yet discovered.

In search of that predator in particular and any large animal life in general, Ting and Harry Nie had gone with some others to the higher elevations, thinking that the dense forests there would provide cover for larger animals. From the helicopter, they discovered several large herbivores, but no carnivores.

However, Ting had seen something big and bulky cross a shadowy clearing. The air had been shimmering in the heat of the afternoon. The humidity had been high and the temperature around 30 degrees centigrade.

New Haven was slightly larger than Earth but had only nine-tenths the gravity. Twenty-one per cent of its surface was land, but most of this was concentrated in one archipelago formed by over a hundred islands of different sizes and shapes. The one they chose for the first settlement was the largest but typical of most. It was about the size of New Zealand and rose abruptly from the ocean to high volcanic peaks that ran down its center from north to south.

The planet, ideally distanced from its parent star, 82 Eridani, had a larger tilt of its axis that gave it more extreme seasons than Earth's. The settlement was about 25 degrees north of the equator where the climate was similar to Stockholm's. They were in the middle of a hot summer.

Ting had figured that she had misjudged the size of the creature due to the heat shimmer, but image processing on the video record confirmed that something about two meters long and one and a third meter wide had crossed the clearing, carrying something smaller in its mouth. The scientists were elated—they had found their large carnivore. Unfortunately, no more sightings had taken place since then.

Takahashi thought the problem was more general than the scientists' search for large animal life on New Haven. Ever since the Annie Li incident, he had made the search for an explanation to the unexplained a hobby of his. In fact, he had become the New Haven reincarnation of the famous British sleuth.

Clarke thought his friend was wasting his time. He only wanted the colony to move forward, which required everybody to do his job, including Takahashi.

"Have you written that report on our adaptability to the local micro-fauna?" he asked Takahashi, trying to change the subject. "I'd like to know if we're going to have to start making and eating Earth cultures."

"I told you that you didn't have to worry about that. As long as our Earth plants and animals are doing well here, we'll be fine. The two ecosystems can exist side-by-side as long as we don't let our Earth system go wild, I'm not sure we have to be that careful, since New Haven's flora and fauna have the numbers advantage."

"You'd better not tell that to Harry Nie," countered Ting.

Ting's coworker was always concerned that the Earth flora and fauna, and especially the microorganisms, could contaminate the whole New Haven biosphere. Takahashi thought the measures they had taken to control this were unnecessary. He believed that the spread of Earth organisms over the planet was only another form of terraforming and had said so in many meetings. Ting was not sure who was right but knew that both would agree that their science didn't have enough experience with these problems.

"At any rate, just write the damn report," said Clarke. "I need hard facts to convince the Council that we're not heading for tragedy. John Wade's bout with diarrhea has scared everybody."

As if that statement had been a cue, a call came in from Wade, who was on duty in the com hut. All received it. Although directed to the mayor, it was on the town public channel.

"Billy, I just received a check-in call from Boris Malenkov. He's out looking at those sink holes and geysers near Lake Placid."

"And?"

"He was cut off in mid conversation. I can't rouse him on any frequency."

***

Takahashi went to school with Boris Malenkov. At Mid-Atlantic University, near the Chesapeake Bay, Takahashi was an introverted and quiet premed student while Malenkov was an outgoing and boisterous planetology major.

While good friends, their professions often separated them over the years. Since their school days, Takahashi was often envious of Malenkov's exploits with the opposite sex, but maturity changed the envy to quiet amusement. In reality, they had little in common beyond their love of beer, old video shows from the 20th century, and Chesapeake Bay crab cakes. However, as often happens, their bond grew over time.

At school and on board the Magellan, they were drinking buddies, often drinking late into the night while discussing the merits of some forgotten episode of *The Lone Ranger* or *I Love Lucy*. Settling down to their respective routines in First Landing had not changed that at all. They both shared a keen interest in explaining the strange incidents that had been occurring in and around the colony and talked about it often over a frothy glass of Raul Gomes' home brew.

Thus, it was with more than idle curiosity that Takahashi accompanied Clarke and Ting over to the com hut. They wanted a better picture about what was happening than the one received over their data link devices.

Wade, now cured of his gambling addiction and a teetotaler, was always protective of his private domain.

"You didn't have to drop what you were doing. I'm capable of handling this, you know." He waved at the screens. "Ines Garcia took one of the RTVs and picked up three other colonists with some firepower, just in case. Hercules has Malenkov's last position down to two meters, thanks to the GPS satellites we have in orbit."

Everyone knew how the coded signals from several of the Global Positioning System satellites that the starship Magellan had established in orbits around New Haven could be cross-correlated in order to determine an accurate position. Such position information regularly was transmitted to the com hut when a person did a routine check-in or when the person was linked. Hercules, the main computer for the colony, would record it in a database for later use. However, knowing where Malenkov had been to two meters circular error probability didn't make Takahashi feel any better.

The equipment in the com hut offered the best that Earth science had to offer, at least the Earth science of 115 years ago. Some of it made the long trip in crates aboard the Magellan, while other components were gutted from the starship's own com center.

Ever since they left Earth, they had been receiving and transmitting information back and forth to the home world and the two other colonies. The information was transmitted at either end via com satellites in geosynchronous orbit. These had 25 square-meter phased array antennas that transmitted a megawatt signal into tight microwave beams using spread spectrum techniques.

The information itself, of a modest bandwidth of 60 kilobits per second, was encoded digitally into the spread spectrum signal of 600 megahertz, making it impervious to most interference. The colonists had laid out these satellites for communications with Earth, together with more usual satellites, including the GPS satellites, while still in orbit around New Haven.

Similar systems orbited around Earth, of course, and the other two colonized planets. Except for the tremendous delay because 82 Eridani was 20.9 light-years from Sol, it would have been possible for a person in, say, Los Angeles, Earth, to call up Gordon Takahashi in First Landing, New Haven. The delay meant that person-to-person conversations were impossible, so communications with Earth were reduced to computers transmitting information back and forth.

Much more information came from Earth, of course, than was sent to it, but Hercules and his other computer allies handled it all. Any of the colonists could use his data link device or a more sophisticated holographic terminal to connect to Hercules and receive the latest twenty-year-old updates.

They all waited as Garcia and her crew drove the five kilometers to where Malenkov had last reported in. She kept up a running chatter over the noise of the rugged terrain vehicle, making light of the whole incident, but her tone changed as they neared Lake Placid.

"There's been a cave-in. Looks like part of the terrain collapsed. Malenkov's CEP center is close to the extreme edge. The caved-in area is about ten meters in radius. We're going down to look for him."

"Garcia, this is Clarke. Leave one person in the RTV, and make sure everyone who's going down has a link to Hercules and a tether to your RTV."

"All right. Nevertheless, there's nothing threatening here. Just a lot of sand and rocks."

"Garcia, Takahashi here. Use extreme caution when lifting him. He may have broken bones. Take a stretcher down with you."

"And ropes. Besides the tethers, I'm going to hook one on to the jeep's wench. Be damned if I'm carrying his womanizing butt up this slope."

Ting winked at her husband. Most knew that Garcia had fallen hard for Malenkov. When he went on to his next conquest, she had started bad-mouthing him.

Takahashi sighed. Malenkov enjoyed her ire and would even take verbal jabs back at Garcia, making the situation worse. Malenkov loved controversy, especially when a woman was involved.

All the preparations were wasted, however. After three hours of digging, Clarke dispatched another team to replace Garcia's. After another two hours, they could come to only one conclusion: Boris Malenkov was not at the bottom of the cave-in.

# Chapter Two

The medical center, including a small hospital, was located on the outskirts of First Landing. Takahashi was removing a basal cell carcinoma from the back of Eric Potts when Malenkov stumbled out of the forest bordering their community. He had a broken leg that had been set in a crude splint and a homemade crutch.

Denise Tombo was taking care of him when Takahashi entered the emergency room after finishing with Potts. Malenkov was trying to tell the doctor something, but she shushed him.

"Your story can wait," said Tombo. "Right now I need to check your leg. So, no talking. We need some x-rays."

Tombo, the oldest of the medical staff, had been working for Eureka L.T.D. for much longer than either Takahashi or Malenkov. She was an excellent neurosurgeon as well as a very protective and compassionate general caregiver. She called Takahashi her dreamer, sometimes in old Swahili, meaning that he wasn't the practical healing machine that she thought every doctor should be.

She removed the makeshift splint and checked the leg, while Takahashi assisted. An x-ray showed that the leg had been set well, so they made a cast. After the brief operation, Takahashi helped her clean him up.

"You're a mess," he told Malenkov.

"No shower, no shave, for three days. What do you expect?"

At that moment, Clarke joined them. "How's the patient?" he asked.

"Somewhat immobilized," said Tombo. "All right, Boris, I guess it's your show. Why don't you tell everyone what happened?"

"Damnedest thing," Malenkov began. "I was snooping around those sink holes, you know. I have this theory that there's drainage from Lake Placid going way down there and hitting lava to make the geysers. The whole area's very unstable." He winked at Takahashi. "Just like me. Anyway, all of a sudden the whole area starts to shake, coinciding with a squirt from one of the geysers, and then I'm going down. I remember a rock smashing into my leg, but the pain didn't last long since another rock knocked me unconscious. The next thing I know is that it's morning and I'm awake on the far shore of Lake Placid. No intranet connection. Weird. Don't know how I got there."

"Well, you did a fair job of setting the leg and making the splint and crutch," said Takahashi. "That's quite a feat."

"That's just it. I didn't."

"Huh?" Takahashi exchanged looks with Clarke. Tombo looked at the ceiling.

"My leg was set and the splint on when I woke up. The crutch was at my side. I didn't make them, guys, honest. Someone did all of that for me, not to mention dragging me out from under a lot of dirt and stone."

"If no one from First Landing helped you, then we have unknown benefactors. We have to get to the bottom of this." Takahashi winked at his friend. "Are you with me?"

The bearded face smiled back. "You bet I am. I want to thank them. They saved my skin, for sure!"

"You two are expressing what a lot of us are thinking but are not willing to say," commented Clarke. "Namely, alien contact. But why are they hiding?"

"Maybe they're scared," said Tombo. "Human beings can be pretty scary. We don't have a good track record when dealing with the local natives."

"But we must communicate," said Clarke. "Imagine the possibilities! Our first contact with other intelligent beings. We can't miss out on this one."

"I'd prefer a more conservative approach," countered Takahashi. "We find them, study them, get to know them as well as we can, all before making contact. In fact, that last step must not happen if they're in a stage of development where contact could be harmful."

"Something doesn't fit," observed Malenkov. "If there is intelligent life here, how did it come to exist, given that the planet is so similar to Earth millions of years ago? I think we need some specialists in on this."

"Not 'til we find the aliens," Takahashi countered.

"How do you propose to do that?"

Takahashi made a face and thought a moment. "Well, they seem to be bent on helping us. Let's create a situation too good for them to pass up. I think Garcia is about to have an accident, which we'll carefully control."

\*\*\*

"At Los Alamos, in 1950, the Italian physicist Enrico Fermi asked Emil Konopinski, Edward Teller, and Herbert York, as well as other physicists working on the atomic bomb project, this provocative question: If life is so common in the universe, why in the hell haven't 'they' shown up on Earth yet?"

Malenkov waited for the laughs to subside, took a sip of water, and continued.

"Fermi noted that there are plenty of stars older than our sun. If life is so plentiful, it would have arisen on planets around these stars billions of years before it arose on Earth. In that case, shouldn't Earth have been visited or colonized by a race much older than our own? Even with a slow means of space travel like we used to come to New Haven, a civilization with a will to homestead could settle the galaxy in a million years or so."

Malenkov looked out at his audience. Gordon Takahashi, sitting in the front row of the cafeteria seats, smiled at him. *So which one of us is Holmes and which one Watson?*

"This is Fermi's Paradox. The 20$^{th}$ century scientists Frank Drake and Carl Sagan explained it away by pointing to the tremendous distances of interstellar space. They suggested that such civilizations would turn to radio communication, but we all know by personal experience that it's hard to hold a conversation with time lags of many years. Well, although we may not resolve Fermi's Paradox, we have a chance to make it an irrelevant question in the sense that we have a plan for making contact with the first alien beings known to Humans."

It was a simple plan. Garcia was to fake helicopter trouble in a remote area, pretending all her com links with Hercules were down. Next, she was to fake a fall that would leave her unconscious long enough for the aliens to risk helping her.

They would wire the remote area to capture all sound and video across a wide spectrum. The trick was to make it appear that they needed all the sensors for something else, so they pretended to be constructing a sensor trap for Linda Ting's large beast.

They left everything alone for two weeks and then sent Garcia out on her fake equipment check.

Back at First Landing, Hercules was monitoring all the sensors and displaying results for the people in the com hut who stopped in to watch the show. In addition to Billy Clark, Linda Ting, Gordon Takahashi, Boris Malenkov, and John Wade, there were present Judy Weinberg, one of the sociologists, and Peter Holst, a cultural anthropologist.

Clarke had over-rode Takahashi and Malenkov's objection about involving others. He was not a very technical person and wanted reasoned opinions from various sources. Weinberg was skeptical and bored about the whole thing, while Holst was nearly dancing with anticipation. Of course, many others that were interested would be listening in or watching on their data link implants.

Those in the com hut watched as Garcia went through her performance. She was good. Although she over-acted at the helicopter, pounding and cursing at the "infernal machine," her tripping on the large tree root seemed real. She went down with an audible thud and was very still.

Five minutes passed. Garcia hadn't stirred.

Clarke was about to call the whole thing off when they all noticed that some close-by foliage began to shake. It parted and they were electronically face-to-face with Ting's beast.

A collective gasp was heard on the net as those outside the com hut tuned into the video transmission saw the beast. What they had tried to make look like a trap for it turned unexpectedly into the real thing.

In shape it was akin to a large domino, even as far as some white circular spots on its oily, black skin. It was carnivorous—an ugly pink drool dripped from a large mouth full of sharp, stained teeth.

"My God, Garcia, run!" came the mayor's warning, "You'll be its next dinner!"

Before Garcia could react, the beast was surrounded by much smaller ellipsoidal fur balls dressed in multicolored suits. The beast expressed his displeasure by giving off an ear-shattering shriek and charging the nearest ones. They stood their ground while some raised weapons.

There were thunderclaps and flashes that saturated both the audio and video pickups. Those tuned in on the net would have headaches for days.

When the video came back on-line, they could see the beast was dead. Some of the fur balls grabbed onto the dead beast with what looked like tentacles and began dragging it off. Others came over to examine Garcia. She startled them by sitting up, and they ran off into the forest.

"I've had enough of this game," Garcia subvocalized over her data link device. "That thing could have killed me."

"Yes, it could have," agreed Holst. "But now we know who our friends are. What do you think, Judy?"

The sociologist was still looking at the screen in disbelief. "Let's hope they are our friends. They may be more advanced than us in some ways."

"You mean the energy weapons?" Clarke asked.

"Correct. We may not be Cristobal Colon and company here. The roles may be reversed."

# About the Author

Born in California, Steve Moore reversed the adage "Go West, young man," living twelve years in South America before settling in Massachusetts. His training as a mathematician and physicist and his interests in robotics, genetics, and scientific ethics are evident in his story telling. Although he writes mostly sci-fi thrillers, it is the human condition that intrigues him—those idiosyncrasies and crazy internal contradictions that plague us all. He also believes that humanity's only salvation is for society to encourage creative individuals who "think outside the box."

Steve grew up "cutting his teeth" on the great dystopian sci-fi thrillers of the 1950s and 60s—*Fahrenheit 451* by Bradbury, *No Blade of Grass* by Christopher, *Not This August* by Kornbluth, and many others. The short stories of Phillip K. Dick—"Do Androids Dream of Electric Sheep?" (the movie *Blade Runner*), "Minority Report," "Paycheck," "The Adjustment Team" (the movie *The Adjustment Bureau*), "Total Recall," and others—inspired him long before they inspired Hollywood. They led him to the "dark classics": Wells' *The Time Machine*, Huxley's *Brave New World*, Koestler's *Darkness at Noon*, and Orwell's *1984*. He is fluent in both English and Spanish and is currently working on Jorge Rodrigues Dos Santos' *El Enigma de Einstein*. His dystopian vision of humanity's possible futures is now associated with his concept of social singularity.

In the latter part of the 20th century and the first part of the 21st, sci-fi authors and futurists talked about a coming singularity. This is a point in human history when machines become sentient and/or humans and machines become one. Frederik Pohl in his Heechee series and Gregory Benford in his Galactic Center series wrote about this long before the *Terminator* movies and Vernor Vinge. In many cases, these conjectures arise from chaos theory, where complex and disordered systems suffer a transition and exhibit simplicity and order. A similar story focused on a computer can be found in the classic *The Moon is a Harsh Mistress* by Robert Heinlein and the movie *2001*.

The three tales contained in *Survivors of the Chaos* are instead about Steve's concept of social singularity: when humanity's social and political structures become incapable of handling the large and complex problems that are created by science and technology; when the present paradigm of one large political state breaks down with the appearance of cohesive and smaller religious or ethnic, almost tribal, units that are unwilling to compromise for the greater good; and when multinational corporations change to the exploitive and fascistic model of Chinese capitalism and step forward to fill the power vacua and control the world economy. These ideas have appeared before in sci-fi, but this concept of social singularity is new.

Steve's three previous novels, *The Midas Bomb, Full Medical*, and *Soldiers of God*, taken in their chronological order (not the order in which they were written), lead up to this singularity. The serialized novel *Evil Agenda* falls between *Full Medical* and *Soldiers of God*. *Soldiers* ends with a bang. *Survivors of the Chaos* describes the whimper. This novel and future ones in this series are hints at what might await us on the other side of the singularity—if human beings can make it that far.

There is always hope that this possible future does not happen or that its effects are mitigated by many good people like Zeb Lane, Jon Lewis, and Billy Clarke, people who have the stamina and motivation to save us from ourselves. This is the message of many of the great dystopian novels. It is also the message in Steve's writing. Unlike the dark classics, in Steve's novels there is always hope.

Steve now dedicates full time to his writing career. His wife and he make their home in New Jersey. Besides his novels, he has written many short stories and over thirty academic publications. Visit him at his website http://stevenmmoore.com where you will find excerpts and other freebies as well as a blog that contains many posts about the coming social singularity. You can also find Steve on Facebook.